The Secrets of Blackthorn House

MARIE MCWILLIAMS

Quill & Crow

The Secrets of Blackthorn House
by Marie McWilliams
Published by Quill & Crow Publishing House

This book is a work of fiction. All incidents, dialogue, and characters, except for some well-known historical and public figures, are either products of the author's imagination or used in a fictitious manner. Any resemblance to actual persons, living or dead, or actual events is purely coincidental.

Printed in the United States of America

Cover Design by Fay Lane

Edited by Lisa Morris, Cassandra L. Thompson

ISBN: 978-1-958228-92-0

ISBN: 978-1-958228-91-3 (ebook)

Publisher's Website: www.quillandcrowpublishinghouse.com

Dedicated to every woman who has been mistreated & underestimated by a man.

They may burn us, but we will always rise triumphant from the ashes.

Publisher's Note

This book contains depictions of graphic violence, including the abuse of women. Please consult the back of the book for content warnings.

Prologue

A scream pierced the silence of night, a dissonant note of fear and despair.

It took the girl a moment to realize the sound had come from her own throat. It was as if her spirit had departed her body the moment she found her little brother dead, and she watched it now from afar, removed by time and space, merely a detached observer. But all at once, she felt herself fall back to Earth, and when the grief and horror hit, it caught in her throat, choking her.

His bedsheet covered him, the outline of his small frame distinct. Deep red seeped slowly from one end, blooming outwards into a bloody rose.

She wanted to go to him, to hold him. She wanted to cry, to run. But her limbs failed her, and instead, she simply stood still, eyes wide with fear as the echoes of her scream reverberated around her in the darkness. The world blurred as tears filled her eyes, and she stifled a second wail with her fist, suddenly aware of the danger. She glanced back at his lifeless form once more, memories threatening to flood to the surface and overshadow the present. But she needed to focus on the now. She needed to stay alive.

As quickly and quietly as she could, she ran through the hallway of her home, desperately trying to calm the fears racing through her mind. The dark, shadowy shapes of tables and lamps, once so familiar, appeared like ships in the fog, each one a potential enemy, a potential killer. He would be on his way back to her brother's room, having heard her scream—she was sure of that. She didn't know where to go or what to do, but she knew she needed to put distance between her and the four-year-old's lifeless body. Thoughts of him threatened to unleash another scream, but she choked it down, swallowing hard.

She had almost reached the back stairs that led to the servants' quarters when she heard his distinct, heavy footsteps approach. She slid behind the hall drapes and pressed against the cold, damp glass. Panic surged through her, and she bit her fist to stifle her cries, tasting the coppery blood she'd drawn. She struggled to control her thoughts as tears forced their way from her eyes.

The footsteps stopped momentarily, and she envisioned him at the doorway to her brother's room, weighing various options in his mind. He would look for her within the wardrobe, among her brother's little shirts and jackets, or beneath the very bed where he now grew cold. She held her breath, straining to listen for his movements over the thrumming of her heartbeat. After what felt like an age, she heard his steps once more as they took the hallway leading west and away from her hiding spot.

Relief washed over her, and briefly, she allowed herself the hope that she would survive the night. But as soon as the thought entered her mind, his steps changed direction, growing in volume with each second. Panic became all-consuming as she debated whether to run and reveal herself or stay behind the curtains. His footsteps grew closer but never faster, always keeping the same, steady pace, knowing neither impatience nor urgency. She suppressed another scream as they continued, one after the other, each one with a distinct sense of purpose. Her mind raced, her limbs shaking as a sob threatened to escape, but still, the steps kept coming, slow and unwavering. They stopped just beyond the fabric wall of her shelter.

The heft of his frame cast a dark shape, even through the thick fabric. She knew then that she would soon meet her end. A whimper escaped her lips as he slowly drew back the curtains. He was calm in spite of everything, an odd look of detachment in his once-kind eyes. The knife flashed in the moonlight as he raised it and paused before slashing it swiftly through the air, the blade easily hitting its mark.

She found her voice long enough to utter two simple words before he drew a line of red across her throat, just as he had her little brother: "*Father, don't!*"

The pain lasted only a moment as she felt her life draining away with her blood, the warmth of its flow distinct from the coldness that now surged through her young body. Her hands scrambled at her neck, a futile act in the face of inevitable death, her blood forcing its way in droves between her fingers and along her arms. It dripped onto the floor in an odd pattern, a message she could not interpret. She wondered, dazed, how she could have so much blood inside her, yet still more came.

Her eyes returned to her father, who stood before her, stoic and determined in his grizzly task. She tried to speak, but the only noise that broke forth was a rasping gurgle. The world began to fade, growing darker at the edges, and she felt herself wavering on her feet. How long had it been? Seconds? Minutes? She felt exhausted. An endless sleep was calling her away from the life she had known only briefly. As her eyes closed and her body crumpled, the last thing she saw was her father placing the same blade against his own throat.

She understood then that Death had three souls to collect that night.

One

They were married at the tail end of summer. The day had been a blur of faces and sounds, and Evelyn found that when she tried to recount its events, it was the smallest, oddest moments that anchored themselves in her memory.

She had worn a long veil over her long, wavy hair, and the way the veil flowed behind her as she walked reminded her of the ebb of the tide on her childhood holidays to Cornwall. She carried a bouquet of yellow roses and white chrysanthemums and recalled the humming of a curious bee that had found its way inside the church and onto the blossoms in her hand. Her father had remarked that the flowers matched her straw-blonde hair perfectly, and being prone to romantic hyperbole, he made her laugh and blush when he told her she "radiated like the spring sunshine."

Her hand had shaken slightly as she extended it to Peter during the exchange of their wedding bands, but he had remained reassuringly sturdy and sure. She vividly remembered the familiar weight of her late mother's pearls around her neck, her way of always keeping her mother with her in her heart, and the echo her shoes made as she walked up the aisle. But as hard as she tried, the rest of the day's events blurred into one another, like looking out of a window through heavy rain, the various shapes of the outside world recognizable yet unfamiliar all the same.

She had awoken the following morning beside her new husband, dazed but contented, as she breathed in the heady musk of his scent, enjoying the weight and heat of his body next to hers. She felt so much older and wiser than she had just twenty-four hours prior when she had risen from her bed riddled with anxiety about the day's events. However, deep down, she knew that more change awaited her as she moved forward with her new life, shedding the old one as she had her name the day before.

She must have succumbed to sleep, for when she opened her eyes again, the sun was higher, casting long, thin shadows across the room. Peter was gone, and his side of their marital bed felt cold. An early riser, she was shocked to see from the ornate mantel clock that it was ten minutes after ten, and she donned her robe, a little hurt despite herself, as to why Peter had not woken her. After all, this was their first day as husband and wife.

A quiet knock at the door interrupted her thoughts. Peter must have gone to fetch breakfast or perhaps the morning paper. She smiled, quickly fixing her hair and pinching her cheeks to bring out their color. But just as quickly as a smile came, it faded with the appearance of a young maid.

"Good morning, ma'am."

"Good morning, Lilly."

If the girl sensed Evelyn's disappointment, she did not acknowledge it, going about her business with a focused determination. Evelyn went to ask about Peter's whereabouts, but thought better of it. She was well aware of the gossiping nature of staff, and being new to the house and its occupants, she remained wary. She hoped the feeling of unease in her new home would shift soon, along with the unfamiliarity of her new status as a wife and lover.

Lilly had been assigned as Evelyn's new lady's maid. At around eighteen or nineteen, she was a little younger than Evelyn, with small dark curls falling about her face, framing green eyes. She may have appeared rather plain on first approach, but her kind eyes and sweet smile made her pretty in her own right. Evelyn liked the girl and felt a warmth in her that she did not sense with any of Peter's other employees.

As Lilly went about helping her dress, Evelyn stared silently into the mirror. The usual face stared back, her porcelain skin and delicate features always making her seem younger than her years. Her eyes, a dark chestnut brown, were her father's, while her yellow-blonde hair, currently hanging in a long braid, was a gift from her mother.

Disappointment rose when she found no difference in her features. A small part of her had expected to see a change come over her as a result of her womanhood. A slight alteration to her mouth, perhaps—a knowing smile. Or a maturity visible within her eyes that had not been there the day prior. But there was no change, no transformation, not even a subtle hint at growth or experience. She appeared as she always had, except now she wore a plain gold band around one slender finger. She pouted slightly in spite of herself, making her appear even younger still.

"Would you like breakfast downstairs, ma'am, or shall I bring it up?"

"Downstairs, thank you."

With a quick nod, Lilly exited as quickly as she had come, leaving Evelyn and her reflection behind. It was not the morning she had envisioned, but she forced a smile, determined to face her new life and home with optimism. Her reflection smiled back, but seemed dubious.

She made her way down the stairs, trying to take in every detail. This building, so strange to her, was now her home and would remain so for many years. It would be her role to manage the staff and ensure that the house was maintained to Peter's exacting standards, a job she looked forward to.

Like everything about Peter, the house was grand and lavish. The walls were covered in paintings—portraits of Peter's ancestors long since dead, their names engraved on brass plaques beneath austere and solemn faces. As she passed them, she amused herself by inventing silly facts about them. *Lord Arthur Black, who kept bees and could not roll his Rs,* or *Lord Montgomery Black the Second, a superstitious man who feared black cats crossing his path and was allergic to blackberries.* It was her attempt at familiarizing herself with Peter's lineage and making a connection with her new family.

The Blacks were a prestigious family renowned for their wealth and reclusive tendencies. Despite also coming from esteem and wealth, Evelyn was honored to be part of such a distinguished heritage, though she found herself intimidated by the faces that glowered at her from their frames. The title of *Lady* lay in her distant future, along with all of its accompanying responsibilities, and even now, she felt the weight of such an undertaking.

Over the years, the presiding Lord and Lady Black stood alongside world leaders and those at the forefront of industrialization. They funded scientific discoveries and churches alike. Wherever there was change and progress, they stood behind it, always present but never the center of attention, allowing those who sought the limelight to have their stage.

They were, after all, above such things. Peter's mother was dead, and his father had many years left, God willing. It was Evelyn's responsibility to acquaint herself with the family's ways and customs and to understand the role she would have and the responsibility that would one day be placed upon her shoulders. She had to learn to be worthy of her title, and it was a task that caused her much anxiety.

Some had seemed surprised when Peter began to court Evelyn, including, to her unease, young women she had considered friends. The raised eyebrows and the slight shock within their voices had only added to her feelings of ineptitude. What if they were right? What if she wasn't good enough?

At a luncheon, a friend's older brother had expressed such surprise. Evelyn had colored slightly, shrinking noticeably. A tiny part of her worried that Peter may take such veiled criticism to heart and perhaps change his mind and choose someone worthier, someone wealthier, someone with a title of their own, or a connection to royalty. Peter must have sensed it as he placed his hand on hers beneath the table, squeezing it gently.

He had spent the entire afternoon complimenting her loudly, inserting any accomplishment of hers or slight talent she possessed into every conversation, staring at her with admiring eyes. In the end, it was her friend's brother who had blushed and stammered. Evelyn had never felt as special or beautiful in her life. That was one of Peter's greatest talents—he could make someone feel as if they were the most important person in the world, and he had never had a more interesting conversation in his life. It was no small wonder he had such influence at Parliament.

In the midst of the many portraits hung a solitary landscape—a dark, cloudy sky hung over a vast wasteland of empty moor. The unending brown and gray was broken only by a handful of large, leafless trees bent and twisted by harsh weather, as a single gray stone house jutted from the earth like a tombstone. The house—a large, old-fashioned manor with a dozen smokeless chimneys and darkened windows—appeared as lifeless as its surroundings, but for a single window on the upper right-hand side which, when closely examined, showed a small shadowy figure lit by the glow of a single light. Evelyn stared hard at the painting, lost in its vast emptiness and wondering who the lone figure was. She didn't know how long she had stood there, lost in her thoughts, but when she felt a hand on her shoulder, she jumped at its touch.

"I'm sorry, ma'am. I didn't mean to frighten you."

It was Lilly who had probably come to see what was taking her so long. Embarrassed, Evelyn turned back to the paintings, heat rising in her cheeks. She was a woman now, a wife, and the lady of the house, and here she was behaving like a child, afraid of its own shadow.

"That's quite alright. Seems I was quite lost in a world of my own."

Lilly smiled sympathetically before leading her toward the dining room and the scent of freshly made tea. Evelyn glanced back at the painting, her eyes falling on that small figure once more before moving to the brass label that adorned its gold gilt frame. The plaque identified a place she had never heard of and was sure she never wanted to visit. She whispered the words to herself, not only to break the spell but also to ensure she would never forget it:

"Blackthorn House."

Lilly led Evelyn into the dining room, where a single place setting lay on the large rectangular table. As Lilly pulled the chair for her to sit, Evelyn was suddenly saddened by the room. She had imagined her first morning with Peter as a pleasant ritual, the first of many meals they would share as husband and wife. Now, she sat alone, the sheer size of the table and its many empty chairs seeming to mock her. Again, she wondered why he had chosen not to wake her, and a small flame of hurt and anger sparked within, bringing color to her cheeks.

A tray was placed before her, the scent of toast and freshly brewed tea making her salivate. She had not realized how hungry she was. Lilly poured her a cup in silence, the steam rising and dissipating around her like a light mist.

The staff here were always so perfunctory, so mechanical, and precise in their duties. It was a stark contrast to the much more informal and friendlier atmosphere of her own home, where staff conversed openly and freely and, having worked for her family for many years, were as much a part of it as herself. On the occasions Evelyn had spent at the house, not a single member of Peter's staff spoke without cause, and rarely did they make direct eye contact. It was something Evelyn had always found rather uncomfortable.

"Would you sit a moment, Lilly?"

"Ma'am?" Her green eyes widened with confusion and perhaps even a sliver of fear.

Evelyn's discomfort increased. "You aren't in any trouble. I just wanted to know you a little better since we will be spending so much time together going forward."

Evelyn wasn't lying when she said this. She had always planned to become more familiar with the many people she now shared her home with. But mostly, the empty chairs seemed to surround her in judgment, and the urge to break the room's silence was overwhelming.

Lilly eyed her suspiciously but obediently and carefully removed the chair from beside Evelyn, sitting delicately on its edge and smoothing her skirts. She had a small burn on one side of her apron, a black iris surrounded by bleeding brown, and a fresh cut on her right index finger, clumsily bandaged. "Tea?"

"No, thank you, ma'am. I never much cared for it myself." Her accent had a lilt to it, a twang which showed she had country roots, which Evelyn couldn't quite place.

"Have you worked for Pet—Mr. Black long?"

"Since August, ma'am."

Evelyn inwardly sighed with relief, realizing Lilly was also a newer addition to the household. There was another in the house who understood her trepidation—an ally of sorts.

"Where did you work prior?"

"This is my first posting, ma'am. I came straight from Saint Mary's."

Evelyn was well aware of Saint Mary's. Part orphanage, part finishing school, it took in young girls in need and taught them the basics required to work as servants for the wealthy families of London and the surrounding areas. She was surprised to learn Peter had hired someone so inexperienced, particularly for such a front-of-house role. Lilly was to be Evelyn's personal maid and, as such, would do everything from helping her lace her corsets to fetching her meals, as she had that morning.

Peter had struck Evelyn as being very particular about the people he surrounded himself with. His conversations with those beyond his focused attention would be polite but perfunctory, and he only accepted invitations from the most prestigious families, snubbing those with "new money," much to their chagrin. Yet here, he had hired someone with no practical job experience. Evelyn realized she knew even less about her new husband than she initially supposed. The thought sat tight in her center, a solid knot like a piece of unchewed food that had been swallowed too quickly.

"And where are you from originally?"

"Leeds, ma'am. My father brought us here for work when I was small, but it's just me now."

A wet sheen appeared over Lilly's green eyes, and Evelyn understood why she had ended up in Saint Mary's. She softened her voice. "And how do you find it here?"

"I'm very grateful to have employment. Many aren't so lucky."

It was an oddly vague and deliberate answer that caught Evelyn a little off guard. She was about to probe her further when she became aware of Peter standing silently by the door, his hat and gloves in hand. Lilly, as surprised as Evelyn to see him there, stood up a little too fast, sending her chair backward with a thud.

"I'm so sorry, Mr. Black. Please forgive me."

Evelyn rose to help the girl, but Lilly had righted the chair before she could and ran from the room in a black and white blur. Evelyn stood there mute, unsure, the mood of the room and the circumstances therein having changed so abruptly. Peter's eyes followed Lilly as she exited before resting on Evelyn's, staring at her the same way he always did, with a look of curiosity and contemplation. It was his eyes that had first drawn Evelyn to him, the way they seemed to reach into her very soul. They were an icy blue, like the shallows of the sea on a clear day. They were arresting.

"Just awake, my love?"

Embarrassed but unsure why, she felt the color rise again to her porcelain cheeks, staining them a cedar rose. But, as always happened when his eyes held her to attention, they swiftly creased into an affectionate smile, immediately putting her at ease and dispelling any worry she possessed. His eyes were what drew her in, but it was his smile that had sealed their betrothal. The knot in her stomach untied, and she returned his smile with her own.

"Yes, unfortunately, my new husband didn't wake me."

"What a rogue!"

He playfully feigned shock as he spoke, closing the gap between them. She felt goose pimples rise on her skin as he leaned in and kissed her, softly at first, then more firmly, a burning reminder of the night before. Evelyn's head spun as heat rose to her chest, surprised and slightly embarrassed at her urge for more.

The housekeeper, Ms. Farrow, interrupted the intimate moment, carrying another tray. Seemingly oblivious to her intrusion, she set another place for Peter, swiftly placing the items with deft, experienced hands. She may have been beautiful once, but her dark hair was now peppered with gray, and her eyes sat heavy in her head. Evelyn wasn't overly fond of Ms. Farrow. Evelyn was told the old housemaid had been with the Black family since Peter was a boy, and she always eyed Evelyn with suspicion, as if she were a bad smell or a stain that needed to be removed from clean fabric. Evelyn always made a point to smile sweetly at her, amused by the clear irritation it caused in the recipient.

She did so now, but as quickly as she had entered, Ms. Farrow was gone again. Peter poured himself his usual cup of tea—black Earl Grey with a squeeze of lemon juice—before fixing his gaze on his young wife again. "I apologize for not being there when you awoke this morning," he said. "However, I received some rather bad news and had to attend to urgent business matters as a result."

"Bad news?"

"Yes. Sadly, my father passed away yesterday afternoon."

Shock and sorrow immediately filled Evelyn's breast. She thought of losing her mother and how painful it had been. Although children are expected to one day bury their parents —that, after all, is the nature of things—it did not make her loss any less heart-wrenching. To lose a parent so young was something Evelyn understood all too well, and her heart broke for Peter.

"I'm...I'm so sorry, Peter."

Evelyn instinctively moved her hand atop his, a small comfort offered freely. She had never met his father, their courtship having been so fast, and to Evelyn's surprise and disappointment, the elusive Lord Black had been unable to pull himself away from his duties to attend their wedding. It was something that had gnawed at her, giving rise to fear of not being "good enough" for the Black family heritage.

Peter had eased her worry when he explained his father's

temperament. Apparently, his father was a reclusive man who rarely left his estate, which had only worsened in the latter years. Added to those tendencies was a prolonged illness, the details of which Peter had been vague in describing, and his father had not left his home for over a year. They had discussed making introductions at some point in the future, along with the many other plans that all newlyweds discuss as happening at some vague and unknown time. Now, sadly, those introductions would never come to pass. Evelyn supposed his bout of ill health had been more serious than initially thought or had perhaps worsened suddenly, and she struggled to find words of comfort for her new husband.

"Yes, it was rather...unexpected."

Peter stared off beyond her line of sight, lost in thought. There was a sadness in his voice, but also something else just beneath the surface she couldn't quite put her finger on. Something akin to anger, perhaps. He had rarely spoken of his father or his family in general. She wondered if there was animosity there, a falling out that would now never be resolved.

She squeezed his hand a little tighter. Emotions were not something men were encouraged to demonstrate, but she wanted him to know he could express his feelings openly and freely with her. But no tears came. He merely stared into the distance a moment before continuing. "Of course, this changes things for us considerably."

Evelyn gave Peter a puzzled look before his meaning hit home, confusion morphing into understanding, the sudden weight of it pressing heavily down on her. Peter was the next in line and, upon his father's death, the new Lord Black and sole heir to the Black family fortune. She was no longer Mrs. Black—she was to be Lady Black, a title that seemed as alien to her as her new name had been.

Her hand slipped from his as she spoke the words inside her mind, trying to make them real. *Lady Black.* The home where they sat—the one she had daydreamed about, where she had created scenarios and imagined scenes of their life together —would no longer be where they lived. They would be moving to his ancestral home, somewhere she had only seen in the painting upstairs and had heard little about. She didn't even know where it was, and the fears that had sat constantly within her chest since the morning of their wedding swelled at the uncertainty of what was to come.

He must have read it in her eyes. He always seemed to understand her without her having to utter a word. She often wondered if his eyes pierced her so deeply because he could reach inside her mind and read her very thoughts. She felt her face flush, embarrassed at her selfishness, engrossed in her own worries, when her husband had just lost his father. He laid his hand upon hers this time and brushed a stray curl from her cheek with a delicate movement of the other.

"Wherever we live, it will be perfect because we will be together."

She smiled, the fear ebbing slightly. He was right, of course. The journey ahead would be something new for them both, and they would traverse it together, whether it was grieving the loss of a loved one or intimidation at inherited responsibilities. Besides, this was her duty as his wife and companion. She had always known she would inherit these things eventually—it had just come sooner than expected, as everything seemed to when it came to Peter.

Their entire relationship had been a whirlwind of chaperoned meetings punctuated with secret letters delivered hastily and hidden from the world, filled with her favorite love poems painstakingly copied for her in his own hand. Of long, knowing gazes and deliberate grazes of her arm as he offered his jacket. Of hasty, secret kisses in the few moments they had alone—kisses which always left her dizzy and breathless. This was just another part of that same pattern. Evelyn wondered when she would have time to stop and catch her breath. Before she could ask one of the dozen questions echoing inside her mind, he removed his hand and rose from the table.

"Forgive me, my love. As you can imagine, I have much planning and many legal matters to attend to."

He kissed her and headed toward the door before she could make sense of her storm of thoughts. They would not quieten —the many questions rising in volume and pitch, confusing words and emotions. Before he could leave the room, she plucked one from the mess and brought it forth into the world with hurried syllables.

"Where will we live?"

It was not the most important of her queries, but it was the first to form fully into spoken words. It would also be the only answer she received that morning. A morsel when a meal was required, but better than nothing at all. He stopped short of the door and fixed his dark and knowing gaze on her again.

"Yorkshire, in the moors. Blackthorn House is its name."

And with that, he was gone.

Two

It was a dull, cold day when her carriage reached the Yorkshire moors. Thick gray fog sat heavy in the air, seeming to cut them off from the rest of the world. It left drops of moisture on everything it touched and sent a chill down Evelyn's spine, reaching deep inside her bones. The air was still like death, no wind whistling about them as the carriage wound deeper into the gray nothingness. Silence engulfed them, save for the padding of the horses' hooves on the mud road and the rumbling of the carriage wheels.

Evelyn sat alone inside the compartment, her only company her thoughts and *The Turn of The Screw* by Henry James, a recent purchase she had abandoned. Peter had left her two weeks prior to get the house ready—at least, that was how he justified his early departure. Evelyn didn't understand what required such an absence so soon. It was not a summer home filled with sheet-covered furniture like silent ghosts lying in wait for their owner's return, but a house that had remained consistently occupied until its owner's recent passing.

The knot inside her throat tightened, resentment taut

around its edges. There was something else, too—a feeling she tried to dismiss, but one that held steadfast despite her best efforts, lurking at the back of her mind. It was something akin to anxiety, and it seemed to stain the edges of every other emotion, though she could not explain the source nor why it was so impervious to reason. In such times as these, she wished she could speak to her mother. Whilst she believed her to be there with her in some form, a guiding angel, she could not directly seek her advice.

Perhaps it was the unusual way the late Lord Black's funeral had been conducted. The arrangements had been unusually secretive, with the burial being attended by blood relatives only at the request of the deceased. As a result, Evelyn was not allowed to attend, giving Peter further reason to travel ahead alone. Such a thing was unheard of in social circles, with the crowds gathered at one's funeral being seen as a mark of influence and status. Instead, the former Lord Black was dispatched with the same brevity shown to common criminals, a handful of mourners by a graveside. The whole thing just seemed too strange, not that she felt comfortable voicing these thoughts to Peter in his current state of mourning.

Evelyn shifted, the wooden seat groaning with every movement. It had been a long and weary journey; her back felt stiff and her head heavy. In order to stave off discomfort, they were breaking the journey into two parts, spending the intervening night in the small village of Whitwick. After so much wilderness and farmland, the sight of houses gathered closely together, and the feeling of a solid, man-made road brought with them a renewed sense of relief. For the first time in hours, Evelyn forgot about the anxieties that had plagued her for so much of the journey.

Whitwick sat a little more than halfway between London and Blackthorn House, and it had acted as a respite for weary travelers for over a century. The White Horse Inn was a seed from which the rest of the village had grown, and it sat at its heart. Evelyn was looking forward to their accommodation immensely. The thought of a hearty meal, a wash basin, and a large, comfortable bed to stretch out upon sounded heavenly after so many hours cramped inside the carriage.

The carriage slowed as the buildings grew closer together until it finally stopped outside the White Horse. Evelyn heard the driver yell instructions to one another before the door opened, sending fresh, cool air into the damp warmth of the carriage. Lilly stood, her face flushed and her hair damp from the rain that had followed them all the way from London. Ms. Farrow had insisted upon Lilly riding up front with the driver as was "her place." Shame washed over Evelyn at not having insisted she ride alongside her. She had wanted to object to Ms. Farrow, but she had found herself unable to protest in the stern and insistent presence of such a formidable woman. She vowed to be more assertive from now on. After all, she was a woman now, a wife, a Lady.

The Inn was a ramshackle, three-story building painted white with black timbers. A wooden sign depicting a white horse raised on its hind legs hung from rusted chains that squeaked as it swayed in the evening breeze. The street was growing dark, and the light emanating from the Inn's windows cast an inviting glow. Evelyn could hear the sound of rowdy chatter beyond the heavy door, and the smell of gravy drifted out, beckoning them inside.

But as soon as the two women entered the building, every head turned to face them. The sound of boisterous, jovial conversation and clinking glasses ceased instantly, replaced with an awkward, heavy silence. Evelyn froze in the doorway, unable to move or speak in the wake of such scrutiny. The room was not large, yet it was stuffed with bodies, all of whom eyed her suspiciously. Evelyn had been told by her friend, who had passed through the village not one year past, that it was friendly and welcoming. She was also aware of the bustling market that welcomed people from the surrounding counties on a weekly basis. Why then had her arrival acted as a black cloud, darkening the place of any light it had once held?

Anxiety pooled inside Evelyn's chest, and every part of her wanted to leave, to turn away from the mistrustful eyes of these strangers and flee. The carriage suddenly seemed so much more comfortable than it had just minutes before, and she yearned for its silent loneliness once more. It was Lilly who broke the awkward silence, approaching the small, elderly man who stood behind the counter.

"We need rooms for the night and a good meal. I believe you will have received notice to expect us from Ms. Farrow in London."

"Aye, that we did. Your rooms are ready."

He handed Lilly three keys with long, gnarled fingers that shook slightly as he moved. "You and the driver are in the back, downstairs. The Lady is on the top floor."

Evelyn, determined to show she was unaffected by the reaction upon their arrival, added a "thank you" in the most casual tone she could muster.

The old man nodded in acknowledgment but would not meet her eye.

Conversation returned to the room, but it was less enthusiastic. The fire of chatter was not completely extinguished but dampened by her arrival. She started forward after Lilly, refusing to acknowledge their whispers and pointed glares as she passed them. She felt the heat of embarrassment painted on her face and the sting of tears threatening to fall from her eyes, but she remained strong, walking straighter and taller than she normally would, her hands gripping her shawl tighter than necessary to hide their shaking. It felt like the longest walk she had ever taken, despite the small size of the space and the hurried pace with which she crossed it. Evelyn hurried up the stairs, slamming and locking the door behind her just in time to hide her tears from the unnerving spectators below.

By the time Lilly returned with her evening meal, Evelyn had cried herself out, and exhaustion and hunger now outweighed the ignominy of their cold welcome. "Will you eat with me, Lilly? I would be grateful for the company and conversation after traveling so far alone."

"Of course, ma'am. I reckon I could use a little conversation, too."

"Is our driver, Mr. Hill, not an adequate conversationalist?"

"Oh no, ma'am, he can talk alright. Problem is, he never stops, so I can't get a word in edgeways."

Evelyn laughed, an honest and hearty laugh, and just like that, the anxieties had eased. Not for the first time, Evelyn was grateful for Lilly.

After a good meal, a change of clothes, and the deep, uninterrupted sleep of exhaustion, Evelyn felt much more herself upon waking. The evening's events had faded with the darkness, and the bright, early morning sunlight brought with it a new sense of purpose and determination. She was ready to take up their journey once more.

As she packed her book and comb, she felt eyes upon her. She turned to find a woman standing in the doorway to her room, watching her with wide, curious eyes. Startled, Evelyn jumped. She had not even heard the door being opened, never mind unlocked. They stood in silence for a moment, both seemingly unable to proceed. Then, the innkeeper's wife broke the silence.

"The driver, he said you was Lady Black. Are you?"

The question was so out of place, so unexpected, that Evelyn had almost answered in the negative, forgetting for a second about her new name and title. "Yes, I am the new Lady Black."

"And you are going to be living at Blackthorn?"

"Yes, that's correct."

The woman sighed heavily. She was a large woman dressed in a simple linen dress and apron with many stains and marks. She was twice Evelyn's age, perhaps in her late forties, and her plump face shone, making her complexion appear slightly greasy. Her hair was pushed back into a simple bun, a small head scarf fixed to stop strays from escaping and sweat from accumulating. Evelyn recognized her from the evening before. She had stood behind the counter, her eyes down and away from Evelyn and Lilly, a direct contrast to the others surrounding them. She looked tired to Evelyn, resigned to a life of hard work and ungrateful customers.

They stood in silence, staring at each other, the room suddenly seeming so much smaller. Evelyn was unsure what to say or how to act, as the motives and intentions of the woman were unknown. She was not threatening nor angry—indeed, her disposition seemed as nervous as her own—but why she had entered the room unannounced and uninvited was something Evelyn could not even guess. Evelyn spoke, unable to tolerate the heavy silence any longer.

"Is there anything the matter?"

The woman made to speak but could not find the words, her mouth opening and closing slightly like a fish pulled from the water, gasping for breath. She wrung her hands, twisting the apron around one so hard that it turned pale. Without speaking, she removed a small parcel, hastily wrapped in brown paper and tied in twine, and set it on the washstand beside her. Evelyn eyed it curiously.

"For you, ma'am."

Evelyn nodded, unsure as to what it could possibly be. It was clearly not a letter or parcel sent by post—there were no markings, no sign of its journey through the mailing system.

The woman only piqued Evelyn's curiosity further when she firmly exclaimed, "Do not open it here—make sure of it."

And with that, she turned and left the room, leaving Evelyn quite bewildered.

Evelyn lifted the small package and squeezed it in her fingers. There was something small and firm within its many layers. It was not heavy, and there was no note accompanying it nor an explanation about where it had come from or who had sent it. Curiosity flooded her as she turned it over in her hand. Still, not wanting to cause any issues or confrontation, nor to delay their leaving, Evelyn did as she was bid and did not open it, instead hiding it within the folds of her skirt.

The bill was settled, the horses readied, and their journey could resume. All the while, Evelyn was aware of the little package that sat in her pocket. The inn was still in sight, them having only just set off, when Evelyn, unable to wait any longer, unwrapped the parcel with the clumsy, hurried hands of a child at Christmas. Inside the brown paper, she found a plain lace handkerchief, clean but stained brown with age, folded neatly into a square. Within its folds was a crudely carved wooden rosary and crucifix, the face of Jesus worn smooth by a million Hail Marys.

Evelyn stared at it, confused. Why had the woman given her this? It was clearly something precious, used well and often, perhaps by the woman herself or a family member. It appeared old, but was clearly important to have been wrapped so precisely and carefully. But Evelyn knew the answers to these questions—the woman had all but told her when she had asked Evelyn her name. *And you are going to be living at Blackthorn?* The image of that painting rose inside Evelyn's mind—the house seeming so desolate, so bleak. She thought about the lone figure staring at her from within and the reaction her arrival had caused.

Evelyn absentmindedly stroked the smooth, featureless face

of Christ. She stared out of the carriage window at the shadowy world beyond, wondering what exactly lay ahead as the carriage continued along its journey, moving ever closer to her new life and home. Moving ever closer to Blackthorn House.

A stone gargoyle emerged from the thick gray curtain of fog like a wild beast, half its face crumbled and moss-covered with age and neglect. The bumps and jolts of infrequently traveled roads became smooth as the carriage trundled along a long and winding drive, the gravel beneath the wheels sounding like broken glass. Evelyn's heartbeat increased as she felt the conveyance slow and roll to a stop.

Outside, she heard voices mixed with the sounds of horses braying and straps being undone. The carriage shifted slightly from side to side as each bag was removed, every part of her life neatly and carefully folded and packed to be shipped to its new destination. She stared out into the ever-decreasing light of late afternoon, searching for clues about what lay beyond, but found only that same thick, gray cloud that seemed to have followed them all the way from London. She wasn't sure what she was waiting for or why she was reluctant to exit the carriage, but something held her back, an invisible hand placed across her torso, silently telling her to remain inside. Her decision was made for her as the door abruptly opened, sending a wave of cold into the compartment.

"We've arrived, ma'am."

Lilly stood clutching her shawl about her slight frame with one hand, the other holding a well-worn leather bag, the contents of which represented the entirety of the maid's possessions.

Evelyn braced herself for the cold November air, her heart still noticeably beating beneath her corset. Alighting from the carriage, she found herself face to face with a large circular fountain, which must have been the turning circle at the top of the house's drive.

Carved from stone and empty of water—not unusual for that time of year—it appeared to have remained unused for quite some time, the stagnant water within the base giving off a smell of rotten leaves. Green moss and black mold coated the once elaborate carvings, giving the depicted figures a look of infection or plague. Evelyn squinted at it, trying to decipher what the carvings represented. It seemed to be some kind of gathering, but was it a party or a battle? She couldn't tell, as the grime was in such abundance, but there were definitely human figures, as well as animals, and a strange selection of symbols she had never seen before. Eager to put her stamp on her new home, she made a mental note to have it cleaned as soon as possible.

Lost in thought, Evelyn hadn't noticed the absence of Lilly and the driver. To her surprise, she stood quite alone in the thick fog, the only things visible to her being the fountain and the carriage itself, the horses nervously pawing at the gravel beneath them. The familiar anxiety began to grow, and she slowly made her way around the animals, careful to give them a wide berth. There was an eeriness to the silence surrounding her as if the fog was so thick that it smothered the noises of any life within. London was infamous for its fog—the smoke and soot of industrialization mixing with the dreary dampness of the British weather, combining to form an ever-present grayness to the city. Still, even when the fog in London was at its worst, it was no comparison to Evelyn's current surroundings.

Carefully, she moved in the direction she believed the house to be. The only sound was the crunch of the gravel beneath her cautious steps and the ragged sound of her own small breaths. She knew there were people nearby—of course, there were—yet she felt so utterly lost and alone. On more than one occasion, she opened her mouth to call out for Lilly or

Peter, but each time, something stopped her. She felt like a child playing a game of hide and seek, afraid to give away her position, but what she was seeking and from whom she was hiding, she did not know. She moved forward slowly, the mist drifting about her like tendrils of some otherworldly being clawing at her clothes and shoes. Unlike the fogs of London, this one was so thick it seemed to have a heft to it, weighing her down and threatening to root her to the spot.

A giggle punctuated the silence. Evelyn spun to see who was behind her, but there was no one, just the same gray nothingness. The carriage and fountain were now merely shadows behind gossamer, but beyond that, there was nothing and no one. Yet that same feeling haunted her, followed her as she turned her head this way and that, trying to make out the shape of a person within the soundless gray cloud. Someone was watching her.

"Hello? Lilly?"

Evelyn didn't know why she had called Lilly's name—she knew it had not been her. The giggle was definitely that of a child, but there were none in sight despite it sounding so very close by. Another followed, this time directly behind her, yet when she whirled to face it, there was no one there. Her heart pounded, and she increased her pace, kicking gravel with every hurried step. It felt as if she had slipped into another world, a realm of shadows and disembodied voices. Another giggle came along with the feeling of someone smaller running by, their hands and skirts grazing her own. Yet when she looked, she saw no one.

"Hello? Who's there?"

She hated how her voice quivered as she spoke; it made her sound so much younger, so much weaker, like the times during childhood when she was convinced that a shadow in the darkness of her bedchamber was some kind of monster come to snatch her in the night. Hurried footsteps approached her from her right without any apparent cause or owner, and once more, something brushed past her, causing her skirts to swish and move by some invisible force. It quickly passed, its footsteps receding into the fog once more.

Fear captured Evelyn and held her tight in its grasp. She felt unable to move, unable to run, or to cry out. She was a statue in the gardens, a woman of stone. Sweat prickled on her face despite the coldness, and her heart thumped within her chest like a drum. An internal monologue ran inside her mind, her own voice listing reasons why what she was experiencing could not be real: she was tired from her journey, the innkeeper and her religious offering spooked her, she was being childish and silly, the fog was playing tricks. None of these seemed to convince her of some earthly explanation. She was simply too afraid.

The rush of her thoughts was suddenly interrupted by another giggle, this one so close to her ear she could feel the breath of whoever made it, yet there was no one and nothing there. This deliberate closeness sent terror surging through her veins and jolted her from her frozen state. All at once, she came back to life, her limbs working freely once more, and she spun away from the invisible source of the noise, eyes darting back and forth, scanning for a person or shape she knew she wouldn't find as a scream built inside her throat. She hurled herself forward, desperate to evade the creature tormenting her. She had become disoriented and no longer knew where the carriage or house was, blindly running forward and praying she would find Lilly, Peter, or any of the staff—anyone with a solid form and a living, beating heart.

She wasn't sure how long she had been running, but sweat now clung to her tired body, and she struggled to catch her breath. A sharp stitch in her side sent a jolt of pain into her body with every clumsy step. She started to fear she was running in the wrong direction, inadvertently heading out into the desolate and treacherous moors, but she still felt the gravel beneath her shoes, kicking a spray of it up and out with every panicked step. The fog surrounded her, a constant wall of nothingness, a blank of gray and shadow. There were no shapes, no landmarks; there were no people or buildings—just a never-ending ocean of nothingness. Panic surged as she feared she would never escape when, without warning, she found herself on stone ground, the house suddenly before her, backlit by the last of the dying sunlight, a vast black rectangle on the canvas of the sky. She let out a small scream as she ran into Peter, who had appeared just as abruptly, catching her as she stumbled to a stop.

"Good Lord, Evelyn, what's the matter? Are you alright?"

She embraced him, grateful for his solid feel, weighting her back into her own world. She had made it. She had escaped that awful void and found her love once more. Relief washed over her, and she felt exhausted, drained of energy and fight.

Peter looked alarmed, his eyebrows scrunched together in confusion and concern.

She turned to point into the fog, to where she had heard the ghostly voice, to explain to him what had happened and relay her terrible ordeal. She stopped short. It was certainly foggy, but the thick, weighted world of gray she had been running through in fear was gone. Instead, small wisps of mist hung around the carriage and fountain, clearly visible and only fifty yards or so from where she stood. Indeed, it was bright enough for her to see most of the driveway, and although the world beyond it remained obscured, the entire front of the house—a large and expansive patch of ground—was clear and open. There was no thick curtain of fog obscuring the world beyond. There was no ocean of nothing surrounding the house, isolating them, cutting them off. There was just a light mist, a dreary day, an ordinary landscape devoid of any creatures or ghostly children. What's more, she could clearly hear the sounds of boxes and bags being carried up the steps to the house. She could see the staff—more than a handful of people —rushing back and forth, carrying out their duties with quiet dedication.

Confusion overwhelmed her as everything blurred through tear-filled eyes. She found her hand instinctively reaching for her mother's pearls and crucifix hidden beneath her blouse, seeking a tether to the here and now, to reality and normality. She thought of her mother and tried to feel her presence, wishing for her to somehow reassure her. She prayed silently there in the cold, under the shadow of her new home. She prayed for answers, for understanding. She prayed for strength. But, most of all, she prayed for her sanity, that she would not lose her mind as her mother had before her. She prayed for her soul.

"Whatever is the matter, Evelyn?"

When she removed her face from his now tear-stained shirt, she could see the confused looks directed at her. Lilly stood nearby, her own face crumpled in concern. The sudden embarrassment of her outburst washed over her, painting her face an ever-deepening shade of crimson.

Quickly, she turned from Peter, wiping the tears from her cheeks and composing herself as best she could.

"Evelyn?" he repeated.

"I'm fine, I'm fine. I'm just exhausted from the journey, and I feel a little odd. I think I need to lie down."

Peter stared at her, brows furrowed in an expression Evelyn couldn't quite interpret. It was clear, however, that he did not believe her. Ever the polite and proper gentleman, he softened it slightly and responded with a diplomatic "Of course" before offering her his arm and leading her toward the front doors.

She took it, grateful he had not pressed the subject and had allowed her to reclaim a modicum of her dignity. As first impressions went, Evelyn had made a poor one on the residents of Blackthorn House.

As they walked, Evelyn tried to take in the details of her new home. A vast gray stone wall rose toward the darkened sky, punctuated by windows reflecting their ghostly frames as they moved past. Tangled ivy and thorn-covered branches clung to the masonry walls, twisting their way upwards. Though impressive in both size and design, there was a certain eeriness to it that Evelyn could not escape. She tried to tell herself it was merely the after-effects of her scare a few moments prior, but she knew it was more than that. The stone in which it was constructed was as gray as the fog surrounding it now, reflecting the dull winter sky above. The notable absence of color gave everything a dour and dreary vibe; even the green of the ivy leaves seemed darkened by its proximity to the house as if everything there lived in perpetual shadow.

The front door was solid, but the black paint had begun to crack and chip away, seemingly as neglected as the fountain beyond. The iron door knocker, peppered with rust, was shaped like some kind of monster's head, the ring held tightly in its toothy mouth, grimacing at her as she passed. Above the doors, carved from the same gray stone as the rest of the house, was the Black family crest—a fierce wolf baring its teeth within a round shield. Its edges were worn from a century of English weather, giving the wolf an emaciated, skeletal appearance.

Evelyn held her breath as she crossed its threshold, something she had done with her brother when they would enter a church or burial ground as children, a sign of respect and of childish fear. A silly superstition adopted by all the children in her family who believed that to breathe freely amongst the dead was an affront to them, a reminder of something they had ceased to do. Why she did so now, she could not explain, but somehow, it felt important to do.

The grand entrance hall made the wealth of the Black

family clear to all who entered. High above, a ceiling rose bloomed outwards, and at its center, a black chandelier made of twisted iron and red glass pendants cast dots of red light about the room. The black and white tiled floor gave Evelyn the impression of a giant chessboard and the feeling of being merely a pawn maneuvered across its surface. Long, red velvet curtains framed the closed double doors to the rooms on each side of her, and the dual staircase ahead was covered in a matching red carpet.

Heavy marble busts atop matching columns dotted the space, and prominently featured on the wall at the top of the staircase was a single painting that Evelyn recognized instantly —Blackthorn House. Identical to the one hanging on the wall of Peter's London home, its much larger size only seemed to magnify the painting's eerie quality. Just like the other painting, the house stood alone among the vast surrounding moors, all darkness apart from the single-lit window, the shadow of a figure peering from within. Evelyn shuddered as she saw it there, though she did not know why. It was only as they continued to move toward it, the image increasing in size as they grew nearer, that she realized it was not, in fact, an exact replica of Peter's painting. Where the lit window in his painting had been on the upper right of the building, this one was on the furthest left window of the second floor. Where his had contained a single shadowy figure, this one contained two, both smaller in stature, standing side by side, facing out of the painting toward her.

Both of them were clearly children.

Three

When Evelyn jolted awake, it was nighttime. She felt as though she had traveled through time, as if the hours that had passed since her arrival had been cut from her day entirely. She sat up slowly, rubbing her eyes as she tried to recall how she had gotten there, sleeping fully clothed atop her new bed.

She remembered Peter leading her toward her room and the hallways of closed doors she passed, a blur of unknown places yet to be explored. Her room was adjacent to her husband's, as was tradition amongst the wealthy at that time, with an adjoining door to allow partners to live together while maintaining their privacy. He had reassured her of its normalcy as he led her to bed as if it somehow provided the closeness from him she yearned for so deeply. The stone and wood between them made her feel more like a neighbor than a wife.

As an adolescent, she recalled asking her chambermaid why married couples chose to live this dichotomous existence. She had responded in a way that Evelyn had found both wise and ominous, "Everyone needs their little secrets, dear."

Evelyn stared at the clock—it was just after two—then glanced at the door separating her from Peter. He would be asleep, of course, and she shouldn't wake him, but she longed to be with him. He was always so confident and self-assured, and that steadfast attitude always steadied her turbulent, anxious mind. He felt like a rock to cling to, and she yearned for that stability now.

She had hoped that marriage would bring with it a sense of maturity, an understanding of the world and its ways, as if every silly young girl merely needed a metal band on her finger to develop and grow. But at that moment, she felt more like a young girl than a woman. She thought of the phantom child she had encountered in the fog, of the disembodied laughter and the invisible eyes. She wanted to dismiss the event as the result of the overactive imagination of a sleep-deprived mind, but it had seemed so real. Her mother had seen things too—she had conversations with invisible people she insisted were there. Could Evelyn have inherited her mother's illness?

"Mother?" she whispered aloud, knowing she would receive no answer.

She closed her eyes tightly, tears threatening to spill forth, and tried to force the thoughts from her mind. To steady her heart and distract her from those sorrowful thoughts, she focused on what she knew was real, what she could see and touch.

Her room was richly furnished, with a mahogany four-poster bed elaborately carved with vines, flowers, and ivy leaves, giving the impression that the natural world from which the wood had been torn was still inside the grain, threatening to burst forth at any moment. It sat in the center of a plush red and navy Persian rug, a vibrant pattern of color and shapes in the middle of the dark wood floor. As with the few parts of the house she had seen so far, red was the primary color of decoration, and heavy red velvet drapes hung around her bed and at the window. They were all held in place with red tassels, the fringing of which moved slightly from a draft passing through the room.

While the color palette was warm, the chill in the atmosphere was distinctive and determined. Evelyn was grateful for the stone fireplace opposite her that contained the last dying embers of a fire. She placed another layer of wood and paper, just as her father had taught her as a child, and encouraged the flames back out from their graves. Soon, heat returned to the space and bathed it in a warm glow. The fireplace itself was carved with a lion motif. Each end of the mantle became the head of a lion, frozen forever in a vicious roar. The firelight cast shadows about their faces, giving Evelyn the uneasy impression that they were watching her, their heads moving slowly to follow her about the room.

A mahogany wardrobe and dresser sat to her right, and the pale reflection of her tired face stared back at her like a ghost. Her long journey and scare had clearly affected her more than she thought, and she wore them on her pallid, gray face. She looked tired, weary.

She also found herself hungry, her stomach audibly protesting its empty state. She glanced again at Peter's door but wouldn't dare wake him at such an hour. Lilly, too, would be asleep and would need her rest as much as Evelyn did. She looked toward the door that led into the hallway beyond and felt her stomach lurch at the thought of exploring Blackthorn alone at night, yet what choice did she have? While her journey to her new room had been a blur, she was sure she could retrace her steps back to the main hall and, from there, to the kitchen. Yet even as she told herself these things, the voice within her mind wavered, her anxieties about what she had experienced in the fog sitting heavy in her stomach like undigested meat. But that same stomach rumbled, unable to be satiated by such folly, so Evelyn slowly turned the handle of her door and stepped into the dark corridor beyond.

The corridor was a vast length of black punctuated by patches of illumination where moonlight had found its way through the heavy velvet drapes. It cast strange shadows and gave ordinary objects an unearthly quality. She had a single candle she had retrieved from her bedside, which provided barely enough light to aid her journey, but in whose humble warmth and glow she found a small amount of comfort. There was a deathly stillness to the place, as if the building itself held its breath. As she moved along, she tried to fill the unnerving silence by humming a nursery rhyme her mother had sung during thunderstorms or after her brother had scared her with a ghost story. *Sing a song of sixpence, a pocketful of rye.* The image of a pie full of singing birds or a maid having her nose pinched by a blackbird had always made her giggle, but at that moment, alone in a strange and unfamiliar place in the dark of night, it brought her little comfort. Her hand moved towards her mother's pearls, too, a gesture which always helped her steady its shaking.

The warm, yellow glow of the candle illuminated the stern faces of various portraits, their eyes seeming to follow her in silent judgment. The entire length of the corridor was adorned with them—an entire jury of men, all with Peter's piercing blue eyes. Those eyes, it seemed, were inherited along with their title. The carpet was a runner, only covering the middle portion of the floor and leaving the hardwood exposed on either side. It gave Evelyn the impression of the red carpets rolled out for royalty, and she wondered if that had been deliberate.

Halfway down, a marble-top table sat, its bright whiteness reflecting the moonlight. At its center sat an ornament carved out of black stone or marble. It depicted a wolf tearing apart a small lamb, its teeth bared in a terrible grimace as the lamb hung lifeless in its mouth, its eyes frozen forever in fear. Evelyn shuddered, partly because of the cold and partly because of the many painted eyes that seemed to watch her, not the least of which was the wolf's own hungry gaze, which also seemed to follow her journey.

Taking a left, she found herself at a dead end. On the door ahead of her, half hidden by a drape, was a sign that read, "Staff" in faded, gold letters. She tutted in disappointment and chastised herself inwardly for having obviously taken a wrong turn somewhere. This door would lead to the servants' quarters and to the various rooms downstairs where they carried out their duties for the Black family. It was not a place to wander into alone, especially at night.

As she turned to walk back, the light of her candle caught the shadow of a figure behind the curtains of a nearby window. Evelyn jumped backward with a small yelp, hitting her shoulder hard on the wall behind her. The candle in her hand shook violently, causing shadows to dance about her. Her heartbeat drummed as fear took hold. She held the candlestick out before her like a weapon, as if its light would somehow protect her. There was definitely a shadow there, distinctly human-shaped, though much shorter than herself.

The house became alive. Creaking footsteps from the opposite end of the corridor drew closer and louder, coming toward her at a determined pace. Thrusting the candlestick outwards, she squinted into the darkness, readying herself to come face to face with whoever it was, but no one ever came, and no movement could be seen. Still, the sounds kept coming closer and closer, louder and louder, as Evelyn shrank back into the corner as far as she could, terrified of what she would see.

They were so close she should be able to see them, or at least their owner's silhouette, but still, there was nothing but the black emptiness of the corridor beyond. Closer and closer they came until the floorboards creaked and moaned mere feet from where she stood, shaking, before they stopped just in front of the window and the mysterious shadow hiding behind the drapes. Goosebumps erupted across Evelyn's skin, the invisible entity bringing a chill like none other she had ever experienced. It seemed to immediately envelop her and permeate her clothing, her very flesh. It struck her so suddenly and with such fierceness that it almost took her breath away.

Evelyn held her breath, her heart pounding so hard she feared it would burst through her chest before the curtains suddenly opened of their own accord to reveal the bright moonlit night beyond. Something inside Evelyn took hold then —be it an ancient survival instinct or a reflexive action.

Forcing herself from the wall, she ran as fast as she could, retracing her steps back to her room, back to the safety of her bed and the warmth of her fireplace. She felt the coldness increase as she passed the window, and for just a moment, she could see her breath. But just as quickly as she had felt it arrive did it ebb away, normal temperature returning as she moved further and further from the window behind her, the brightness of the moonlight fading back to familiar darkness once she had turned the corner. But she never slowed, never stopped until she reached her room and turned the key within the lock before collapsing against the door as her legs gave way. The instinctual burst of energy, having served its purpose, now dissipated, and she found herself exhausted.

She placed the candle, burned almost completely down to the brass holder, onto the nightstand with trembling hands and gathered herself under the covers as she had as a child, the blankets offering the illusion and comfort of protection from the unknown beyond. She lay there shivering, her mother's pearls clutched in one hand, the other holding her knees to her chest. She played what had just happened over and over again inside her mind. She tried to tell herself it had been her imagination playing tricks and that she was tired and didn't really know what she had experienced. But Evelyn could not shake the thoughts from her mind now, no matter how desperately she tried. Thoughts of footsteps without a person to make them, of a shadow cast without a person to cast it, of a deathly cold like none other she had experienced, and worst of all, of a voice so small, so quiet it was barely audible above Evelyn's ragged breathing. Yet she knew she had heard it.

"Father, don't."

Four

Evelyn awoke to the sound of Lilly's quiet knock. Daylight crept beneath the velvet drapes and brought a yearning for comfort. But despite the daylight chasing away the shadows, Evelyn could not shake the things she had experienced or the sense of dread and foreboding that accompanied them. She smiled weakly at the young maid as she carefully placed Evelyn's breakfast tray on the edge of her bed. The weight of sleep still hung heavy on her weary body, and the thought of food now made her nauseous.

Evelyn had replayed what she had experienced repeatedly until her exhausted mind succumbed to sleep, but she was still unable to find a logical explanation. As much as she wanted to dismiss them as the temporary visions of a sleep-deprived mind or some kind of nightmare with a real and existing cause, something curable or fixable, she couldn't do so. It had simply felt too real, too vivid to be explained away as nothing. She thought about the shadowy figure in the window, of the footsteps with no owner, and the small, terrified voice: *Father, don't.*

She shivered, the mere memory of that coldness enough to cause a physical reaction.

Lilly watched her, concern noticeable on her furrowed brow.

"I didn't sleep very well," Evelyn explained. "I wish to be dressed first; I'm not hungry just yet."

Lilly looked at her a moment longer, but if she suspected something was wrong, she held her tongue, instead obediently retrieving Evelyn's various items of clothing before dressing her with gentle hands. Unable, or perhaps more accurately, unwilling to talk of her experiences, Evelyn remained silent throughout, only speaking again to dismiss Lilly with thanks. Their normal morning routine consisted of chatter and smiles, but her mind could think of nothing but that shadow, that voice.

Father, don't.

Evelyn twisted and molded her thoughts until they were tangled, and now she was left with only two possibilities. The first was that Blackthorn House was haunted. Evelyn had always told herself she did not believe in ghosts—she had even shouted it indignantly at her brother on more than one occasion when he had sought to scare her with one of his stories. But in truth, Evelyn had always felt there was something beyond this world. It was the reason she always wore her mother's pearls. They were a physical connection between her and her mother, wherever she was now. Was it possible the building was truly haunted? She laughed out loud to herself at the absurdity of such a notion.

But, just as quickly, her smile fell and turned into a face marred by fear and grief, for the alternative was much more horrifying. This is how it had started with her mother—this was how she came to die. Could it be that Evelyn was destined to meet the same terrible fate?

Evelyn's mother, Grace, had been the epitome of her name.

She was beloved by friends and family alike, and it was always said she would light up every room she entered. Evelyn saw her mother through the lens of time, twelve years having passed since she died, and as she knew, time had a way of softening and filtering memories. Often, she would remember events as a third-party observer of her own life, things slightly differently each time, some details added by her memories and some by the remembrance of others, gained from stories told around the fire. Despite knowing all this, Evelyn swore she could see the light emanating from her mother even back then. Grace had a glow that grew in intensity when she smiled. To the young Evelyn, she had been like an angel or a star, a celestial being who had drawn Evelyn into her orbit and kept her there long after she had died. And, although she believed her mother had remained with her, in some form, that light had disappeared. It had become a black hole, an aching void where love had once been.

Evelyn dug through her small leather bag, the one she had insisted remain with her, having refused to allow it to suffer the indignity of being strapped atop the carriage. This was where she had carried her most precious objects. None of the things within were particularly valuable, but to her, they were priceless. Inside was a book gifted to her by her father, which he had received from his father, *Ulysses* by Lord Tennyson. It had sparked in Evelyn a love of literature and poetry and had connected her to her father in a way that only they shared, as if they were two members of a secret club. The bag also contained a handful of battered, well-used lead soldiers, which she now placed on the mantle—her very own army. To settle her restless hands and mind, she began to unpack, adding her little treasures to the room to make it her own.

The smallest things triggered the most intense memories, like the smell of honeysuckle or the taste of elderflower cordial, her mother's specialty. She could recall moments with such clarity, which seemed so innocuous and ordinary at the time, but now she saw them for what they were—stitches in a beautiful yet sadly unfinished tapestry.

It had started small. Her mother had always had nightmares, but toward the end, they increased both in frequency and intensity. Grace began to sleepwalk, exploring the house and grounds at night in only her nightdress. She'd be discovered the next day, shivering in some far-off closet, with dirty feet and no memory of where she had been. She talked to herself and saw things that weren't there. Slowly, her interactions with social engagements and clubs—the events and people she loved—began to lessen until she had closed herself off from the world. The bags beneath her eyes grew darker, and her smile became sadder.

Evelyn was still young. She didn't understand what was happening, and when she would ask, her father and older brother would merely tell her that Mama was sick and just needed her rest. Doctors visited more frequently, dosing her mother with every concoction and potion they carried in their big leather bags. Evelyn hated the bottles and vials that littered her mother's bathroom cabinets, which were filled with foul-smelling elixirs and tablets that looked like pieces of chalk. They had made her mother so detached from everything, as if she were trapped inside her body, slow to react and understand, sleeping most of the day. They made her a shadow, a pale reflection of who she had once been.

So, when Evelyn had discovered a little pile of those chalky pills hidden inside one of her mother's jewelry boxes, she had sworn to her mother she would never tell anyone. After all, her mother seemed so much more alive, so much more herself without them. And Evelyn had been glad to have her back, to look into her mother's eyes and see her there once more. She didn't understand what the medications had been for. The words she had overheard the doctors whisper to her father, such as *hysteria,* had meant nothing to her. She had no notion of mental illness, of hallucinations or seizures—she just knew her mother.

Not a day had passed since then that Evelyn hadn't wished she had broken her promise. But hindsight is a curse that brings no comfort, and Evelyn would have to carry that guilt, rightly or wrongly, for the rest of her life.

The last thing Grace had done before taking her final walk through the gardens was to give Evelyn the pearls she had always worn, even while confined to bed (she had always said that any outfit, even a ratty old nightgown, could be made instantly glamorous with a set of pearls—something which never failed to make Evelyn laugh). She had placed them gently in Evelyn's hand, closing her tiny fingers around them and cupping Evelyn's fist in her own. She whispered, "Remember who you are, my love. You have the power inside you, as I did, and you alone decide your fate. Wear these and I will be with you, wherever you are, I will be walking by your side."

To the young, naive Evelyn, it sounded like her mother was planning to journey somewhere. She had even thought it a good idea for her mother to get respite somewhere beautiful with lots of fresh air. She had envisioned a trip to the seaside. It never occurred to her that her mother's plans were more permanent, more destructive.

Then she had kissed Evelyn tenderly—not a simple kiss, displaying affection and love, but one that lingered several heartbeats too long while she inhaled the scent of Evelyn's hair.

It was the last kiss. It was a kiss goodbye.

Fifteen minutes later, she was dead.

She had walked immediately to the barn and stacked crates atop one another, high enough to throw a rope around one of the beams. After tying a noose around her neck, she stepped off the crate and transformed from a woman, a wife, and a mother to something lifeless and empty, a broken doll.

Evelyn couldn't help but draw the parallels between herself and her mother now. Hallucinations had plagued Grace towards the end. Could she be walking a similar path? She stared at her pale, gaunt reflection and saw her mother looking back. With the same large, brown eyes and the same sad smile half-heartedly forced upon her face, it was hard not to believe she was losing her mind.

She thought of Peter. Her mother's illness and subsequent death had marred her father in a very real, permanent way. A part of him died along with her, and he never recovered from that loss. How would Peter react if she were to be similarly afflicted? The thought alone filled her with shame and anxiety.

A short, sharp knock pulled her back to reality, and Peter entered her room without awaiting an invitation as if summoned by her thoughts. "Good morning, darling. How did you sleep?"

Evelyn visibly winced at the question but quickly painted a smile back on her face, determined not to let him see her worrying. "It was good. I feel better." It wasn't a lie exactly, but it was hardly the entire truth.

She thought again about what her maid had told her as a child: "*Everyone needs their secrets.*" She continued before she could allow more memories to cloud her present. "I was hoping you could give me a tour of Blackthorn today. I would love to get to know it better."

The house seemed to creak and groan in response, and she felt the hairs on her neck rise ever so slightly.

"Oh, darling, you don't know how much I wish I could, but I have a few appointments in the village I simply must keep. There are still some matters regarding the estate that need to be settled. You understand, don't you?"

The pang of disappointment, becoming more familiar to Evelyn with each passing day, caused her mask to fall. It had been so long since they had spent any time together, and Evelyn couldn't help but interpret his answer as rejection.

As always, he read this plainly on her face—a talent she was increasingly wishing he did not possess. He sat beside her and placed his hand atop her own, his face immediately softening. "I'm sorry. I know it has been hard for you these past weeks, and I can assure you it's been just as hard for me. I will be back late this afternoon, and we can have dinner together. Our first as Lord and Lady Black in Blackthorn House."

Lord and Lady Black.

The titles still sounded foreign to her, like someone mispronouncing her name. But the thought of real, quality time with him that evening raised her spirits slightly. She nodded in tacit agreement, and he kissed her tenderly in response, drawing her close and enveloping her in his arms. His scent and the feel of his lips against hers brought the warmth she craved, and she yearned for more. She ran her fingers along his neck and into his hair, leaning deeper into the kiss, but before anything more could happen, a knock interrupted their affections, breaking the link that had momentarily formed between them.

Peter pulled back instantly, leaving Evelyn feeling unfulfilled and resentful.

"Enter."

Peter rose, disappointment and frustration dampening the embers glowing between them.

A woman entered the room, and Evelyn vaguely remembered seeing her outside Blackthorn House upon her arrival the day before. She was much older than Evelyn—in her fifties, perhaps—with a stern, plain face and small, sharp eyes that reminded Evelyn of a bird's. Her dark hair, peppered with white, was tied back in a tight bun. She wore a plain black dress with an off-white apron and a single, carved mourning brooch pinned to her lapel. The brooch, while much in fashion at the time for widows to wear, had a symbol on it that Evelyn couldn't quite place. The woman pursed her lips in a frown, looking very much like someone holding many secrets behind that bitter expression.

"Ah, Ms. Winters, just the person I needed. I would like to formally introduce you to my wife, Evelyn, the new Lady Black."

Evelyn rose to stand beside Peter, smiling at the stern face before her. The woman's eyes moved briefly to Evelyn's, her lips pursing as her hand tightened slightly around the large set of keys that hung from her apron belt. It was a subtle gesture many would miss, but Evelyn saw it nonetheless. Ms. Winters clearly did not approve of the new Lady Black. The similarity in temperament between Ms. Winters and Ms. Farrow was immediately apparent to Evelyn as if every man in the Black family required a strict, humorless woman to maintain their homes. She stifled a smile at the thought.

"Evelyn has requested a tour of the house—an excellent idea—but one I am sadly unable to assist with. Perhaps you could oblige?"

Ms. Winters sniffed slightly. "Of course, Milord."

Peter clapped his hands enthusiastically, the problem now satisfactorily solved, and kissed Evelyn's hand under the watchful, disapproving glance of Ms. Winters. "Until tonight," he whispered, and just like that, he was gone, leaving both women to stand in awkward silence.

Evelyn opened her mouth to speak but stopped when Lilly entered with her breakfast tray. Lilly kept her head down, never making eye contact with Evelyn, working in silence. Ms. Winters watched Lilly intently, assessing her every move, and Evelyn could sense immediately that she was not the only person Ms. Winters disapproved of. Clearly, the staff of Blackthorn House were not accustomed to strangers.

When Lilly had completed her tasks, she stood stiffly by the table, a soldier awaiting orders from their commanding officer. She was not the Lilly that Evelyn had become accustomed to.

Clearly, Ms. Winters managed her staff with a stern hand, and Evelyn found herself angered by the woman's snobbish air and haughty attitude. The arrogance of her to look down her nose at Evelyn when she knew nothing about her. And how *dare* she so blatantly attempt to crush the gentle spirit of a young girl like Lilly? Color rose to Evelyn's cheeks as heat rose within her.

Ms. Winters broke this train of thought by clearing her throat and addressing Lilly in a curt, impatient tone. "That will be all, girl. Go about your chores."

"Actually, Ms. Winters, that will not be all. I have further need of Lilly."

Ms. Winters stood in silence, clearly taken aback by Evelyn's assured and authoritative tone. Evelyn saw shock on her puckered face and even a hint of outrage, but, ever the professional, Ms. Winters quickly regained her composure and nodded in understanding. Emboldened by her success, Evelyn continued, a little surprised by her confidence.

"As my lady's maid, I will need Lilly throughout the day. Please ensure she is available. Further, I would like her to accompany us on the house tour since this is a new home for her as well. Shall we say an hour from now, Ms. Winters?"

The hand Ms. Winters had clasped around her keys was now white with tension, her mouth slightly agape. Perhaps she was not used to being given direction by someone so much younger, but there was stark disapproval behind the woman's eyes, maybe even disdain.

"Of course, milady."

Ms. Winters swiftly left before Evelyn had time to say anything more.

There was something about the woman, not just her snooty attitude—it ran deeper. She reminded Evelyn of a fairy tale in a book her mother used to read to her, of a witch living in a gingerbread house that lured children in to eat them. The book contained a woodcut image of the seemingly frail and harmless old woman, her dark, beady eyes staring toward the reader, inviting them into her quaint little home for tea. Ms. Winters bore more than a passing resemblance to that image.

Evelyn recalled something her mother had told her when she read that particular tale: "Always trust your instincts, my love. Often, evil hides behind the most unassuming masks."

Five

Evelyn had learned over the years that houses are not just reflections of the people who live within their walls but a historical record of those who have come before. Some history is presented deliberately—like the austere portraits painted of ancestors long dead or prizes once hunted and won, then stuffed and mounted on walls, their dead eyes replaced with glass, forever trapped within their final moments. But there was always a less visible history, its meaning lost with death or time, or perhaps, even deliberately hidden or painted over.

This was the history that fascinated Evelyn. It was the lines drawn on door frames, each one marking the increasing height and age of a beloved child, or a section of beam unceremoniously removed from a barn, the markings made by a rope too painful a reminder of the life lost at its end. This was the true history of a family and its home, the unedited version not intended for public consumption. This was the history Evelyn now sought out among the rooms of Blackthorn House.

Ms. Winters arrived exactly one hour after their conversation and said very little to either Evelyn or Lilly before beginning her tour of the vast, extravagant property. Her descriptions were perfunctory and irritatingly lacking in detail, and she moved at an impatient pace, introducing each room with a quick wave of her hand. Ms. Winters responded to every question Evelyn asked but never fully answered them, as if she only spoke in riddles, Blackthorn's very own sphinx.

"How long ago was Blackthorn House built, Ms. Winters?"

"Oh, the Black family has been on this patch of land for many centuries."

"And this building specifically?"

"Oh, several generations."

It was infuriating, and eventually, Evelyn ceased asking anything at all and merely did her best to take in the details of every room. She felt both impressed and overwhelmed. It seemed strange that this house was her own now—that it belonged, in part, to her. She had been to many grand properties in her lifetime, and indeed, her family owned many, but there was a grandeur to Blackthorn House that Evelyn had never encountered before. It was larger than most estates, of course, the height of the ceiling evoking a sense of awe in all who entered. But it was more than size. Every piece of furniture, every drape, every curio, and every painting was of the highest quality—solid and imposing. The house and its contents were deliberately chosen to present a particular image. Blackthorn was a carefully constructed and curated museum, its artifacts displayed to impress upon its visitors wealth, power, and, of course, taste.

Each bedroom used a slightly different color palette, with the house's overall red and black theme brought in through the elaborate patterns of the fabrics, the paintings, and the rugs and tapestries. One room was a dark and luxurious forest green, while another was a rich sapphire blue. A four-poster bed sat at the center of each one, each elaborately carved in various patterns and motifs—some simple geometric patterns and others thematic of natural elements, animals, or plants. Thick velvet curtains hung from the posters on the frames, allowing whoever slept within to cocoon themselves in complete darkness and warmth. The beds sat atop a thick patterned rug in the same colors as the drapes and bedding, and each faced a huge fireplace carved with predators baring their teeth.

In some rooms, the hunted adorned the floors. Their pelts and skins lay flush against the hardwood floors whilst their heads sat upright, glass eyes watching those tramped upon their backs. To Evelyn, it gave the rather unnerving impression that they were merely playing dead, their mouths and teeth bared in an eternal growl, ready to strike the foot of any who came near. As such, she gave them a wide berth.

Oil paintings depicting stern faces or dark, brooding landscapes adorned the walls, interspersed with the occasional gilt mirror or piece of taxidermy, creating the impression of many eyes, an audience for whoever slept within. Dark wood furniture stood guard around the bed, which only added to the sense of crowding. Even more unsettling, when one examined the artwork more closely, it became apparent that many were not as innocuous as they first appeared. In one painting depicting a fox hunt, a man lay amongst the usual image of horseback hunters donning their shotguns, his face twisted in pain and a red blotch across his chest denoting some kind of terrible injury. The dogs stood around him, some baring their teeth, others merely observing, whilst the hunters simply looked on, unmoved. Was it a hunting accident? Had some poor man been mistaken for a deer or taken a stray bullet? Or had the dogs been set upon him? Whatever had happened to the man, it appeared that the hunters cared little for him and his fate.

In another painting, a farming scene depicted what at first

appeared to be a mother nursing her child whilst her husband tilled the soil nearby. Upon closer inspection, the frozen expression of pain on the mother's face and the tightness of the child's swaddling revealed something much worse. A mother clutched her dead infant, her face twisted with grief, as her husband dug a grave amongst a patch of other stones and markers. It perturbed Evelyn in a way she was unprepared for, and she made a mental note to replace the paintings as she was able.

Thick hand-painted wallpaper in a dozen elaborate patterns and prints lined the hallways. Some corridors boasted jungle scenes, with exotic animals or flowers in bloom. Others were *fleur-de-lis* or simple stripes. But throughout, the same red carpet ran through the center of the floor, a river of blood snaking through every part of the house.

Chandeliers of exquisite French crystal hung in every room, and matching wall sconces ran along the length of the corridors. But despite this and the huge windows in every room, there never seemed to be enough light. Perhaps the dark color scheme and the thickness of the various fabrics somehow absorbed the light, but there was a darkness there, present in every space, regardless of the time and brightness of the day. Regardless, everything about Blackthorn—from the fabric of the drapes to the individual ornaments and paintings chosen for each room—had a resplendence about it. Each room was a showroom, and each item a gilded piece of art. The house felt like a museum, with each exhibit a display of the wealth, success, and taste of the Black family.

Blackthorn was impressive, but as the tour continued at Ms. Winters's hurried pace, Evelyn began to feel an ever-increasing sense of uneasiness. They moved from one jewel-colored bedroom to another, then to a music room filled with every instrument Evelyn could name and several she couldn't. An invisible orchestra, a black grand piano at its center, awaited the directions of a conductor. The sewing room was filled with every color of ribbon and fabric, with several chairs sitting ready with sewing easels and frames, but they seemed rarely used. There were multiple reading and sitting rooms, all with inviting plush chairs and a small polished table beside each, awaiting a drink or book.

Eventually, they reached the smoking room, which was decorated in a much more masculine way than the rest of the house, smelling of rich tobacco and leather. Multiple taxidermy heads were mounted along the walls alongside the brass guns, which had brought about their end. Cut crystal decanters of varying heights sat atop a polished cabinet, holding liquids in a myriad of colors and shades, and green leather club chairs accompanied raised, free-standing brass ashtrays dotted between.

But every room remained shaded and darkly colored, reflecting the dreary moors beyond. Each piece of fabric or upholstery was thick and heavy, stifling the light and air. The thick carpeting muffled their footsteps, and the heavy, walnut-stained furniture crowded every space. The walls were consistently cluttered with somber, lightless paintings, portrait after portrait, scene after scene.

There was a heaviness to the place, as if there was a stronger pull of gravity within its walls, a force that grew stronger the deeper into the house they moved. It began to push down on Evelyn with every step, her breathing becoming more labored until her mind was as full as the house.

Evelyn envisioned the house as some great, hulking creature and the blood-red carpeted corridors its veins. She and Lilly were traveling along inside it, moving deeper and deeper until they were digested or engulfed. Feeling dizzy, she hurried over to a nearby chaise and sank into it. "This is such a grand room; shall we sit a moment and take in its splendor?"

Lilly, kind and attentive as ever, rushed to the window and

opened the sash a couple of inches, allowing the cold, damp air of the moors to leak into the room. Ms. Winters stood by the door, clearly irked at the interruption and further extension of the tour. Her lips were pursed so tightly, Evelyn thought they might never unstick, like a knot tied too tightly.

The house creaked in the silence, and for a moment, she swore the walls were moving inwards somehow, closing in on them like a mousetrap snapping shut. Lilly stared at the same wall as if she, too, sensed its movement. The house, it seemed, was breathing.

Evelyn didn't know why such morbid thoughts crowded her mind, but a part of her, the part inherited from her mother, knew that places and buildings were often affected by the things that happened within them. *Echoes,* her mother had called them. The more emotive the events, the louder the echoes left behind.

She thought of the dilapidated cottage on the edge of her family's estate. The homestead had burned down long before her grandfather was born, and little was known about the place by the time Evelyn had come along. Only a few pieces of broken wall jutting out from the weeds like grave stones and part of a crumbling chimney tangled in ivy and thorns were left.

Evelyn recalled one bright summer day when she and her brother had been playing and came upon the old stones and hunks of charred, weathered wood, remnants of someone's life. Her brother Thomas had climbed on what was left of one of the walls, paying no heed to what it had once been, but Evelyn would not venture on that ground. She felt something emanating from it, a vibration that stopped her dead in her tracks. The place seemed to reside in permanent shadow despite the clear, sunny skies of that August day. Even in the heat of the sun, it felt cold. Thomas had beckoned her to play and even mocked her when she shook her head, adamant she would not go there. That was the day Evelyn had understood what her mother meant by *echoes*.

"Ms. Winters, how many rooms does Blackthorn have in total?"

Ms. Winters inhaled sharply, the question clearly testing her patience further. "One hundred or so."

"So many rooms…so many." Evelyn said it more to herself than to the other women, her mind whirring. To have so many rooms, most to be left untouched, unused, and empty, all felt so overwhelming.

Perhaps not empty, not truly. The thought formed undeterred by her best efforts, and she heard the small voice of the child once more, the sound of laughter and footsteps with no owner. The rooms may be devoid of life, she thought, but they were not empty.

Despite no answer being required or wanted, Ms. Winters snorted a terse, "Indeed," before stomping towards the window and slamming it shut. Without another word, she turned and walked back into the corridor. The tour, it seemed, had resumed, whether Evelyn was ready or not.

They soon turned a corner and entered a corridor that Evelyn knew all too well. The door at the far end, with the faded word "Staff" just visible in cracked, gold lettering, was still partially covered with a curtain. The window directly to its right had its heavy drapes closed once more despite the hour. It was the only window along their journey that remained covered, and Ms. Winters, realizing the same thing, tutted loudly before marching forward and violently pulling them apart.

Evelyn let out an involuntary gasp, her hand moving towards her mother's pearls. She hadn't known what she was expecting to see, especially in the bright light of mid-morning, but the events of the previous evening still sat fresh within her memory. She could almost hear that small, terrified squeak of a voice: "*Father, don't!*"

But there was nothing there, no ghosts or ghouls, no headless specters or wailing banshees. There was just an ordinary window with an ordinary view beyond.

Ms. Winters had not noticed Evelyn's reaction as she busied herself with the drapes, but Lilly had. She looked at Evelyn with wide-eyed understanding, a gaze Evelyn couldn't meet just then, embarrassment and fear churning within her. She took a few cautious steps forward to look inside better in hopes that it would put her childish fancies to bed once and for all. As she did, she noticed the plush, red runner, which had lined every length of every hall they had walked, suddenly give way to bare floorboards. Upon closer inspection, the end of the rug was rough and fraying, clearly showing where it had been quickly cut. The shape of the absent runner was distinct and obvious, the edges being treated and varnished, whereas the large rectangle between was untreated and bare. Small, visible holes along the edges of the varnish indicated where carpet tacks had once been deposited. In one of two spots, the tack remained still, the dents surrounding them indicating an impatient hand being unable to pull them free that had instead hammered them deeper into the wood to prevent injuries.

Evelyn stared in quiet contemplation. Every part of the house, without exception, showed no signs of wear and tear. There were no spots of wall where a naughty child had drawn a self-portrait. There were no curls of loosened wallpaper or chipped vases on wobbly plinths. Everything had been curated, carefully cleaned, and maintained. How then had there been a large portion of the carpet, perhaps six or seven feet in length, missing from its home, ripped away like a piece of flesh, revealing the bones of the house beneath?

"What happened to the rug?"

She spoke softly, almost to herself. Ms. Winters continued

her task of folding the drapes neatly into their tie-backs, undeterred.

"Ms. Winters."

The woman turned with a jolt as if she had forgotten they were even there and stared at Evelyn with that same impatient, stern look.

"What happened to the rug?"

As if to illustrate her point, Evelyn pointed at the rough wood floor, and Ms. Winters stepped backward, her face shifting a moment to reveal something else, something akin to fear. But just as quickly as the mask fell, it was neatly replaced, and the stern, cold eyes stared back at Evelyn once more. "A stain couldn't be removed, so the rug was instead."

"What kind of stain?"

"It happened so long ago that it's difficult to remember, but I believe it was paint."

"How long ago?"

"Several years back. Shall we get back to the tour?"

Evelyn nodded absentmindedly as she continued to stare at the floorboards. The housekeeper was obviously lying. Fibers remained from when the rug was cut, and the now-exposed and untreated wood looked clean, untarnished by footsteps or sunlight. Why would the woman lie about something so meaningless?

As they began to walk away, with Ms. Winters walking at an even faster pace than before, Evelyn looked at the floor and the window beside it again, knowing that the detail was important but not knowing why. It was like finding the answer to a riddle as yet unknown.

Father, don't!

Evelyn had spent so long worrying over her mental health, fearing she might follow her mother in life and then death, that she had spent little time pondering the other possibility that perhaps everything she had experienced was real.

Her mother had called them echoes. What if such "echoes" went far beyond a mere bad atmosphere or cold spot? What if they had form? What if they had a voice? And if it was an echo, what kind of echo was it? Who was the child she had heard speak as clearly as she heard Ms. Winters now, as she announced the purpose of each room and what had happened to them? The questions turned over inside her head and tumbled about, striking one another like thunder, a storm within her mind. So many questions, but as of yet, no answers. That was something Evelyn was determined to change.

Ms. Winters marched down the corridor without a word, presumably expecting both women to follow her, her manner cold and abrupt. Evelyn thought she was perfectly suited to Blackthorn House, their lack of warmth and comfort mirroring one another. As she hurried after her, she could not help but feel eyes on them all.

Father, don't!

They turned the corner and almost ran straight into Peter, who was emerging from a door on their immediate left. Lilly let out a panicked gasp, and Evelyn felt her heart pounding so hard that she thought she might burst. He had scared them half to death, appearing in the shadow of the corridor like some kind of specter.

Ms. Winters came to her senses first. "Milord...I..."

Peter raised his hand, immediately silencing her. Ms. Winters clasped her hand to her chest in a fist and lowered her eyes to the floor.

She's afraid.

Lilly, too, lowered her eyes, shrinking back against the wall beside her as a child might when caught with their hand in the cookie jar. Only Evelyn looked up into his face, and she saw something there, a darkness she had not noticed before. His features shifted slightly as if he were placing a mask upon them, and several seconds passed in uncomfortable silence before he spoke, his words slicing through the stagnant air. "Is there a reason for this ambush?"

Evelyn was taken aback. His tone was so cold, so sharp, that had she not seen his lips move, she would never have believed he had spoken. It was not a voice she recognized—it was not the voice of her husband. His eyes moved to Ms. Winters, who shrank beneath their gaze as if each syllable had actual weight to it.

"Sincerest apologies, Milord. I was showing Lady Black around Blackthorn, and I..." Her words decreased in volume until they were barely audible before they trailed off into silence.

Confusion clouded Evelyn's mind as she did not recognize the man before her. Desperation prompted her to speak to end the awkward confrontation, little of which she truly understood, and to bring the Peter she knew back to that moment. "Ms. Winters was kindly showing me about. The tour, remember?"

Her tone was pleading, and she hated how childlike she sounded and how childlike she felt. Only then did he tear his eyes from the cowering Ms. Winters to meet her gaze as if he had only just realized she was there.

"The tour. Of course."

He was irritated, that was clear, but there was more, something Evelyn could not discern. Slowly, he turned back to the door, locking it with a brass key he promptly placed back inside his breast pocket. Returning his gaze to Evelyn, his face gave the impression of politeness, of reciprocity, but his eyes remained dark and distant. Coldness snaked its way down Evelyn's spine, and she struggled not to shudder.

"I would prefer if the tour gave my office a wide berth. There is nothing here for wives or servants." His words were spoken carefully, deliberately, and Evelyn felt the blow of their meaning like a physical punch. Gone were his pet names of *dear* or *darling*; gone was any sign of affection or care. Even her very name had been stripped from her as she was merely labeled by her new role—*wife.*

The message was clear: this house may be where she resided now, but it was and would forever be Peter's house. She was only there as an extension of him, there to serve a specific role, and in this instance, she had stepped out of line, entering space reserved for only him. Ms. Winters understood, too—Evelyn could tell from her wringing hands and quivering lip. She had made a mistake, a bad one, and there would be some kind of repercussion for it, although what form that would take was unclear.

Everyone seemed to be holding their breath as he looked from one to the other, ensuring his words and the intent behind them were fully understood before he spoke again, his voice returning to his usual cheerful tone in an instant. "I suggest you take them back towards the east wing, Ms. Winters. Those rooms have the best view of the gardens."

"Of...of course, Milord."

With that, Ms. Winters stomped back the way they came, albeit with distinctly less confidence in her step, and Lilly and Evelyn followed.

Evelyn felt bewildered by what had just happened. Though nothing particularly dramatic or untoward had occurred, the man in front of her had momentarily ceased to be her husband. He was a stranger—someone completely unknown and completely without feeling. The entire exchange had left her unnerved and shaken.

As the three women walked in silent unison, Evelyn stole a glance back at Peter. He was half hidden by the shadows, but she could feel his eyes on them, watching to make sure they left, and for just a moment, it felt worse than the invisible eyes of that dreaded hallway.

The day passed by in a blur of rooms and hallways. Blackthorn House was larger than any estate Evelyn had visited, a fact which intimidated her, despite her best efforts. Further, it was laid out in a very strange and awkward manner. Long corridors wound around the outside of the house in a spiral and sliced through it in multiple directions. The effect was a confusing, maze-like design, which made Evelyn feel dizzy. It was an enigma, a puzzle without a solution, and she found that the harder she tried to solve it, to understand and remember it, the further away the answer seemed.

After almost two hours of Ms. Winters's brisk tour, not including the kitchens or the staff areas and quarters, Evelyn was exhausted and in desperate need of a chair. She knew exactly where she would rest.

Of all the rooms they had seen that day—and they had seen many—the one that made the greatest impression on Evelyn was the library. An avid devourer of books of all kinds from the moment she learned to read, Evelyn had immediately fallen in love with the room. She couldn't wait to explore its many books and to while away the hours engrossed in their pages.

"We have kept you long enough, Ms. Winters."

The housekeeper, unable to hide her relief at Evelyn's statement, simply muttered, "Indeed, ma'am."

"I don't know about you, Lilly, but I could definitely use a cup of tea."

Lilly enthusiastically agreed, a smile spreading across her weary face.

"Ms. Winters, could you get the kitchen to put something together for us both? Lilly, if you could bring it to the library, I will meet you there."

Lilly nodded and began to walk away, her footsteps noticeably perkier. Ms. Winters, however, looked more irritated at having been so abruptly dismissed than she had at being forced into giving the tour. She paused a moment, her mouth twitching, before she nodded in acknowledgement and trudged after Lilly. It was apparent to Evelyn that she was a woman whom few could please.

Evelyn wound her way backward, the many books calling her back to them. Her father had always told her that any problem could be solved with a cup of tea, and now, more than ever, she hoped that he was right. Evelyn wasn't sure tea would be potent enough to solve her particular woes, but the memory made her smile briefly before her mind wandered back to the bottles and vials littering her mother's shelves.

"No."

She didn't know why she said it out loud or to whom it was directed, but the urge to defy her own mind's determination to maintain a sorrowful state of existence was strong, so she declared it openly to the world around her. Just then, she heard it—barely audible but clearly there. It was the giggle of a child, half-stifled. She stopped and held her breath, partly to hear better but mostly so as not to give her own position away, although from whom she was hiding, she had little idea. Then it came again, this time louder, as if the child was losing a battle against themselves to stay quiet.

It was a game of hide and seek, and Evelyn had walked into the middle of it.

"Hello?"

The giggle came once more, this time with no attempt to quiet it.

Evelyn, recalling the laughter in the fog, prayed that this time, there was a source for the sounds. She walked cautiously forward, the boards beneath her creaking ever so slightly as she moved. She only managed a few steps when the small frame of a boy burst forth from behind a bureau, a brown-haired blur moving with hurried feet and happy laughter toward the corridor on the left. Evelyn smiled with relief and quickly joined in the merriment, her laughter mixing with the young boy's as she began to chase him in a game known universally to all children and remembered fondly by all adults. Assuming he was the child of a guest or one of the staff, she was grateful for the distraction.

It was not lost on her that for the first time since her arrival at Blackthorn House, she was smiling.

She turned the corridor just in time to see him enter one of the bedrooms on the right. She burst into the room to find it empty, and her smile wavered slightly as she caught her breath. Painted a sky blue, with a single wardrobe and a bare bed frame in the center, the plain room was a stark contrast to the rest of the manor. Evelyn heard another giggle, this time coming from within the wardrobe, and relieved, she stifled a laugh of her own.

"Where, oh, where could he be?" she asked as she tiptoed toward the wardrobe doors.

The young boy's laughter increased in volume as she moved closer, and she found herself excited to win their little game.

"No, not beneath the bed..."

She crept closer and closer, treading as lightly as she could so she could truly surprise the young boy.

"And not behind the curtains! Where could he be hiding?"

The laughter always increased after she spoke, the lad clearly pleased with the cleverness of his hiding spot. Closer she approached until she stood before the doors between her and her prey. She grabbed a handle in each hand and silently counted to three before throwing the doors wide.

"Found you!"

But the wardrobe was empty. There was nothing and no one inside, and the constant happy giggles of the boy ceased the second she flung open the doors. How was this possible? Where did he go?

Her smile quickly faded as she frantically felt the wood inside the cupboard, seeking some kind of trap door or hidden drawer she knew deep down didn't exist. She slumped onto the floor, half in and half out of the heavy mahogany box, tears filling her eyes and tracing lines along her face before darkening the wood beneath her in small, damp pools. Her fears about her sanity overwhelmed her, and she couldn't help but wonder if she, too, would swing from the end of a rope. She touched her mother's pearls, aching to feel her presence there somehow, to feel the weight of her reassuring hold once more.

Something stopped the tears—something barely visible in the shadowy interior of the wardrobe. Evelyn climbed in further and squinted, her eyes adjusting to the gloom. It was a crude little drawing etched into the wood by a young child's hand. It depicted a family: a mother made distinct from the father by the line tracing out long hair and the triangle of a dress, and two children—one a boy and one a girl—who were distinguished in the same way. Below it, carved in a small, unsteady hand, was the name "Emmett."

Evelyn reached out her hand and traced the crude letters with her fingertips.

Emmett.

"Milady?"

Evelyn, startled by the visitor, bumped her head on the wardrobe door as she clambered out. Lilly stood watching her with large, curious eyes and a tray in her hand. Evelyn hurriedly wiped away her tears with the back of her hands. Embarrassment burned bright beneath her skin, and she could barely make sense of the thoughts and feelings boiling and bubbling beneath its surface.

"I...I just..." She trailed off, unsure how to finish the sentence in such a way as to make the situation seem normal.

How could she explain being half inside a wardrobe in some random bedroom? How could she explain her disheveled appearance? How could she explain her tearful eyes and terrified expression?

She opened her mouth a second time, unsure what she would say, but knowing she must say something—anything to break the awkward, painful silence that filled the empty bedroom. But before she could speak, Lilly's voice filled the space with only a handful of words, which instantly brought Evelyn a flood of emotions. Words that brought her back from the brink with a snap.

"You've seen them too, haven't you?"

Six

The bright light of early afternoon flooded through the library windows, illuminating the unsettled dust as it floated about the room. The green leather armchair where Evelyn sat was unusually large, making her feel small, like some fragile porcelain doll. Lilly stoked the freshly lit fire, carefully placing sticks and wood in an intricate grid-like pattern to encourage the flame. The tray sat between their chairs, their two cups already drained and refilled, but the scones untouched, neither being in the mood for eating.

It wasn't usual for a maid and mistress to share cake and tea, of course, but then there was nothing usual about this situation or the conversation to come. Lilly had tried to refuse Evelyn's requests to sit, not as a maid, but as her friend and equal, but Evelyn had insisted. Despite her predominantly meek and mild-mannered ways, she could be forceful when needed. Her father had always joked that the half she had inherited from her mother was a stubborn one.

Double doors opened into a large, bright room with a dizzyingly high ceiling painted with a mural of a starry night sky. Dark wood shelves lined the walls both on the bottom and on the second mezzanine floor. The mezzanine wrapped around the outside of the room, held aloft by a series of ornately carved dark wood columns, accessed by a wrought iron staircase that spiraled between the two like a vast black snake. Dotted along the shelves were dark wood ladders on brass runners so even the shortest of readers could access the tomes on the top shelf.

In the center of the room, placed thoughtfully about the large green Persian rug, were a number of leather club chairs in a dark fern green. Several desks toward the outer edges of the rug were paired with matching green leather tops and smaller club chairs perched on shining brass wheels. Beside the large marble fireplace sat a small sofa and a large plush armchair, both in a plush red velvet pattern—the perfect place to curl up with a good book. More books lined the shelves—in every color and binding imaginable—than anyone could ever hope to read in their lifetime.

When the flames had taken hold and the library was filled with the warm glow of firelight, Lilly sat awkwardly in an armchair identical to Evelyn's. She perched herself on the edge, her back straight and formal, rather than relaxing into the chair as Evelyn had, a clear insistence of "knowing her place." She lifted the teacup to her lips and drained the remnants, eyeing Evelyn cautiously over the rim.

Evelyn had decided to wait for Lilly to speak first, partly because she had no idea how even to begin such a discussion, but mainly because she was afraid the girl would think her mad. So, she emanated an impatient energy until Lilly began her story.

"When I was little, I saw things that no one else could see, people that weren't there, people that were dead. The sight—that's what me mum called it. She said my grandmother had it too, and her mother before her, and so on—that all the women in our family had it. She said it was a gift, but sometimes it felt more like a curse. I didn't mind most of the spirits; they were just lonely and wanted someone to talk to. Some weren't so nice. They had usually died in a horrible way, or maybe they had just been unhappy people and so became unhappy ghosts, but those ones, they scared me."

Evelyn listened with bated breath, her hands clasping her skirts so hard they drained of color.

Lilly continued, "I asked me mum once why they didn't leave like the others. I'd known plenty of death as a child, family members and neighbors and the like, but none stayed behind. They moved on to whatever comes next. My mother told me that most had things they needed done, things that bothered them, and they couldn't move on 'til they was put right. I learned after she died not to talk about them no more. It scared folks and made some whisper of witches and devils, so I began to ignore them, to pick my moments. But I try to help them when I can, poor things." She took a sip of tea, closing her eyes a moment as if steadying herself to continue.

"I had a man ask me to tell his missus about a letter that had slipped behind their fireplace. I don't know what was in it, but it must have been important for him to hang on like that. Many just have a message needing passed, a *thank you,* or an *I love you,* and such like—simple things, really, nice things. Others just aren't ready to let go of their lives, which I s'pose I understand. But that other kind, the ones I said scared me, those ones are altogether different. They're stuck, they're confused, and they're angry. 'Tortured souls' is what my grandma had called them. There are such spirits in this house. I've seen 'em, and I think you've seen them too. Am I right?" Lilly tilted her head slightly and stared at Evelyn inquisitively, the serious expression on her face enforcing the weight of what she had just said and what she had just asked.

Evelyn swallowed hard, her mouth dry despite the tea. Everything about this was ridiculous. It flew in the face of everything she had been raised to know and believe. There was no such thing as ghosts—everyone knew that. And yet, she had seen things, heard things. Objects moved by invisible hands, laughter, and footsteps without an owner, a foggy plane that only she had entered. And then there was the house itself, grand and beautiful on the outside but heavy with a sense of foreboding. Wasn't the possibility of spirits better than the other, the idea that she may be losing her grip on her sanity, just as her mother had? Of that, she wasn't sure. But what she did know, regardless of what was happening to her, was that having someone who understood in some way, someone she could confide in without risking judgment, was everything in that moment. And so, with a heavy sigh, she whispered, "Yes."

Lilly nodded knowingly, her suspicions confirmed, and stood to pour them another cup of tea. Evelyn noticed she always heaped her own with sugar, glugging the sickly-sweet potion enthusiastically. It was another reminder of how different their situations in life truly were. Sugar was a small thing, but one of so many small things that Evelyn gave little consideration to. But to Lilly, it was something rare, something special.

They had bonded over their shared losses. Lilly, too, had lost her mother young, having also been the one to find her, though she had died from influenza rather than by her own hand. But unlike Evelyn, she had no father to support her through her grief, hers having died when she was only a few months old. She had no money with which she could ease her pain a little. She was left poor, homeless, and alone, and thus, at only ten years old, ended up at a girl's orphanage, destined for a life of servitude and poverty.

Lilly spoke again after she had drained her third cup. "This house, there's something different about it, something wrong. Have you felt it?"

Evelyn nodded silently, her eyes fixed on the dancing flames of the fire.

Lilly continued, "I've never felt so many in one place. So many souls, so much hurt and anger, so much loss. I've seen at least four since we arrived and felt a few more. Some don't show themselves—they hide, or maybe they don't know how, I'm not sure, but they're there, alright. This house...this house."

Lilly shook her head the way an exasperated parent would when describing their children's bad habits.

Evelyn nodded again in agreement. *This house, indeed.* "I thought I was losing my mind, like my..."

"Like your mother?"

Evelyn stared at her through wide, surprised eyes. "How did you know?"

"The way you talk about her, the words you use. Her 'illness' or 'difficulties,' her 'passing.' So careful, so considered. When people discuss diseases of the body, they always name the thing, like it's an explanation in itself. To name it means they understand it. But when it's a disease of the mind, they always speak so vague. Same with why they died. People'll just say how it happened, like, 'she fell from her horse' or 'he got smallpox.' But not so when their death was something unnatural, something 'wrong.' I've been around death my whole life, just as much as I've been around the grieving, and you learn to understand these things."

Tears began to fall from Evelyn's eyes, snaking their way down her cheeks in hurried lines.

"I'm sorry, ma'am, I shouldn't have said that; it's not me place. I just—I don't get to talk to people about these things. They don't understand. Forgive me."

"Don't apologize—you haven't said anything wrong. I'm not crying because of that. Well, not that exactly." Evelyn didn't explain to Lilly why she was crying—she didn't feel she had to for Lilly to know.

She seemed to understand so much without anything being spoken aloud. Evelyn wasn't crying because she still missed and grieved for her mother, although both of those things were true. She cried because she hadn't realized until that moment how ashamed she had been of her mother's suicide, a realization which brought with it another wave of shame.

Grace had been ill—it wasn't her fault—and yet wasn't Evelyn taught by the very minister who had conducted her mother's funeral that suicide was a sin? Evelyn had clung to her mother's words, to the belief that she was indeed with her somehow, walking by her side, unseen, as the alternative meant she was in Hell. None of her family openly discussed how her mother died, not with each other and certainly not with outsiders. It was simply glossed over, like her prior mental deterioration, as if to admit such things happened would somehow sully her memory. But they *had* happened, and they were as much a part of her mother's story as everything else.

Evelyn had tried in the beginning, being an inquisitive, precocious child, and more importantly, having been the one to find her lifeless and swinging from a knot she had tied with her own hands. She had asked and begged for answers, desperate to understand. But her father, who had loved her mother dearly, was utterly heartbroken by her loss, and so he chose to visit only the happy, smiling memories and ignore the dark, painful ones. Her brother simply shrugged his shoulders and went along with it.

Evelyn later understood why they had chosen that path, but by then, the damage was done. After years of never addressing her mother's illness or suicide, after years of unanswered questions and refused explanations, Evelyn had come to two conclusions. The first was that to suffer any infliction of the mind was a fate worse than death—something she feared for herself greatly in general, but lately, more than ever. The second was that her mother's suicide was her fault, having failed to raise the alarm about the medications hidden in her mother's jewelry box.

These realizations had left Evelyn in a perpetual state of anxiety, constantly fearful that she would end up just like Grace, as well as a sense of unending, sometimes overwhelming, shame. Shame for that very thought, as if being like her mother was a death sentence. If her mother did indeed walk with her, she did not want to let her down. She felt she must live a life her mother would approve of and become a person she would be proud of.

She sighed again, her thoughts weighing heavily on her mind along with Lilly's revelations. Everything seemed to press down on her, just like Blackthorn House did, and she suddenly longed to be outside in fresh air and open fields.

Lilly interrupted these melancholy thoughts with another question. "Did your mother have the sight, too?"

Evelyn sat up a little straighter. "I'm sorry?"

"Did she see these things too? Is that why she..."

Lilly didn't need to finish the sentence. They both knew what the absence of words meant, the implication hanging in the air between them. *Is that why she killed herself?*

Evelyn's heart and mind began to race. She thought back to her mother's conversations with thin air, of her refusal to go to certain places or take certain paths because of things she feared there. She thought about hushed conversations between doctors and her father about her mother's "hallucinations." Could it be that her mother had not been crazy after all? That she simply saw what others couldn't?

"What makes you say that?"

"My mam said that it was passed along from mother to daughter, so because you have it, you must have got it from her. She must have had the sight, too."

Evelyn's tears increased as this pronouncement and all it implied flooded over her. Her mother had the sight—she must have—and because of the things she saw and heard, because of the loneliness and fear it brought, she had taken her own life. Her mother had the sight, and now Evelyn did too. She never thought she would be in a position where she was glad that spirits, lost souls, or whatever they were called, were real. Hope and relief filled her heart as much as fear did. Could it really be so? Could she and her mother share an ability to see a world that others could not? She wished more than ever to ask her those questions.

"She never said anything about what she saw, and my father won't talk about it." Evelyn stared into the fire. A log, now blackened and cracked by the flames, crumbled into ash, indicating just how long they had been sitting there.

Everything turns to dust.

A thought occurred to Evelyn. "Can you see my mother?"

Lilly merely shook her head.

Disappointment swelled through Evelyn as she thought back to the times she had been sure her mother had been there, when she had suddenly smelled her perfume or felt an invisible hand on her own. Most recently, on her wedding day, she had seen a shadow close by that did not seem to belong to her, taking every step with her down the aisle.

But she had not once seen her.

As if sensing her thoughts, Lilly spoke. "It isn't the same for every spirit. Some are silent, but you can see 'em, others are sound alone, without an actual shape. Some are stronger than others and can make things move or interact with us, while others are more like an echo, just replaying an event over and over, unaware we are here. Just 'cus we can't see her, don't mean she ain't here."

Evelyn nodded, though she remained disappointed.

Lilly continued. "I have felt something 'round you before, something akin to a warmth or a light. I knew it were good though I didn't know what it was. That could be her."

Evelyn smiled, tears filling her eyes once more. "Yes, that's her." She held her mother's pearls and smiled.

Lilly's face dropped, the energy shifting noticeably.

"What is it?"

Lilly looked at her hands, not meeting Evelyn's eyes. "But..."

"But what?" Evelyn prompted her, urging her to continue.

"But...I haven't felt it since we got here, since we got to Blackthorn I mean."

Evelyn's smile fell, too. What could that mean for her? What could it mean for her mother?

Lilly watched her over the tea-stained cups, the pot long since cold. Neither spoke for quite some time, the only sound being the occasional pop from within the grate. Evelyn's mind was filled with so many questions and memories that she feared they might burst.

"What do we do?"

"I don't rightly know, ma'am. I normally ask them what they want and help them move on, but there are so many here. And then there's this house..."

This house.

"If we start having conversations with thin air, they'll think we're mad."

Evelyn thought about the pills and medicines, the vials and needles. She thought about her mother's once vibrant, sharp eyes, which turned foggy and absent. She remembered how she would lie there for hours, staring into space, unaware of her surroundings, of her own sense of self. To Evelyn, that felt like a fate worse than death.

Lilly let out a resigned sigh and fixed Evelyn with serious, knowing eyes. “I learned early on, ma'am, that if you don’t listen to their whispers, you force them to scream.”

Seven

Evelyn chewed her food in silence, unable to broach the subject consuming her every thought. Peter spoke of legal matters—of wills and deeds and his plans for the house—and Evelyn smiled, nodded when required, and answered any questions he asked: Yes, she was enjoying the meal. Yes, she had been given her tour as requested. No, she hadn't explored the grounds yet. Yes, the library was magnificent.

These were not the questions that sat on the edge of Evelyn's tongue, begging to be freed and said aloud, yet Evelyn carried on, unsure how to begin. Peter provided the opportunity when he raised the subject of his father.

"Father loved his library. I wouldn't be surprised if he had read every book there."

"Did your father ever remarry?"

Peter looked at her, a little surprised by her question.

During their courtship, when she had yearned to know all of him, she flooded him with a million questions about every aspect of his life, but he had always remained caged, aloof. Evelyn assumed speaking of such matters was distressing to him; after all, she understood better than anyone how painful the loss of one's mother could be. Peter's had died in childbirth, leaving his father a young widower with an infant son to care for. He rarely mentioned his father, and when he did, his words had sharp edges, jagged and raw, like something torn apart rather than cut cleanly. It was clear there was animosity there, a division that had widened with the years. Evelyn, not wishing to cause Peter any discomfort, politely steered the conversation in a new direction. She had vowed to be a patient wife, not one of the boorish nags she had heard her brother's friends complain about. She had assumed that the slow unpicking of such tangled tapestries would bring them closer together. Indeed, she had found the air of mystery surrounding Peter attractive—thrilling, even.

But now, mere days after arriving at Blackthorn, Evelyn found her patience had worn thin. There were too many secrets locked within Blackthorn's many rooms, too many unanswered questions left floating in the air, along with the lazy dust motes and the spirits of the dead. When she thought of how Peter's vague responses and half-truths had once excited her, her face colored with embarrassment. She understood then what a naive young bride she had been, and her foolishness filled her with shame.

"He did, yes," Peter said. "A lovely woman by all accounts. Sadly, she died during childbirth."

Evelyn looked up from her food, unable to hide her surprise. "He had other children?"

Peter had never mentioned any siblings, not once. Where was this child? She thought about the boy and the drawings in the wardrobe. She thought about the laughter in the fog.

Peter cleared his throat and shuffled slightly in his seat. Was he uncomfortable? Was this the reason for his and his father's disagreement? Whatever he had felt, it was there only a moment before he righted himself, his expression shifting to that same charming smile that told Evelyn everything and nothing.

"No, sadly, the child passed as well."

"Oh, how terrible!"

"Yes, very tragic. Father was never the same after that. He had so loved that wife."

What an odd turn of phrase—*that wife*—as if he were referring to one of many, an item in a vast collection. And was that bitterness in Peter's voice? He sounded so cold, so distanced from the topic on which he spoke, robotic even.

It made Evelyn shudder.

He moved on quickly, resuming their conversation about his plans for renovation. Evelyn chose to move with him rather than try to steer the conversation back. Her father told her that many things in life were like the ebb and flow of the sea—one could either resist and fight the waves or let them take you out to sea. On this occasion, the sea was very much what she wanted to discuss.

"Tell me more about the house."

He flashed her that same surprised look before a smile replaced it—this time a genuine one, one that showed his enthusiasm for the topic.

"What would you like to know?"

"Oh, everything. When was it built? How long has it been in your family? Everything!"

"It's an interesting subject, actually. The Black family originated from Scandinavia; did you know that?"

Evelyn shook her head. His clear blue eyes spoke of an origin far from their current shores, but she had never considered where.

"They came in long boats, clad in animal skins and wielding hammers, swords, and axes, and took this land as their own. They weren't called Black then, of course—they had their own language, their own name, now lost with time. But they declared this land to be *dyster,* which translates as gloomy and somber, but it can also mean the color black. I assume that is how they came upon the name, but I cannot say for certain. What I know is, they tore through this county like a plague and spilled the blood of many a local until they had the respect of all." He smiled when he said this as if the discussion of mass murder was somehow akin to recalling a pleasant memory of years gone by.

Evelyn felt a slight shiver run down her spine, and for the first time since their meeting, she wondered just how well she knew the man she had married. "Local...as in the village?"

His expression shifted into one of disgust. "Ah, yes, the village...awful place. They resisted at first—of course, they did —farmers and their kin are hardly of the educational standard required to understand the necessity and benefits of change. People like *that* are so short-sighted, so incapable of looking ahead. They resisted, but they burned for it. Where do you think the name of the village, Black Skull, came from?"

Evelyn merely shook her head slightly, transfixed by the way his face shifted slowly into a joyous sneer.

"Why, after their fire-blackened bones, of course." He spoke as if the fact were evident to anyone with half a mind, as if it were natural for a village to be named after the burned corpses of their ancestors.

"They killed them?"

"Of course. It's the only language such simpletons understand. If a dog bites your hand, you must give it your boot and not stop until it cowers in an understanding of its place. My ancestors ravaged and burned their way through those people until they understood their place and cowered before their betters." He paused, raising his glass slightly before draining its contents.

He continued. "They took a man from each family—sometimes the head of the house, the father or grandfather—but where there were no adult males, they took a son, a babe even, dragging them out into the village center to make examples of them all." He paused, watching her, making sure she was listening before continuing, "Each was slaughtered, their head removed from their shoulders, their skulls cleaved into the dirt, and their bodies piled high and set alight in a glorious bonfire." His eyes shifted now as if he were recalling some happy memory. Evelyn felt bile rising in her throat. He refilled his glass, lifting it once more before stating, "It is said that the fat of their flesh made the fire burn hot for many days. The women left behind were ravaged, taken with force until the warriors had their fill, though I imagine they put up little fight in the light of their husbands' flaming corpses!" He scoffed, amused at this grotesque image.

"The locals' mud huts and wooden lodges they burned to ash, and anything of value they removed and kept for themselves. Those allowed to live became their servants and built the very first of my family's homes to reside in this exact spot so many centuries ago." His story ended, and he once more raised his glass, this time a little higher, making a clear salute to the ancestors he had just described before drinking heartily. Evelyn shuddered as a small drop of red wine escaped his smirking lips and snaked its way down his chin.

Evelyn was horrified, not only for the vivid, vile language Peter used but also by the glee he had in telling it. Her discomfort must have been plain from her expression, for he smiled knowingly, staring at her coldly until she cast her eyes downward, unable to look into his eyes any longer. Once, they had seemed so beautiful to her—a deep pool of water, changing with the light of the sky. Now, they were almost soulless, the painted glass eyes of a waxwork dummy.

"Don't climb on your high horse too quickly, my love. They were invaders, after all. The clue is in their title. It was a different time. What was once accomplished with axes and swords is now accomplished with the swish of a pen. Either way, the results are the same in many ways."

He continued, unbothered by her discomfort. "Throughout the centuries, the Blacks asserted themselves as leaders and rulers. They maintained their status and wealth as well as the respect they had spilled blood to gain. But always, they remained here, where their story had begun. First, they built a house of wood and mud, then of rocks and stone, and on and on until the building you find yourself in was constructed nearly two centuries ago in 1710: Blackthorn House."

He waved his hand and cast his eyes about the room as if to emphasize his point, as if she might have somehow forgotten where they sat. "Of course, every owner has added to the place—put their stamp on it, as it were—but the spirits of my ancestors remain."

Evelyn thought this was another strange choice of words, but said nothing.

"There have been many who have stood against us over the years—power brings with it many enemies. But every soul who rose to fight the Black family fell on our sword, and we only became stronger as a result. And the village? Well, they understood and accepted their place beneath the shadow of Blackthorn, and they continue to serve us to this day." His face brimmed with pride, talking about murder and violence as if it were a medal to pin to one's chest. "That legacy, that responsibility, has now fallen onto my shoulders, and I do not take it lightly."

It seemed almost performative now. It was like he was speaking to someone else, not to her, and the discomfort Evelyn felt began to increase. The legacy he described was the bloody history of invaders and despots. It was a history most modern gentlemen would seek to downplay or even deny altogether. It was a story of those who took rather than gave, and it wasn't something that resonated with her at all—never mind one that made her proud to bear that name.

Lady Black.

"It is a legacy I look forward to passing on to our future son." His ice-blue stare penetrated her, making her squirm beneath his gaze. She had always wanted children and had even fantasized about it in the lead-up to their wedding. But when she tried to imagine them now, running through the halls of Blackthorn House with the ghosts of other children, it made her stomach churn.

It seemed fitting for him to bring up a new life after his discussion of death. Perhaps, she thought, children could bring joy and vibrancy to the house and its surroundings. Perhaps she just needed to get used to the place before she could imagine their lives there. But deep down, she knew no child could remedy what was wrong with her new home. Lilly was right—something was very wrong about Blackthorn, and Evelyn was determined to find out exactly what that was.

He watched her intently, smirking, as if aware of her thoughts yet uncaring as to their meaning. Unsure of what to say and unwilling to show him the true extent of her discomfort, she merely said, "Indeed," before glugging down the remainder of her wine, the warmth of the alcohol bringing little comfort.

That evening, Peter came to her chamber.

She had longed for him since their wedding night, when she felt closer to him than she ever thought possible with another human being. From Evelyn's perspective, they had connected emotionally just as much as they had done so physically, and that closeness brought with it even more pleasure than the act itself. She had felt like two souls entwined, uniting to create new life, a new soul perhaps.

But then his father had died. He had left, and she had spent every night alone since then. And for the first time since her mother had died, she felt lonely. Now, as he held her hand and led her toward her bed, that same heat rose from her core, resting eventually on her flushed cheeks. Anticipation washed over her, causing her entire body to tingle as if charged by an electrical current.

But something was wrong. Instead of the synchronized, yearning motions of their wedding night, every movement felt awkward and stunted. It was as if they had not already spent an entire night in each other's embrace, tracing every line of the other's body, learning their reactions, their desires. He stared at her as a stranger might look at an obstacle he must overcome and treated her with the same impatient annoyance. He pawed at her dress, pulling at it hastily and yanking so hard that she struggled to keep her balance, her corsets unlaced and pulled with the same unsympathetic force.

He made no effort to undress himself, and when she reached a hand toward his shirt, he swatted it away as if she were a persistent insect. His lack of nakedness only served to make her painfully aware of her own and perhaps even slightly embarrassed by it. He undressed her final undergarments the way a clinician would undress a patient and observed her naked form like she were cattle to be inspected, touching her with the unfamiliarity of a complete stranger and not the intimacy of a loving husband. She wanted to say something, to ask what she had done to cause such a noticeable shift in his behavior toward her, but she could not find her voice. It had been tossed thoughtlessly to the floor along with her clothing.

He laid her down on the bed without any pretense of tenderness or desire, but with a gruffness which made her painfully conscious of her vulnerability. A single, awful thought filled her with fear and dread.

He can do what he wants to me, and there is nothing I can do to stop him.

Tears stung her eyes as he unbuckled his belt and climbed on top of her, mounting her like he would a mare. Gone were the longing kisses, the soft and languishing touches of before. In their place, she found only the short, sharp thrusts of a deed performed with rigid, indifferent efficiency, with no regard for her or her desires. She looked into his eyes, hoping to connect once more, but he did not look back. His thoughts and consciousness were elsewhere, and that same familiar loneliness washed over Evelyn once more.

She placed her hand on the side of his face, hoping to bring him back to her, to connect with him as they had their first time, but his eyes remained fixed at some point in time beyond that moment, not even registering the warmth and weight of her touch. The rebuff was almost too much to bear, and her hand soon fell limp by her side. The painful silence was only broken by the occasional grunt of his efforts or the creak of the bed beneath them. Evelyn closed her eyes tightly, forcing a tear to fall, and waited for it to be over.

It only took a few minutes. The task completed, he arose from the bed without the slightest hesitation and panted a brief good night as he went into his own bedroom, tucking his shirt into his trousers as he went. Evelyn said nothing, not even stirring, as he closed the door between their two bedchambers. The sound of the key turning had been like a knife to her chest. She released her sorrow in a torrent of silent, blinding tears.

She lay for some time staring into the dark, empty space of her ceiling, lying immobile in the same position he had left her, used up and discarded. She replayed every interaction they had had leading up to that morning she had awoken alone in his London bedroom, tracing their history through her mind, looking for some kind of clue for an answer to a question not yet formed. Every conversation, every stolen kiss, their first night together, played out before her, and she was left wanting.

Something had shifted between them, something fundamental, and no matter how many times she traced their shared timeline, it always came down to the same moment: his father's death. Evelyn understood how grief could mar and deform a person, but this felt different somehow. Was it the pressure of the title coming so much sooner than expected? Was it the timing of it happening so soon after they were married? Or was it merely grief at the loss of a beloved parent, or perhaps the regret of a feud left unresolved? Perhaps it was a combination of all four.

Despite her best efforts, Evelyn could think of no explanation that seemed to sit comfortably within their new narrative. Emotional pain and suffering without cause or explanation cuts far deeper than one that can be explained away, packed inside a neat little box with an appropriate label. Wasn't that exactly why her entire family, herself included, along with every physician in the area, had chosen to paint her mother with the title of hysterical and mentally ill? It is an understandable reaction when one observes it from afar. To not identify, to not explain means that the cause is without explanation, without understanding or identification. It is other. It is foreign. And there is no greater fear to mankind than the fear of what could be hiding within the shadows or beneath our beds, the terror felt toward the unknown. So, Evelyn chose to once again explain away her concerns and her instincts, which screamed defiance within her, simply because it was easier.

But the conscious mind cannot force such pretenses onto the subconscious mind, which lives and breathes by its own set of rules. No sooner had Evelyn given in to slumber did her dreams pull back the veil to reveal its terrors. Leaving her sleeping body behind, Evelyn found herself walking through the darkened halls of Blackthorn House. An unnatural silence draped over every doorway and window, and only the small creaks of her slow and steady footsteps and her own ragged, fearful breathing were audible in the darkness.

She was barefoot, but the carpet did not have the expected texture of woven cloth. Instead, her feet squelched and trudged through it as if it were the wet, soggy moors beyond the walls, her weight pushing her feet into the cold sludge. She shivered, the cold permeating her white nightdress with ease and causing her entire body to erupt in gooseflesh. Every breath sent a whispered cloud of smoke into the air. Her hair was loose, falling long about her shoulders, shifting slightly with a breeze that should not exist.

Before her stood a door carved crudely from plain, unfinished wood. Unlike the doors to the various rooms leading off the corridor, this one stood independent of any walls or structure, seeming to hover inside the house, a mirage in a desert of shadows and brick. All around the frame were strange symbols carved with sharp, jagged lines, each painted with the streaks of hurried hands in red and brown. Evelyn knew instinctively it was blood, some fresh, some much older.

Without fear—for why should she fear a dream—she reached her hand out to push the door open. Logically, it should have revealed the rest of the corridor. Still, Evelyn somehow knew this door was unlike any other—that this door would not lead merely to another room but somewhere beyond the known universe, to a plain of existence and a place in time disconnected from her mortal world.

It opened with a painful creak and exhaled a cold, forceful breath. Inside the frame was a world of shadow, where thick, foggy tendrils twisted about as if alive. Despite the overwhelming cold, fires burned deep purple and blue, flames that gave off no heat, no light, and no comfort. It was a world of darkness and gloom. As the mist shifted, Evelyn saw glimpses of movement, feeling the weighty stare of invisible eyes upon her. Waves of desperation and hopelessness gripped her and tried to drag her into the sea of fog.

She yearned to run, to flee from that terrible place, but she felt transfixed as if something, or someone, were calling her to it. Just as she began to gather the courage to turn and run, a path parted through the fog, revealing the silhouette of a woman hanging in mid-air. Her head lolled lifelessly and unnaturally to one side, and her arms hung limp by her sides, a marionette with its strings cut. Even without the figure's features being visible, Evelyn instantly recognized her mother, hanging just as she had found her that day inside the barn. Tears flowed from her eyes, and she felt just as she had when she was a child—the same horror, the same grief and helplessness swelling in her chest, ready to burst forth in a pained scream. But before it could escape her quivering lips, the form twitched and contorted in a vile and unnatural way, like the spasms of a dying creature.

It moved toward her, revealing its features in an eerie blue light. It looked like her mother, yet it was not her. There were two faces there—one alive and human, the face of her mother, the face of any woman, of every woman all at once. The other, which somehow lay atop the first like a gauzy mask, was the rotten flesh of a corpse long since expired. Green and blue meat clung in desperate clumps to the skull beneath, and holes where cheeks had once been exposed, yellow teeth. The jaw hung from the skull in a lopsided, broken way, and as the specter moved toward Evelyn, it shook like some kind of grotesque puppet show. The tongue, black and swollen, hung out of the gaping mouth, revealing maggots inside its yawn, squirming and writhing as they feasted on what remained of the flesh. A gaping hole stared at Evelyn where one of the eyes should have been. The other eye stared blankly at Evelyn; it was fogged over as if whitewashed. Instead of the wet sheen of a healthy eye, it was dry and matte, and the eyelid stuck behind it as it bulged out of the socket, a full and bloodless orb.

The being lurched toward Evelyn, jerking its legs forward on an invisible path in mid-air as it reached its long, pale arms out to her, one with flesh, the other blackened bone and rotten sinew. Evelyn opened her mouth to scream, but fog poured inside her throat. Her arms and legs grew stiff and frozen, turning her into an ice statue, her mouth agape, her eyes streaming tears, unable to move or scream, only able to see the living dead thing twitch its way toward her and place its rotten hand about her throat.

Evelyn awoke with a start.

She was sitting up in bed, the covers and blankets twisted about her like rope. She panted, sweat coating her skin, making her feel cold and unclean. Her throat was dry, and she ached as if she had been running or climbing, her muscles fatigued from thrashing around in her sleep.

She placed her hand upon her chest and attempted to get her breathing under control, forcing the image of her mother's corpse—of that thing—from her mind. She focused on the objects inside the room, on the real and the permanent. She listed them to herself, in order— "chair, fireplace, wardrobe"—as if by doing so she were manifesting the room into being. Her heart rate came down, and her breathing slowed—"tapestry, dresser, mirror—" She stopped with a start, the sight of her reflection serving to undo her calm.

She scrambled out of bed and ran to the looking glass, inspecting what she saw with disbelief. She was as white as a sheet, the blue and purple lines of her veins visible beneath skin so pale it seemed transparent. There about her neck were five bruises, the distinct markings of four fingers on one side and a thumb on the other. The shadowy mark of a palm rested over her windpipe. She placed her own hand there and gently rubbed, hoping it was somehow a trick of the light or something that could be removed like rouge, but the markings stayed firm. Her hand sat so small within the large width of the handprint, a grip wide enough to hold her entire throat with ease.

She knew then that the creature and its icy hand of rotten flesh had been no mere nightmare. She recalled what Lilly had said in the library, how the glow of her mother was gone since arriving at Blackthorn. Whatever that thing was, it had taken her mother. It had defiled her memory—her form—though to what end, Evelyn did not know.

But the creature was very real, and somehow, it was a part of Blackthorn House.

Eight

Throughout her life, Evelyn had found solace in facts and figures, in words typed neatly in books, in the curved lines of graphs, or in the polka dots of the night sky on star charts. She found comfort in the Latin names of animals and vegetation, as if to name a thing was to have power over it. And when her head ached from cramming in all the newfound information, and her heart cried out for enrichment instead, she turned to books filled with fairy tales and impossible adventures, their pages scrawled with the imaginings of flighty minds and creative souls. She looked to lines of iambic pentameter and soliloquies of such longing and beauty that they'd bring tears to the eyes of even the sternest of souls.

Unable to find answers to the dozens of questions that tore at her mind with the painful ease of sharpened claws, she lost herself in the worlds and wonders found inside the pages of books. She ingested them at a rate unnatural for a child of her age, building a world for herself—half fantasy, half fact, of the real and the imagined, and she enclosed herself within it, a caterpillar within its cocoon, protected from the world outside, transforming completely within. Whenever she found herself afraid or facing a difficult choice, she would seek answers in libraries and bookshops.

Now, more than ever, she needed the solace and comfort that a library brought her as well as the answers the books within it contained. It was the only place she could think of to go to calm her panicked mind and find the truths she so desperately needed.

She'd changed from her sweat-dampened nightgown into fresh clothing, but it did little to fight the chill as she moved through the slumbering house. She clutched her robe a bit tighter, hoping her tiptoed footsteps wouldn't rouse suspicion. The nightmare still gripped her like the horrible creature that had left its mark on her neck, and she wasn't sure she'd be able to explain to anyone why she now walked the halls in the middle of the night.

The familiar, calming scent of wood, leather, and old paper hit her as she entered the library, bringing her instant comfort. The gas lamps left burning, cast a low yellow glow about the room, enough for Evelyn to discern its beauty, even if they weren't bright enough for her to truly appreciate it.

Evelyn often thought of the library in a home like its mind, each of the books contained within representing a thought or memory. The bedroom would normally represent the heart, a place where people met the sweet embrace of dreams and of lovers, but for Evelyn, neither of those things was true. Her heart, just like her bedroom, had begun to feel abandoned. Every corridor and hallway snaking within would be the veins, and the kitchen, of course, would be the stomach. Evelyn smiled at this thought as she walked around the various shelves, her hand lightly skimming the spines of every book as she passed. She thought her metaphor clever and poetic until she began to wonder what the people inside the building represented, and the unease she continually felt inside Blackthorn began creeping up within her once more.

At first, she had supposed herself and the other residents to be blood cells, moving through the hallway veins and entering the various organ rooms of the house. But then a darker and more repulsive notion seeped inside her mind: what if they were a virus? An uninvited and unwanted guest inside Blackthorn's body, something to be eliminated and removed? Or perhaps they were food, small creatures ingested by the wide-mouthed front door, slowly being digested within.

Evelyn shuddered at the idea.

The candle she held flickered, casting strange shadows as she passed from one shelf to the other. She didn't want to risk making the lamps burn brighter, resigned to using the candlelight—something she was used to doing, having scurried away to unknown, shadowy corners of her childhood home to escape the pitying stare of guests or the anxious questions of her father.

There was a thick layer of dust on many of the books, along with the familiar signs of bookworms. It seemed she was not the only intruder within Blackthorn. She held her breath a moment, imagining she could hear them feasting on the various tomes. A pity indeed to imagine such destruction. She sighed heavily. Like everything else in Blackthorn, beneath the shining surface, there was rot.

The dark wood shelves were densely packed with hundreds of books covering every topic imaginable. Everything from history to biology, from poetry to astronomy, was neatly packed side-by-side in cloth and leather covers in every color, all faded by age and sunlight. She ran her hand over their spines, brushing them gently with her fingertips, wondering how many lifetimes it would take for someone to read each and every one. They were like friends she had not yet met, and each one made her feel a little less lonely.

Mid-thought, her hand stopped suddenly and wavered over a worn, brown leather spine. The book was titled *Ancient Runes*, and along its length were the simple, lined shapes of a language Evelyn did not know but had seen in her dream, etched and blood-soaked on a doorway to another world.

Her hand remained motionless and removed, as if touching the book would transport her back to that terrible place, back to the dead and rotting woman. Thoughts and memories flitted through her mind, frantic and random, as an attempt to find a rational and real-world explanation for what must surely be a coincidence. She had never seen such symbols before—not that she could recall—and yet she had recreated them so perfectly inside her mind. How was that possible?

The only conclusion—and a flimsy one at that—was that she must have glanced at them on one of her many library visits, on a monument while traveling, or perhaps in an exhibit in a museum or the wall of a gallery. The images, the symbols, once seen, however swiftly, must have lodged themselves deep within her subconscious only to emerge now in her nightmares. But even as she told herself this and tried to convince herself that it was true, she knew deep down that it was something else, something otherworldly. Could it be the sight that Lilly had described? Could she truly have such abilities?

Slowly and carefully, like a prospector removing dynamite from his pouch, Evelyn pulled the book from its home on the shelf. She held it away from her as if it could explode and gently placed it on a nearby table, examining the cover with anxious curiosity. It had the same patina as the spine, the book having been read and re-read many times over. In patches, leather had been worn completely away, revealing the card beneath. It reminded Evelyn of a sick animal, balding and mangy. Taking a deep breath, she opened the cover and began to read, suddenly hungry for the possible revelations within. She read aloud in a hushed tone, lest Blackthorn itself may hear:

"These primitive symbols may appear as simple lines and shapes to the untrained eye; however, they represent a rich and varied culture with a history stretching back millennia. Each symbol represents letters and concepts in a set of related alphabets native to the Germanic people, known as Runic alphabets, dating as far back as 150 AD."

Pausing, she searched her mind for any instances in which she may have encountered such an alphabet but was once more left wanting. As confused as she was with the relationship between herself and these symbols, she also pondered their connection to Blackthorn. What relevance would the symbols of an ancient Germanic language have to a stately manor house in nineteenth-century England?

She read on: "Although several nations and cultures used these alphabets, they are most associated with the Viking invaders of Northern Europe." The words of her husband's unnervingly enthusiastic retelling of his family's violent past came to her mind, and she immediately understood the connection.

Reading at a frantic pace, she finished the chapters on etymology, history, and origins in mere minutes, trying to absorb the information as quickly as possible. She flicked through page after page with desperate veracity when she abruptly came to a stop on a chapter entitled "Magical or Divinatory Use." Of all the chapters, this appeared to be the most read, its pages loose, its corners dog-eared and worn.

She whispered the words aloud, casting a spell of her own. "Runes were often used for magic and charms by these ancient peoples, as part of ceremonies and worship of their many gods, or to abate the fears caused by their superstitious beliefs. Examples have been found across Europe of their use in everything from divining the future to cursing enemies, from protecting homes and loved ones to fertility rituals. In every example, it is clear to historians and archaeologists that to these ancient races, these symbols were more than mere words and letters: they transcended language and communication to become powerful talismans all their own."

Evelyn mulled this over in her mind, the ramifications weighing heavily on her heart. She had known the symbols were something beyond mere lines—why else would they have been carved there? But to see her fears made manifest, written neatly and so matter-of-factly, sent a coldness snaking down her spine. Clearly, the symbols had been placed there with intention, a deliberate design. They were not mere decoration but a declaration, a prayer to gods long dead, a spell cast by ancient means. But the reason behind such action remained a mystery, so she continued to flick through the pages with desperate hands, absorbing the information with fervor.

She read through various instances of legend where the symbols were used to raise the dead, to smite enemies with powerful affliction, and to enlist or incite the wrath and power of ancient gods and goddesses whose names meant nothing to Evelyn with her traditional Christian upbringing. She found herself both fascinated and enthralled by this ancient culture. The stories were poetic and vivid and made her imagination roam toward ancient battlefields and crumbling castles.

Eventually, she came to a page that listed the symbols themselves, as well as their translations, pronunciations, and meanings—a traveler's handbook for a land long lost to time. Her hand began to shake as she immediately recognized the runes she had seen in her dream, the image of their blood-smeared carvings forever imprinted inside her mind.

There was one that looked to Evelyn to be a drunken, slanted capital F, which, according to the table, meant *wealth*. The next was another less pronounced but equally drunken F, this time its two horizontal arms slanting down rather than up, which meant *god*. An elongated X, which meant *gift,* followed, and finally, a sharp-edged knot, as if someone had drawn an X without lifting their pen from paper, which meant *possession* or *estate*. There had been another symbol, the largest and most prominently placed directly above the center of the door, which Evelyn frustratingly could find no example of within the guide. She said the meanings aloud, hoping she could derive some meaning from them by doing so. "Wealth, god, gift, possession, estate."

Why, of all the symbols, were these the ones she had seen in her dream? And realistically, was there any meaning to derive, or were these images long since buried in her subconscious, a random selection of the many within her mind, appearing for no reason or purpose? The question was maddening, and for a long time, she continued to stare at the table, willing an answer to appear and make itself known to her. As if her silent prayers were answered, the book slipped from her hands and fell open to reveal pages covered in the hurried scribbles of a frantic hand. Some of it was illegible and looked more like scribbles than actual writing, but among the inky scrawl, Evelyn could discern words.

"Hel will have her vengeance."

"Save their souls."

"Forgive me."

"Penance."

The clear desperation with which they had been written, combined with their regretful, religious rhetoric and mournful tone, made anxiety tighten and knot within Evelyn's chest, her breathing growing shallow and rapid. What did this mean? Who wrote it? Who was Hel, and why would she be seeking revenge?

A dozen questions screamed inside her head, but it was not these questions nor the words from which they grew like thorny vines that caused panic to cloud her vision and the room to spin. It was a name surrounded by the scratched ink, a name that Evelyn had already found etched into Blackthorn, representing a side of her of which she was afraid: *Emmett.*

Conflicting emotions bubbled within her. She had come to the library to seek answers, and that was exactly what she had found within the ragged book held in her shaking hand. But the book seemed to raise more questions than it provided. Her frustration and confusion vastly overshadowed these answers and her sense of achievement.

She thought of Hansel and Gretel from the tale told by her mother. They had laid pebbles along the path to find their way home. Evelyn was working her way along a path through a dark and strange place, too, and the book seemed to be a pebble, a marker to guide her. But, she thought, it could easily be a breadcrumb, something fleeting, consumed by the birds to lead her further into the dark. The image of the young ghost boy came to her mind, running happily around a home where he was forever lost. Was he Emmett? Had he led her to his name to help guide her or to confuse her further so he might have a playmate among the lost souls of Blackthorn?

She shuddered, the fire having long since died away within the grate, leaving the room without warmth, light, or cheer. She tightened her grip on the book.

You cannot have this breadcrumb.

Whatever had happened within Blackthorn's past and whatever was happening now, she would follow the trail until she found her answers. What choice did she have?

Lilly held the book delicately with her eyes closed, a hand placed palm down on either side of it, as if in prayer with the family Bible. She said nothing; her only movement was her chest's slow and rhythmic rise and fall. Her eyelids fluttered slightly, her eyes moving rapidly at first, then slowly beneath the delicate skin of her lids, as if she could somehow read the words inside. Evelyn realized she was holding her breath. The room was eerily quiet; the only sound was the soft movement of the fire's flames and the occasional pop of a damp log within. Eventually, Lilly opened her eyes, the green stark and bright despite her being in shadow.

"Anything?"

Ever since Evelyn had hurriedly shown Lilly the book and updated her regarding her nightmare and the strange markings on her neck, still tender and currently hidden behind the high lace neck of her blouse, she had been desperate to hear her thoughts on the subject. Lilly felt like her only real friend within a house of strangers, including, it seemed, her own husband. Other members of the staff were cold and distant, eyeing her with disdain as if she were a bad smell or a foreign invader that needed to be overthrown. She had attempted to engage them in innocent, innocuous conversation about the weather or the book she read, but they acted as if they had not heard her. Even when she merely enquired their name or thanked them for their services, they refused to acknowledge her beyond a curt nod. In four months at Blackthorn, apart from a handful of words, Ms. Winters was the only servant to speak to her, though it was more of a reluctant grunt. Sometimes, she compared their silence toward her to the existence of the spirits of Blackthorn. This, she thought, must be how they feel—invisible, unseen. Peter's abrupt change made it all worse—this new version of him, so cold and uncaring, a stark contrast from the affectionate and loving man she had fallen in love with. Indeed, if it weren't for Lilly, she would have surely lost her mind. Involuntarily, her eye flitted toward the ceiling, imagining a rope, a noose at its end. She shuddered despite the heat of the fire.

"It's hard to distinguish much of anything other than the

emotion," Lilly said finally. "It's so strong—the grief, the anguish, the fear. I feel those things a lot in this house. Blackthorn is steeped in it."

Evelyn moved her eyes around the walls of the small parlor and understood exactly what Lilly meant. A person didn't need psychic powers to sense the negative emotions radiating from the building like heat from a flame. It was palpable and unmistakable.

"Can you sense anything that may help us?"

"It was a man who wrote it; I can hear his sobbing. He sounds older. He sounds in pain."

Evelyn let out a frustrated puff of air.

Since her nightmare and subsequent discovery in the library, she had embarked on a fervent search for answers. She'd spent hours pulling books from the library shelves, looking for one with more writing inside and more clues, but found none.

In her own home, the family Bible had been handed down from father to father and contained her entire family tree. They had boxes of letters, memento mori cards, and wedding invitations, all stained yellow at the touch of passing time. But within Blackthorn House, she could find no such mementos. When she asked Peter about their family Bible, he fixed her with a look so cold and disdainful that she positively withered beneath it. "We have none," was all he had said, and not wishing to pursue what was clearly a controversial topic, she sought no clarification.

She had walked the length and breadth of the house a dozen times and found nothing save for hundreds of portraits of the male heirs to the Black family name and their male relatives, with no trace of any women anywhere. No mothers, no sisters, no family portraits—just stern, square-jawed men with receding hairlines or young teenage boys showing off their horse or sword, all with the same sandy blond hair and ice-blue eyes that seemed to pass through the bloodline as consistently as the Black name and title.

The only room she had not been able to explore fully was her husband's office, one he had made clear to her that she was not to enter. She knew there would be answers within those four walls—she could sense it—but she was not ready to risk Peter's wrath. A man capable of such dichotomous emotions and such abrupt and inexplicable shifts was not someone she wanted to test just yet.

Even Lilly had been unable to produce any information from the other staff members who treated her with the same disdain and coldness as Evelyn, albeit in a more openly hostile way. They refused to speak with her except to bark orders.

Evelyn's hand moved to her mother's pearls, catching the small crucifix hidden within her blouse. She thought of the woman at the inn, of her reaction to the name Black, of the silent warning behind her fearful stare. "We need to ask the locals in the nearby villages," she said.

Lilly, who had seemed lost in thought since placing the book down, turned her gaze to Evelyn. "Ms. Winters won't let me go with the others to get supplies, and when anything gets delivered, she shoos me away from them like I were a naughty child. The one time I got speaking to a boy—the one who brings the meat—I only got in a few words before she came flying out in a rage, yelling at me like I were being indecent or summit. I've tried, ma'am, I have."

"Well, I haven't. Wives go into town all the time to shop and to make visits."

"Who would you visit?"

Evelyn sagged a little at that, for she had no one. No friends or family lived nearby, and despite sending multiple letters to her brother and father, she had yet to receive a single response. She often wondered if, by taking a new name and home, the old Evelyn had somehow been erased, forgotten. That Lady

Black, as she now was—a woman who lived in a house she was afraid of with a husband she did not know—was utterly and completely alone. Once more, she was struck with the understanding that without Lilly, she would have succumbed to those dark feelings and thoughts that picked and scratched at her insides.

"I have no one, but we could still say I wish to explore, to shop. I haven't left this godforsaken house since we arrived. Even the walks I have tried to take have been thwarted time and time again by the seemingly never-ending rain. We will come up with something."

"But then, what do we say when we get there? Who will we talk to? It's not like we can tell them the truth, is it?"

Evelyn smirked, imagining herself going up to some stranger on the street.

Hello there. I think the house I live in is haunted, and my husband is hiding something terrible from me. Do you know of any psychics or ghost hunters nearby who could assist?

No doubt she would end up on the same numbing drugs as her poor mother or be hauled off to some asylum for troubled wives somewhere, where ice baths are administered daily, and the women inside have retreated into their minds to avoid the true horrors of their existence.

"I don't know what we will say or to whom we will speak, but we aren't getting any answers here, so we must try."

Nine

For two weeks, Evelyn tried every avenue she could think of to convince Peter to allow her to go to the village. Each conversation would go much the same, regardless of how or in what context the topic was introduced. She would raise the subject, suggest it casually, or perhaps ask outright, and he would shrug off her requests with the same platitudes spoken with indifference.

"I was hoping to go into the village this week."

"Is there something you need?" He stared at her above his newspaper, eyebrows knotted in the middle in confusion—or was it irritation? She could no longer tell.

"No, I have no need of anything specific…"

"Precisely! You have everything you could possibly need here at Blackthorn. Why go elsewhere?" He returned to his paper as if the matter were now resolved, boxed neatly, and tidied away with her other nonsense ideas.

She pressed on.

"I would like to know the area where we live to see all it has to offer."

"It has nothing to offer people like us."

She wasn't sure what he meant by that statement. His tone seemed to intimate that more than mere class separated him from the local villagers, but Evelyn thought it wise not to inquire further.

"I believe a change of surroundings would do me good."

The newspaper was lowered slowly now, deliberately. It was more than just a movement to enable eye contact with her—it was a statement in and of itself.

I've said the wrong thing.

"Is there something wrong with Blackthorn?" His entire visage shifted. He stared at her, eyes darkened by anger as his hands clenched around the edges of the newspaper, far too hard, crumpling it along with her will to object.

She wanted to scream, *Yes! There is something very wrong with Blackthorn. There is something terribly wrong with you as well, with all that dwells here, both living and dead.*

The question, however, was an obvious trap. If she were to answer in the negative, the conversation would be over, ending in defeat once more. And, if she said yes, it would result in an argument, and Evelyn feared what that would mean for her.

He stared at her now like a predator watching its prey. She feared his anger more than she feared Blackthorn itself, so she changed the subject, and Peter returned to his paper.

So it continued every time she asked him. She would broach the subject tentatively, and he would return her question with impatience and then anger, almost daring her to continue to see what would happen. When she mentioned wanting to visit the seamstress, new dresses appeared in her room. When she spoke of wanting to find a new hobby, embroidery hoops and music books were left by her door. When she wished to explore or get some air, even just into the house's moors, she was told the weather was too wet and too cold. She would get ill. She would get lost.

Tension finally reached a fever pitch on a blustery Saturday afternoon as they took tea in the parlor. Evelyn gently stirred her tea as she spoke as casually as she could muster. "I always found church to be such a peaceful place. Perhaps I could meet with the reverend tomorrow ahead of this week's Sunday service and get better acquainted?"

Peter slammed his fist onto the table with such ferocity that his teacup jumped within its saucer.

Fear paralyzed Evelyn, her breath bated in anticipation of what was to come. She recalled coming upon a rabbit once in the forest near her home. It had come to a sudden stop before her, a statue apart from its twitching nose. She had opened her mouth to reassure the creature, to let it know she meant no harm, right before the silence was punctured with a sudden pop. Blood and sinew erupted from the startled creature in small sprays, its eyes frozen in pain before it fell lifeless and still. Her brother and his friends had been hunting—something Evelyn still abhorred to that day. At that moment, she was the rabbit, waiting for the shot to come.

Peter stared at her intensely, his once handsome face contorted with fury, his fist resting where it had dropped. He spat out words that filled her with dread: "There is no god at Blackthorn but me!"

Seconds seemed to stretch into forever as he held her gaze, and Evelyn remained still, a rabbit in the sights of a gun. Then his features softened, his stance became relaxed, and in a tone that one might even consider warm, he politely excused himself and left her to weep alone.

The walls of Blackthorn, once so vast, so grand, began to close and tighten around her. She felt like a prisoner in her own home, at the mercy of a man she did not recognize and guarded by a staff whose loyalties had been made clear. She felt suffocated, stifled, subdued. She went to the window to stare out at the vast moors, the road to the village, and the birds that flew freely above it until the feeling became overwhelming.

In an instant, it felt as if her very breath had been stolen from her. She gasped and retched, clawing at her corsets with fevered, desperate hands. Lilly, who had come to clear the tea, rushed to her side, saying words Evelyn could no longer hear—she sounded so far away. Others appeared, and someone caught her as she fell, the room spinning and darkening before her. Ms. Winters yelled something she couldn't make out, and someone placed a firm hand across her chest—too hard, too strong. Couldn't they see she was dying?

She pulled at her laces and tore at her dress, but they only held her more firmly until terror gave way to overwhelming exhaustion. The last thing she saw before she willingly succumbed to the black void of unconsciousness was the face of her warden, her husband.

Good, she thought before she passed out completely. *At least he can see what he has wrought.*

She awoke in bed surrounded by staff and flanked by men she didn't recognize, one being her husband.

"My name is Dr. Wells," said the other, holding her wrist with his sweaty hands. "From Whitwick."

Still dazed, she didn't bother to ask why Peter did not seek the help of Black Skull's physician, though she knew the locals had good cause to steer clear of the Black family and their home. Even this man, Dr. Wells, seemed fidgety and nervous, his hand shaking as he checked the cadence of her heartbeat.

She thought of the White Horse Inn and the woman there who had, in her own way, tried to warn her. Evelyn understood that the stain of the Black family spread far and wide, bleeding out from Blackthorn, tainting everything it touched, and spreading fear like a virus. The doctor was afraid, and when their eyes met briefly as he went about his examination, she could tell he understood that she was as well.

"It is psychological, I'm afraid—an attack of the nerves," he told Peter. "Quite common among women of a certain age, particularly when they go through a great change, like getting married or moving home. I recommend she get out of the house and get some fresh air."

Peter made no effort to conceal his disgust, spitting his words at the doctor with such vigor that the man recoiled as if they might somehow take form and strike him once they were uttered. "Fresh air? Your prescription is fresh air?"

Everyone in the room—Evelyn, the doctor, Lilly, and the other staff—held their breaths, and it felt to Evelyn, not for the first time, that Blackthorn itself held its breath as well.

"W-w-well, y-yes, it's ah, it's quite common among—you know—and yes, often the little things help most." He mopped the sweat from his brow with a shaking hand before continuing, "An iron-rich diet, plenty of rest, staying hydrated, and um —you know—ah, fresh air. A change of-of-um, scenery, as it were."

Peter seethed, emanating a silent but palpable hatred. He was a furnace, slowly overheating, ready to burst at any moment. Evelyn felt Lilly's hand tighten around her own. He opened his mouth, and Evelyn flinched, readying herself for the verbal attack. However, before he could utter a syllable, the doctor spoke again.

"Of course, you could, uh, seek a second opinion if you so wished."

The effect was instantaneous. The wrath evaporated, and Peter visibly sagged, angry but defeated. Evelyn understood then that Doctor Wells was the only nearby physician willing to go behind the walls of Blackthorn House. Peter had no choice but to take his diagnosis, knowing none other was forthcoming. And she understood something else as well—the doctor was trying to help her. It filled her heart with hope and optimism she had not felt in quite some time.

Peter straightened himself, swallowing his anger like a child taking its medicine. "I see. What happens with this condition if it goes untreated?"

Evelyn's hope disappeared as quickly as it had come. He intended to ignore the doctor, to keep her trapped like some sad wild bird forced into a cage.

I'll never be able to leave this place.

"Well," Doctor Wells shifted uncomfortably as understanding settled in. "It can lead to greater mental illness, even to insanity and hysteria."

Peter stared at him unsympathetically.

"B-bu-but it, ah, it can lead to physical issues as well."

That seemed to reach Peter, and he stood a little straighter. "Physical issues? What kinds of physical issues?"

Doctor Wells cast toward the carpet.

Poor man.

"Well, eh, there are a multitude of issues which can occur —er, ah, physically—everything from, um, from temporary blindness, headaches, nausea..."

Peter seemed unperturbed.

The doctor went on. "To, um, fertility issues, to..."

"What?" Peter balled his fists, his eyes bulging. He was furious; that much was clear, but there was more there. Concern, maybe even fear?

"Are you telling me that she may not be able to conceive a child?"

The doctor seemed surprised—he clearly hadn't thought he would be able to persuade Peter of anything, and the notion gave him new confidence. He stood straighter and looked Peter in the eye, his tone changing to a wobbly confidence it had not possessed seconds earlier. "Well, yes. She needs rest, good nutrition, and exercise, and it is my formal diagnosis that a change of scenery will benefit her overall health." He nodded slightly at the end of the sentence as if to affirm what he had said.

And just like that, Evelyn was allowed to leave Blackthorn House.

As the carriage rattled away from Blackthorn's shadow, the weight of the place began to lift. Evelyn sighed, closing her eyes and leaning back into her seat. Lilly must have understood the meaning of the gesture, for she responded in kind with the removal of her bonnet and the unwinding of her rigid back.

"It feels good to be away from that place, even if it's only a while."

Evelyn nodded. "I tried to arrange a visit to my father's, but Peter would have none of it. He was so angry at the mere suggestion that I didn't dare push further."

This time, it was Lilly's turn to nod.

Evelyn continued, "The village is better than nothing, as you say, and at least this way, we may get some answers."

Lilly straightened her back, her face taking on a more serious expression. "What are our plans?"

Evelyn thought for a moment. "We must ask around, see if any of the villagers will speak to us. It's all we can do."

"What of Harrison? He won't approve of the conversations we need to have. And I doubt he'll let us out of his sight."

Harrison, one of Blackthorn's stable hands, was indeed a problem. Peter had insisted that the women be accompanied at all times by a member of his staff. Although he had looked as unhappy about his role as prison guard as Evelyn had, she knew he would do whatever had been asked of him with diligence, just as all the staff at Blackthorn did when Peter gave an order.

Evelyn looked at Lilly slyly. "Do not fret on that, for I have a plan."

Lilly appeared puzzled, but as Evelyn reached into her

skirts and removed a small vial, her expression changed to understanding and even admiration. It was laudanum, provided by the kindly Doctor Winchester. "A few drops of this in his drink, and he will sleep like a newborn babe." Both women grinned, co-conspirators in a grand scheme.

The carriage rolled and rocked like a ship on choppy seas, the uneven marshland passing by in a brown and gray blur. Lilly gripped the seat with whitened knuckles, her face pale and clammy, motion sickness lodged stubbornly in her throat, while Evelyn stared out the window. As the moors passed by, Evelyn could understand and appreciate their beauty. It was a wild and untamed world of trees twisted and coiled after years of beating winds, of coarse grass as tall as herself. A lonely and picturesque landscape painted in the darkest greens, intense browns, and mottled grays. Even the dreariness of the winter rains, with its gray skies, complemented the fierceness of it all; the ever-changing light and shadow cast about the land as the clouds rolled and tumbled above. As she watched, the sky lightened with the midmorning sun, shafts of it cutting deep, straight lines through the clouds and highlighting points of the earth like spotlights. It was beautiful.

Evelyn sighed. "I forget how isolated we are at Blackthorn."

Lilly murmured understanding, moving her eyes briefly to the blur of wilderness rolling past them, the window framing it like a moody oil painting.

"I used to pray for snow every winter. My brother and I would sled down steep hills or throw snowballs at one another. One year, we built a snowman and put our father's good jacket and hat upon it, along with his reading glasses. He was not too happy about that one, but how we both laughed." Her face fell, memories once happy, making her feel nothing but grief and loneliness. She missed her family terribly. "Now, I fear snow more than anything. I am already a prisoner within my own home. The snow would be the final turn of the key on my cell door. We would have no escape."

Lilly leaned toward her, taking both of her hands in her own and squeezing them tightly.

Evelyn appreciated the gesture more than Lilly could ever know, and as she squeezed her in return, her heart swelled with love for the girl.

"How long until Black Skull?"

Black Skull. Even the village had their name. Every time she heard it, it filled her head with visions of vicious pirates and flags with skulls and crossbones, of blood and battle. Of course, the village name had nothing to do with pirates, but to Evelyn's overactive imagination after a lifetime of reading, it was a ship full of buccaneers.

"I would say at least another thirty minutes hence," Evelyn replied.

Lilly took the opportunity to lean back into her seat and close her eyes.

As Evelyn watched the desolate landscape beyond the carriage window, she thought of her dinner with Peter. Of him reveling in the bloody and violent history of the Black family and the poor villagers who met the sharp end of their swords. She wondered how he could so nonchalantly discuss mass murder. To Evelyn, the past shaped who they were. Even ancient history still altered the world around them, through traditions, the origins of which were long forgotten, and the language and expressions used, right up to the names they bore and passed down to the next generation. Good or bad, its touch was inescapable, and Peter, it seemed, delighted in it, regardless of how dark and terrible it may have been.

The Blacks apparently felt quite comfortable with one foot forever static within their long and bloody history, and Blackthorn House was that past made manifest. A museum of the Black family and a self-aggrandizing exhibition—a monument to their achievements and sense of self-importance. She now hated the portraits, busts, and items placed carefully under glass cloches with tiny brass plaques commemorating their importance and meaning. Blackthorn was a prison with golden bars, but a prison nonetheless.

Lilly, her face still a pasty white, weakly asked, "How long now?"

"It appears we have arrived."

The vast moors were interrupted by the appearance of stone walls and neatly trimmed bushes, of flower beds and vegetable patches, and stone cottages and thatched roofs. The pitch and turn of the waves gave way to slower and stiller waters, and the carriage leveled out and quieted, much to Lilly's obvious relief. Eventually, the soft, water-logged noises made by the turn of the wheels and the sploshing of the horse's hooves gave way to the steady, sharp thrum of stone. The houses began to crowd together in narrower and taller quarters, like children vying to get to the front of a line, eager to be the first out the door.

By the time the carriage rolled to a steady stop, Evelyn was hungry and eager for lunch. Lilly, however, looked decidedly queasy at the idea but was fully on board with the concept of a static seat. They walked side by side toward the village pub, their driver and reluctant escort Harrison trailing behind them.

Evelyn loathed that she had to be guarded and watched, and she couldn't work out if it was for her own protection, as Peter had stated, or if it was to maintain control of her even when outside the walls of Blackthorn. Either she was a precious porcelain doll incapable of looking after herself, or something to be owned and possessed, and both ideations ignited sparks of rage within her. She shot a look of contempt back at her newly inherited shadow.

He was an extremely tall man—a good head taller than Peter—and despite being relatively thin, the outline of muscle bulged and stretched the fabric of his gray shirt, rolled up just below his elbow, revealing tanned skin, a clear indication of outdoor labor. He had a square head and jaw, a thicket of coarse black hair peppered with gray, and a strong brow. He must have been in his thirties—no older than thirty-five—yet he had a haunted look to his gray eyes, which spoke of having seen enough for more than one lifetime, making him seem older than his years. He furrowed his brow constantly and rubbed his stubbled chin as if perpetually pondering a question no one asked. When not rubbing his chin, his hands were wiped at the back of his neck with a red kerchief. They were calloused and rough, each finger at an odder angle than the next, a map of injuries and breaks going back years. He clomped behind them with large, heavy strides and watched them with an air of discontent.

He appeared as irritated by his new duties as Evelyn was. When she glanced back at him a second time, his eyes met hers briefly before he cast them down again, like a child caught spying.

The local pub, unimaginatively called Black Skull Inn, displayed a wooden sign hanging perpendicular to the building depicting a skull lying in the dying ashes of a fire, partly blackened from the heat. The sign swung on squeaking hinges as they made their way beneath it, and Evelyn briefly imagined the damage it would do to their skulls were it to come loose from its post and crash down upon their heads. Inside, a brick fireplace cast its cozy glow about the room, the smell of burning peat mixing with scents of food and ale. Red brick peeped out from cracks and holes dotted about the white plaster walls, and the only picture—a map of Britain—hung askew in a battered frame. A wood and black iron light fixture hung from thick ropes above their head, cobwebs shifting like gossamer in the draft. There were a handful of wood top tables, scratched and stained by a thousand glasses and plates, and mismatched chairs—many with obvious repairs—sat atop a bare stone floor. It was the pub of a poor village, imperfect and well-worn but comfortable nonetheless.

To the left was a dark wood counter, just as scratched and aged as the tables it served. Several pumps of brass and stained wood rose from behind it like the fingers of some creature reaching out from the darkness beneath. On the wall behind the counter stood dusty bottles, glasses, and mugs on wooden shelves, all of which surrounded the mounted head of a stag. Its antlers were tangled with the same delicate webs as the light, its black glass eyes caught forever in its last, panicked state. Its fur had been worn in patches as if it had mange and lightened considerably on the side where it had caught decades of sunlight through the dirty windows.

Beneath the stag, a rotund man stood drying a pitcher with great concentration, sweat dotting the edge of his receding hair-line. He wore a half-apron, stained and fraying, below a brown shirt. His collar was open to reveal a blue kerchief, neatly tied and tucked beneath the shirt. He looked at them when they entered, and his hand stopped mid-wipe, his dark brown eyes slowly moving between the three of them as recognition hard-ened his features. It was clear he knew exactly who Evelyn was and where they had come from, and it seemed to instill him with a nervous kind of resignation. Her presence would be tolerated, not welcomed.

It appeared to be a running theme.

Only four other patrons were inside the inn at that time, and all four paused in solidarity with the barman, although slightly delayed in their reaction. It was as if a spell had been cast about the place, turning them from flesh to statues of wax. A pipe stopped midway, a forkful of pie crust never made it to a mouth, a hand limp in mid-air, and a young boy, no older than ten, who also wore a dirty half apron, held the glass he had just collected in front of him like a shield. It was a painting, a still-life capture of the bar at that exact moment in time.

Of course, the locals knew who she was, for who else would she be? They did not need to see the grand carriage parked outside with the Black family crest carved neatly in its doors to know she was from Blackthorn House. She was now painted with the same blood-soaked brush as all others who held the Black family name, and like it or not, she would now induce the apprehension and discomfort the name wrought in others.

It was the second time her presence had elicited such a reaction, and Evelyn was still not used to such unnerving attention. Her face flushed, and the familiar pangs of anxiety clawed at her chest once more. She desperately searched for a way to break the tension, to end the silence that hung over them like the spiderwebs, but her mind was a racing mass of thoughts and feelings. She barely managed a timid squeak, which quickly became a cough, only serving to draw further attention to them.

From her conversations with Peter, as well as her own research conducted prior to her move, she had learned that Black Skull was not a thoroughfare—it was not a village frequented by travelers or those passing through. Black Skull was the last sign of life on the very edge of a vast wilderness, apart, of course, from Blackthorn. The only strangers who ventured there had business there, and few of them were of the higher classes.

Just when she thought she would have to turn and run from the place, unable to take the focused gaze of strangers much longer, Harrison's booming voice came from behind her and firmly but politely requested a table. This seemed to break the spell, and all concerned simply sputtered back to life again, an engine successfully turned over. The barkeep tipped his head toward a table by the leaded window, and all three carefully maneuvered toward it, hoping not to draw further attention to themselves with the echoing sound of their boots. Harrison took their coats, and Evelyn and Lilly took a seat on either side of the indicated table. Harrison chose a small one-seater table nearby, half hidden by shadow. Clearly, while he understood and continued with his duties, he still respected and maintained propriety toward Evelyn and her title. For that, she was grateful, not wanting her and Lilly's conversation to be overheard.

"I seem to cause quite a stir wherever I go these days."

"It's not you, ma'am; it's your name."

Evelyn silently let the implications of those words settle over her. It was something she had already known but would not utter aloud for fear of what it truly meant. Lilly, unlike Evelyn, spoke plainly and openly, her heart ever present on her sleeve, her intuitions understood and identified. These were qualities Evelyn did not possess. She seemed to stumble through life, confused and anxious, constantly trying to decipher its meanings. Lilly walked ahead, her head up, her heart sure. If these things could be taught, Evelyn would have asked for instruction, but as it stood, she could only watch the girl in quiet admiration.

A slight woman approached their table and gave Evelyn a slight bow of her head, recognition of her title and status. Evelyn immediately felt uncomfortable, color rising to her cheeks.

She had never experienced this kind of submission before. Having grown up in a wealthy family, she was no stranger to being treated with a certain amount of esteem by hired staff or the lower classes. Status and wealth afforded such regard, whether deserved or not, but Evelyn's family had always mirrored that respect in return.

The way people treated her now, however, was on an entirely different level. It was not just the respect of her title—there was a distinct fear to it as if she could bellow "off with their heads" at any moment. As if she were the Queen of Hearts, and they were the lowly playing cards whom she could have executed on a whim. Evelyn found it unbearable.

The woman was older than Evelyn, with tired, sagging eyes ringed in dark circles and a mouth pinched tight. She wrung her hands on a small towel, pulling at it like a child clinging to a safety blanket. She sputtered when she spoke, fear at the edge of her soft and mumbled voice. "We don't have much on offer, my lady. I'm afraid we aren't used to catering for finer folks here."

Evelyn smiled warmly, trying to put the woman at ease. "I'm sure whatever you have will be wonderful. We aren't fussy."

The woman seemed taken aback, her brow furrowing as if she had been unprepared to continue the conversation beyond her initial statement. "Well...we have game pie and lamb. Comes with potatoes and carrots."

"Both sound wonderful. I think I will have the lamb. What would you like, Lilly? And don't bother saying you aren't hungry—I insist upon it. Same for you, Harrison." Evelyn shot Harrison a look that he briefly met.

He appeared uncomfortable and unsure how to respond, his mouth twitching as if to speak, but he remained silent, having thought better of it. With no response from Harrison, Evelyn took it upon herself to order for all of them. "It appears all three of us would like the lamb, thank you."

Lilly smiled in approval, perhaps at the order but more likely at Evelyn's handling of Harrison and the innkeeper's wife.

Their orders taken and the woman hurrying away like a frightened cat, Evelyn removed her bonnet. Then she picked up her glass of wine and lowered her voice and her head conspiratorially toward Lilly. They had come to the village for answers, and answers they would get.

Ten

It had been significantly easier to ditch Harrison than either woman anticipated. Lilly had easily slipped the laudanum into his ale under the pretense of serving him. He had eaten and drunk greedily, and after half an hour or so, his eyes grew heavy, and he fell into a deep, heady sleep. Evelyn paid the barkeep a generous tip to ensure he was not disturbed while they left.

She had felt a prickle of guilt—drugging someone did not exactly sit comfortably within her sense of morals. However, as things stood, she felt she had no choice. Desperate people, after all, have been known to render desperate deeds. Lilly, however, felt no discomfort at their actions, commenting that people had done far worse to escape their prisons. Not for the first time, Evelyn was struck by Lilly's tenacity and strength of conviction. She was gladder than ever to have Lilly as an ally.

Lilly had spoken with their waitress when Harrison was distracted with his meal, attempting to raise questions about Blackthorn House and the Black family, and the girl had shaken her head fervently and placed a hand on either ear as if she were a child refusing to listen to a scary story. She ran from Lilly like a deer chased by hunters, the other bar patrons following suit. Even the barkeep point-blank refused to discuss any such matters with them. "We don't talk about the Blacks here," was his cryptic and final response.

They had almost given up hope when the young lad they had seen upon entering caught Evelyn's eye and beckoned her to the rear rooms with a quick jolt of his head. With Harrison now slumped and dozing, Evelyn knew it was time to move. She caught Lilly's eyes. "Will you watch over him?"

Lilly nodded.

Evelyn quickly retrieved her coat and hastily followed the boy into a rear courtyard dotted with rotting wooden casks and weeds. It was only drizzling, but the sky hung heavy and gray above their heads, angry clouds heavy with a burden they threatened to unleash at any moment. It seemed the drizzle was just a hint of the torrent to come. Though she still wore her hat, the boy did not, and Evelyn stepped under the overhang to offer them shelter.

"What is your name?" she asked him gently.

"Charlie, ma'am."

"And how old are you, Charlie?"

"Eleven, ma'am. The barkeep's my pa." He looked from her to the inn's door and back again, fidgeting nervously as if, at any moment, his father would appear with a reprimand. To Evelyn, he looked like a hare who had caught the scent of hounds in the air.

She waited patiently for him to settle, and when both felt comfortable that no one had noticed their disappearance, she spoke. "I'm looking for information about Blackthorn House and the Black...I mean, my family history. Can you tell me anything?"

"I don't know much, miss. Just stories I heard from the other kids in school."

"What kind of stories?"

He looked at her sheepishly, a glint of embarrassment and mischief in his eye. "Scary stories, miss. Ghost stories and alike. We try to scare each other with them."

"Go on."

The boy glanced once more at the door and swallowed hard. "They say Blackthorn House is haunted, ma'am. That the Blacks brought death with them when they came here all them years ago and trapped it in the house. They feed it people."

Evelyn sighed heavily. The stories whispered among playmates in the playground were just that—stories. The boy could not help her.

"I-I bet that happened to the last Lady and her kids."

That drew her attention. "What Lady?"

The boy looked at her guiltily, his eyes wider now, fear tinging the edges with tears that threatened to fall. He suddenly looked so much younger than eleven. "I ain't s'posed to talk about it, ma'am."

She withdrew a coin from her pocket and lowered herself onto her haunches so she could look him straight in the eye. "Please, Charlie—this is important. What Lady? What kids?"

He took it but looked away, suddenly fascinated by his own foot, before he mumbled his response. "The last Lady Black and her children. There was a girl and a younger boy. I don't know their names; they didn't go to our school."

A younger boy.

Evelyn could hear the disembodied laughter echoing inside her racing mind. She could see the young lad and his scrawled drawings.

Emmett.

"What happened to them?"

"I dunno about the children, but the lady died. I remember hearing my dad talking to the Doctor 'bout it, but I never heard nothing about the kids. Maybe they went away after their mum died? I only saw 'em once, when I went with Pa to deliver wine to Blackthorn. He normally doesn't take me there—always told me to stay away from it—but he'd hurt his back, and there was no one else to help with the unloading. I saw 'em at the window, all three."

"When was this?"

"Last year, miss. The Lady died not long after, I think."

Evelyn's heart pounded, and her head roared with a thousand questions, all threatening to burst forth at once. Peter had told her he was an only child—that his stepmother had passed in childbirth along with their only child. She had asked him outright, and he had lied to her unflinchingly and unapologetically. He had looked her directly in her eyes and told her a story, a fiction. Anger flared within her chest, burning away the anxiety. She spoke more harshly to the boy than she intended, grabbing his small arm when he backed away. "What else? What else?"

"I don't know. Please, I don't know nothing else." Tears began to fall from his eyes, dampening the collar of his shirt. He looked at her with terror and fear, like she was one of the Blacks from his stories, a monster or a murderer.

Instantly, her flames were quenched by his tears, and she let go of his arm. "Forgive me," she murmured. She placed a comforting hand on his shoulder as she stood. He ran off the second she removed it, and she made no effort to stop him, having done more than enough already.

He paused just before wrenching the door open. "You need to speak to the old woman who lives alone in the moors east of here, but be careful, ma'am. She's a witch." And with that, he was gone.

Evelyn hurried back into the tavern, her heart hammering in her throat. She ignored the curious looks of the patrons as she walked toward Lilly and bent to whisper in her ear. "We must go now before he wakes. Follow me."

Lilly wordlessly retrieved her coat while Evelyn approached the barkeep and produced yet another monetary bribe. “I will need directions to the old woman’s house in the moors.” When he gave her a blank look, she added, “The witch.”

He raised an eyebrow but retrieved a pencil and paper from behind the bar.

“Where are we going?” Lilly said quietly beside her.

“Are you able to untether the horses from the carriage?”

“Yes, ma’am.”

“Good, we’ll need to move quickly. I’ll explain everything en route.” Evelyn nodded thanks to the barkeep as she retrieved the hastily drawn map and led Lilly out the front door.

The cold of winter—much starker compared to the velvety warmth of the pub’s interior—winded Evelyn as they stepped out onto the cobbled street. A few people milled about, but not many. Black Skull was a sleepy, quiet place with little happening save the monthly market. Isolated by the moors and blanketed by the fog and chill of the season, it hibernated, patiently awaiting spring.

It hadn’t taken long to reach the cottage. Evelyn hadn’t ridden a horse bareback since she was a child, and she had forgotten just how uncomfortable it could be. Her thighs ached, and her neck hurt, her stress tensing her so she could not move along with the horse. Lilly had struggled to mount hers at first, but by the time they rode clear of the village, she seemed to have gotten the hang of it, establishing a quiet truce between both parties. Both horses were sweet and accustomed to riders, so neither made much of a fuss, and they reached the small stone building without incident.

Their destination was a dark-stoned cottage with a

thatched roof. It squatted in the tall grass, with no wall, fence, or row of bushes discerning its own land from the moors surrounding it. Smoke billowed from the stubby chimney as a few crows huddled near it for warmth, eyeing both women suspiciously as they approached. Like Blackthorn, this place had an aura about it, a feeling which sat heavy in the air and permeated the soul. It did not evoke in her the same sense of dread and sorrow as Blackthorn, however. Where Blackthorn's silent song was a wail of lamentation, this little structure's tune was more a tutting of disapproval, a warning to tread carefully.

Evelyn and Lilly dismounted and approached the door with slow, unsure steps. The bones of small animals hung from strings in strange patterns, wind chimes of death making hollow noises in the wind. A ram's skull hung above the door, staring at them from hollow sockets. Evelyn went to knock but stopped before her small fist made contact with the weathered wood. It hung there a moment, unsure, then knocked three times in a short, sharp burst. She stepped backward as soon as she had, fearing what would answer. She heard shuffling and clattering inside before the sound of deadbolts and latches on the other side of the door signaled an answer to Evelyn's call.

The door creaked open to reveal a glassy, white eye and a dark one, both staring at Evelyn from a wrinkled, square face topped with a bushel of coarse gray hair. Similar hair sprang from her ears and chin alongside a wart. Liver spots dusted the pale, dry face. She shielded her body with the door at first, a barrier of protection between herself and her uninvited visitors. But as soon as her eyes fell upon Evelyn's, she pulled it open entirely before shuffling back inside the house, a silent but universal invitation to follow.

They were forced to duck through the small doorway, but the ceiling allowed them space to stand. The one-room cottage had a wrought iron stove, atop which sat a bubbling pot, filling the stale, warm, and musty air with the scent of bone broth.

On the other side lay a small cot, blankets piled on a mattress stuffed with straw. A small table and chair sat beneath the cottage's only window and source of natural light, the smeared, dirty square no bigger than two feet wide. Glass jars and bottles containing dried plants and strange-colored liquids filled a nearby cabinet, while dried herbs and plants hung from the rafters in fragrant bushels. Evelyn walked straight into one, distracted by the possible contents of the jars and bottles.

The old woman limped toward a rocking chair. She was as short and squat as her home, her square, broad shoulders and wide arms draped with sagging skin showing the strength the woman had once possessed in her youth. She wore a black tunic dotted with patches and lumped stitching—a timeline detailing decades of improvised repairs. In one hand, she held a yellowing handkerchief into which she coughed loudly, her raspy, wheezing breath returning once she had overcome the attack. As Evelyn took in the woman and her home, she could understand why the local children believed her to be a witch.

She lowered herself into her rocking chair, her bones creaking as she did. For several seconds, no one spoke; Evelyn and Lilly stood in awkward silence as the woman creaked back and forth in her chair, angling her head to stare at them with her good eye. She smacked her lips, a slight smirk on her face. It was the old woman who broke the silence.

"You're the new Lady Black."

It wasn't a question, more a statement of fact, but Evelyn needed to respond anyway, nodding nervously. The old woman answered Evelyn's nod with her own, continuing to rock back and forth. The creak and tap of the chair and the bubbling brew on the stove were the only sounds within the cottage.

Evelyn held her breath, preparing for bad news.

The old woman continued, "You're not the first to come to me for answers."

"Not the first of the Black family, you mean?"

The woman nodded again before spitting onto the dirt floor, continuing her rocking motion throughout. She offered no further information, so Evelyn pressed on, desperate for answers.

"Who came before me?"

"Oh, there have been many over the decades, but the one before you was the last Lord Black himself."

Evelyn's eyes widened, her heartbeat quickening.

Why would Peter's father have come to this place? What could he have possibly wanted?

"What did he want?"

"He wanted the impossible, as you do, I imagine." The woman smacked her lips, placing her hands on her chest as she continued rocking back and forth.

Evelyn grew flushed with frustration. She began to wonder if this old woman could even help them. She was clearly in no hurry to provide them with any information—if she possessed any to begin with—and Evelyn did not have the patience or the time to play games. She was painfully aware that Harrison would be looking for them soon. She needed answers, and she needed them *now*.

"What was impossible?" she pressed. "What did he ask about?"

"He wanted to know how to break a contract that cannot be broken."

"What contract? With whom?"

"With Death herself, my dear. With Death herself."

Evelyn let out a loud and exasperated sigh, anger bubbling beneath her skin. The woman just sat there, rocking back and forth, back and forth, the creak-tap, creak-tap of her chair drilling into Evelyn's skull, testing every nerve she had. She didn't have time for children's stories or snake oil salesmen. "I don't have time for riddles—I need answers!"

The old woman huffed a short laugh as Evelyn paced in the

small cottage. She began to get the impression that the old woman was enjoying the interaction and that she was playing with her, teasing her. She wanted to scream at her to stop rocking, to answer her, to tell her what was happening to her, what was happening at Blackthorn.

"You ain't asking the right questions."

Evelyn felt a scornful yell forming on her lips, but Lilly spoke before she could voice her anger. "What is wrong with Blackthorn? Why do the dead remain there in such numbers?"

The old woman abruptly stopped rocking and turned her good eye to face Lilly. "A doorway was opened many years ago, a door to the other side."

"Who opened the door?"

"The Black family, of course, though they had a different name then."

"Why would they do such a thing?"

"The same reason all folks do bad things. For power."

"How did they do it?"

"They brought their magic with them from whence they came. They brought their gods. They came and took everything from our people, our land, our lives, and eventually, our magic. They mixed it with their own to open that door, something that should never be done. They corrupted that place with darkness and blood. Blackthorn is cursed." She turned her dark eye back toward Evelyn before speaking again, driving home the gravity of her words. "The Black family is cursed."

Evelyn's hand instinctively moved toward her mother's pearls and the crucifix beneath as if they were a talisman that could protect her from such things. Part of her wanted to laugh and storm out indignantly, embarrassed for going there in the first place. But she had seen things, felt things, at Blackthorn, which gave the old crone's words a mark of truth. She felt torn in half between belief and skepticism, between the Evelyn prior to arriving at Blackthorn and the one now. Between nightmares and reality.

Lilly spoke for them both. "What should we do?"

The old woman did not stop to think. There was no pause before her answer came, her voice sure and steady: "You should run."

Evelyn's mind raced with questions, so many that she could not seem to untangle them. Before she could utter another word, their parley was interrupted by the fervent sound of approaching hooves. It seemed their time was up.

She inhaled, readying herself for some kind of altercation with Harrison, grasping at the edges of a not-yet-fully formed excuse for their impromptu excursion to the strange, remote little home. However, her breath, along with all her courage, was immediately knocked from her when she opened the cottage door and came face to face with Peter.

Panic surged instantly through her body, the hairs on her arms standing up and her breathing growing quicker, more shallow.

"Peter...I—" was all she could manage. Her mind had become a blank canvas, with all thought and reason having escaped with her courage. She could think of no excuse, no reason, no explanation, for she knew that it was fruitless. She thought once more of that frightened rabbit on the path.

"My Lady, I am so glad I found you. We were all terribly worried, weren't we, Harrison?"

"Yes, Milord."

Peter made no move to turn to face Harrison, who stood several paces behind him, his head hung low, shoulders sagging. He looked utterly deflated, like some kind of human ragdoll, limp and lifeless. Fresh blood stained one of his cuffs, and he cradled one arm to his chest with the other.

Peter stood unnervingly rigid like a snake readying itself to strike. He did not make eye contact with Evelyn as he addressed her; instead, he looked past her and Lilly to the old woman. His face appeared calm, but the smile that hung upon it was tainted with malice. He made no attempt to disguise the revulsion, anger, and disdain emanating from him in waves, made all the more disturbing by that unwavering smile.

"I..."

Peter interrupted, "I think it's time to leave, don't you, dear?"

His voice was so flat, so toneless, yet filled with a sort of repressed energy, each word barely containing the torrent of emotion they held back. His smile remained fixed in place, though his fists were balled so tightly by his sides that they had drained completely of their color. He was some kind of grotesque clown, a painted smile hiding the sinister truth beneath. He never took his eyes off the old woman behind her, making the interaction all the more unnerving. Evelyn knew better than to argue, and as if Lilly had heard her very thoughts, she approached, placing a hand gently on Evelyn's elbow and steering them both out of the cottage.

Evelyn glanced back, her eyes falling immediately onto the old woman who stood frozen, her features twisted in what could only be described as abject terror, while Peter remained rigid—silent and still. And although Evelyn could no longer see his face, she knew he still wore that smile. He took two sure steps inside the cottage, the woman backing away as he did before the door closed with a slow creak. The last thing Evelyn saw before she heard the faint click of the latch was the old woman's terrified face.

Harrison was already working on harnessing the two horses they had borrowed back in place with the other pair. Now that she was closer to him, she could see the redness on his face, the swelling of his cheek and lip, and the faint shadow of bruises freshly painted on his skin. His hands shook badly, making his work with the horses take twice as long.

Evelyn realized hers shook, too, and she grabbed Lilly's. They stared at one another with wide, terrified eyes. No words were uttered between them, yet a silent conversation took place all the same, each knowing the thoughts and fears of the other as clearly as if they had been their own.

"We are discovered!"

"Yes, and we should assume he knows all, not just about this."

"He will not let us leave again, will he?"

"No."

"Will he hurt us? Kill us, even? Is he really capable of such things?"

"Perhaps, I do not know."

"Perhaps it is enough."

"Yes, it is."

"What do we do?"

"We escape."

"How?"

"I do not know."

All was expressed with the quiver of a lip, the slight nod of a head, and the squeeze of a hand. They were in danger—that much was obvious—but to what extent, they could not know for sure. It was clear from Harrison's newly acquired limp that Peter was capable of violence, but would he really harm her? Was he capable of murder?

Both women looked back toward the cottage. From within came muffled sounds, but they were not distinct enough to make out completely. Evelyn strained, trying to hear a stray word or noise that would indicate what was happening inside. There were voices—that was certain—not screaming, but still loud enough for their sharpest tones to reach the road beyond the garden.

No, Evelyn thought. *Not voices.* A *voice. Peter's voice.*

An abrupt noise reached her that caused her heart to skip —perhaps some kind of bang or the sound of something breaking. Evelyn could not be sure, and she cursed her cowardice. If only she were brave enough to creep up and peer through the cottage window. She held her breath as if doing so might allow her to hear more.

Evelyn realized the voice had stopped when another sound erupted from the cottage, this time loud and distinct enough for them all to hear and understand. All three of them—Evelyn, Lilly, and Harrison—turned to face the source. Harrison had dropped the holster he was holding just as Lilly had squeezed Evelyn's hand tighter than ever, and Evelyn had brought her hand to her chest. This noise, which had so fully captured the attention and fear of all three onlookers, could only be described as a woman's scream—a wet, gurgling scream filled with pain and terror, and it had lasted only a second before it was cut short, leaving only silence in its wake.

All three stood staring at the cottage door, an audience awaiting the actor to enter on stage. Evelyn swallowed hard. Somehow, the silence was worse than the muffled noises. It hung about them, thick and heavy like the fog, telling all yet revealing nothing.

Without any warning, Peter flung the door open. How long had he been in there? Evelyn could not be sure. Time had held its breath alongside them, and only now did it gasp to life once more. He still wore the smile, but it was altered—almost manic. A thin layer of perspiration coated his skin, and he appeared slightly out of breath as if he had just been on a brisk walk rather than having a conversation. She noticed one of his cufflinks had come undone, the sleeve now hanging free as if pulled from his jacket, and most disturbing of all, he was wiping his hands on his kerchief, which, having once been pure white, was now stained red.

Evelyn was instantly reminded of Lady Macbeth trying to remove the mark of blood and death, which had permanently stained her hands after her terrible deed had been done, and she shuddered. She looked behind Peter, where she had last seen the old woman, but the woman was no longer there. What she could see of the small one-room cottage appeared still and undisturbed, but this filled Evelyn's heart with little comfort. She longed to see the old woman—she needed to know if the suspicions, the fears that clawed at her chest, exposing a terrified and broken heart beneath, were correct. But the door simply closed behind him, and all was still; it was quiet.

Peter walked toward them, and she felt Lilly grow tense beside her. Harrison moved behind the horses like a dog, trying to avoid a hard kick. With every step toward them, Evelyn's terror grew until she felt ready to burst. Peter stared at her, his eyes bright with a furious fire, his stride sure and unwavering, and his smile, that terrible, twisted smile that conveyed anything but happiness.

Evelyn opened and closed her mouth to speak more than once, a fish gasping for air, but words failed her. What could she say? Her mind raced and whirred, and she readied herself for violence, her body tensing in anticipation of an assault. Yet, when he reached her, he took her hand and steered her toward the carriage door, gesturing his head toward Lilly and giving her a silent but clear order: *Sit up front, NOW!*

Lilly complied and hurried toward the front seat, where Harrison had already planted himself behind the reins. Peter never took his eyes off Evelyn. He opened the door and removed the stairs with practiced ease, but just as she went to step up onto it, he tugged her hand slightly, indicating she should stop.

Evelyn complied, fearing what further disobedience would bring.

Slowly, he moved toward her until his lips met her ear. He was so close she could smell his sweat underlined with the musk of his cologne and something else—something sweet and acrid that she could not place. His breath fell slow and humid onto her cheek, and she shuddered despite her efforts to control her terror. He whispered softly into her ear in an almost affectionate tone, "This will be the one and only reprieve you ever get, my darling wife. If you ever step so much as a toe out of line again, I will murder you. I will kill you, Lady Black, and I will bury you so deep that no one will ever find your mangled corpse. Do I make myself clear?"

He still held her hand, and now he squeezed it painfully, twisting her wrist until she cried out in pain, her knees buckling slightly with the force. He held her there a moment, staring down at her with that manic grin, twisting her arm until she was sure she would feel it break. Evelyn looked at him with tear-filled, pleading eyes, and she knew with horror that he meant every single word of what he had said. She nodded as silent tears fell, and seemingly satisfied with her response, he dropped her hand and strode away without another word.

It took every ounce of Evelyn's willpower not to crumble then and there, to fall to her knees and scream out. He would kill her—she knew that now. She finally understood what he was capable of. As she forced herself up into the carriage, she looked back at the cottage and began to cry without restraint or apology. She let the tears fall in large, desperate gulps as her sorrow and helplessness overwhelmed her. She cried for herself, she cried for Lilly, and she cried for the old woman, for she did not need to see behind the cottage door to know what violence lay beyond it.

Eleven

Evelyn sat across the large mahogany dining table from Peter as he silently ate, occasionally watching her as he sipped his wine or chewed. The table was intended to seat ten —not an insignificant distance between them—and yet, every time his eyes met hers, she felt the room close in around her, humiliation and panic surging through her veins. Each time, she would pull her gaze away and stare down at her plate as if the contents fascinated her.

When she first moved to Blackthorn and found their place settings so far apart, she asked if they could be moved to adjacent seats. Initially, Peter and Ms. Winters humored her. But, gradually, over the months since that had passed, the settings were moved farther and farther apart until they were back where they had started. Evelyn had protested once or twice, but Ms. Winters insisted that decorum and propriety must be maintained, and to Evelyn's dismay, Peter agreed. It was unseemly for a couple to show public affection of any kind, and apparently, that included proximity while they ate, even in private. Now, however, she was glad of the distance. She felt sure that if he were beside her and that icy gaze fell upon her, she would fall into it and be lost forever.

After their disastrous trip to the village, she felt like a child who had been caught with their hand inside the candy dish. She had done nothing wrong—she knew that—and yet, she felt an overwhelming amount of guilt, as if she had somehow betrayed Peter, betrayed the Black family legacy in some terrible and unforgivable way. Worse, the guilt of her being the cause of any harm or suffering to the old woman or any of the villagers hung around her neck like a millstone. Even the house itself had shifted somehow upon her return, a sense of anger and reproach marrying with the other despondent emotions leaching out of its walls.

The meal she ate beneath his gaze tasted of betrayal—bitter and difficult to swallow. She so wanted to break the silence, to say something that would make everything alright, but she could think of no such magic spell. She would surely be punished for her actions—she knew that—but somehow, it was the unspoken nature of Peter's anger that ate at her the most. She saw it behind his eyes, a flame ignited, burning fierce and hot.

Evelyn had not seen Lilly since the moment they returned, and Ms. Winters had led her away. Another maid brought Evelyn her tea and helped her change for dinner, and her queries as to Lilly's whereabouts were only met with an indifferent shrug and cold silence.

Even Harrison, whose eyes would not meet Evelyn's when he opened her carriage door, had been led away by other staff, his head bowed low. He had gone to unhitch the horses and had been sternly told by Peter to leave them and return to his quarters. "I will come and see you shortly. We have much to discuss."

When Evelyn watched Harrison walk away, he looked pathetic and small, deflated by a few words from his master. Evelyn's mind, fraught with dread, had immediately likened the scene to a prisoner being escorted toward his execution.

The thought made her shudder.

She couldn't help but wonder exactly what Peter and Harrison had talked about. Despite her indifference toward Harrison, him being no friend of hers, she wished no harm upon him. After all, *she* had been responsible for the incapacitated state Peter had found him in. She worried he had been let go, his home and livelihood gone in one fell swoop—or worse. She thought of his injuries, of the old woman's terror-stricken face, and the blood on Peter's shirt, and she felt regret and fear swell within her. And what of Lilly? Was she also let go, thrown out into the night to fend for herself, miles from everything she knew? Or perhaps given the same treatment as the others, beaten or made to disappear into the fog? She dropped her fork onto the plate, the noise puncturing the heavy silence like a gunshot.

"Did you enjoy your time in the village?"

Evelyn looked up, startled, unsure of how to respond. He wore that same smile of superiority and assuredness, of silent reproach and assured punishment. It was the smile of a poker player with the winning hand or a hunter who had cornered his prey. Someone who knew a secret he would never tell to someone who desperately needed to hear it. It was a cruel smile, a cold and haughty sneer, and it bore down on Evelyn with great and unending weight, stealing her voice, stealing her very breath.

She swallowed, her mouth dry, before uttering a quiet, mousey: "Y—yes."

What else could she say? She longed to scream at him, to yell and throw her plates, to demand answers. She wanted to make him say aloud what he had done, what she knew in her heart he had done. But how could she? This was his game, and for now, she had no choice but to play it.

"Of course you did! What was your favorite part?"

"The...the people."

"The people? How so?"

"They were very kind."

His laughter was abrupt and mocking, its falseness emphasized by the silence that followed its quick cessation. He continued without explanation, "Which of the villagers offered you kindness? I would love to repay it."

Gooseflesh erupted on her skin, the implication of his words hanging heavy between them. He swirled the wine within his glass before downing its contents, a small dribble of red wine escaping the side of his mouth and staining his white collar. An image of the red-stained kerchief flashed suddenly in her mind, and fear began to crawl up her throat.

"I—I cannot recall their names."

"Hmm, I'm sure." It was clear he did not believe her, but he did not press the point further.

Evelyn's mind raced. Was he letting it go because he did not care and was merely goading her? Or was it because he already knew?

He carried on, clearly amused by her reaction. "The villagers are such a strange and superstitious lot. They tell such strange and ghastly fictions about my family, about my home." With this last word, he gestured with his wine glass to the room as if including Blackthorn in their conversation.

Evelyn didn't know what to say. She sat dumbly staring at him, her hand holding the fork midway toward her plate, frozen in place by his commanding stare and the flame ever visible within his eyes.

"They talk of dark magic, of murder and curses. They talk

of human sacrifices and deals with the devil. Have you ever heard such nonsense?"

The question was rhetorical. He did not want a response, and Evelyn didn't wish to give him one. It was for effect, a way to let her know that he knew her motives and fears, that her innermost secrets were laid bare, and she could hide nothing from him.

"Superstitions can make people do irrational things," he continued. "How many have been killed or hurt by the small-minded in the name of a 'greater good' or a 'higher power'? How many women have been burned by those who would call them witches? I shudder to think what would have happened to you had I not found you when I did."

Did Peter know that she could see and hear the dead? That Lilly had the sight, too? The implied threat, real or imagined, clung to Evelyn like spiderwebs.

He rose, dabbing his mouth with his napkin before walking toward her. Her heart thrummed inside her chest, and her hand shook, the knife tinkling off her plate, a small, sad bell. Slowly, he made his way behind her chair and placed a firm hand on each of her shoulders. Evelyn dared not move, dared not look up at him; she just stared ahead, her breathing heavy, her pulse racing. He lowered his mouth to her ear, his breath hot and wet against her neck.

"I think any future excursions beyond Blackthorn are unnecessary and unproductive, don't you? Best you just remain here from now on, where I can keep you safe."

He squeezed her shoulders tighter, his fingers digging into her collarbone on either side, and she sank into her chair involuntarily in response. Then, without another word, he left, the sound of his boots echoing as he crossed the room out into the hall beyond. The entire time, she simply stared ahead at his now vacant chair, afraid to turn around, afraid to look at him.

Relief washed over her as soon as he was gone, and her body, which had been so tense and upright just a moment before, crumpled as silent tears came in a rush. Was this how her life was to be from now on? Was it to be spent in fear, hiding from the one person she was supposed to trust the most? Walking on eggshells, afraid to misspeak or step out of line? Evelyn knew she could never live in such a way. Abuse, whether physical or emotional, would chip away at her until there was nothing left.

But what was she to do? Her only reprieve from the shadow of Blackthorn had ended in disaster, and now, she lived in constant surveillance. Her father and brother were yet to respond to any of her letters. Her only ally at Blackthorn was being kept from her. She felt wretchedly helpless, a spider caught within Blackthorn's sticky web. She just hoped she could find a way out before she was consumed.

Five days passed without Evelyn seeing Lilly. Five days of worry and dread. Five days of her mind creating dozens of scenarios of what had befallen her dear friend and confidante. Perhaps she had been let go, sent away without notice or pay. Maybe she had been locked away in some far-off part of Blackthorn where Evelyn could not hear her screams.

There had been moments when Evelyn was feeling her lowest that she had imagined worse things, such as injury or death. Her husband was a stranger to her, a cold and detached stranger who kept her locked away from the outside world. He had lied to her for reasons unknown about children—his own siblings—who were now mysteriously absent without explanation, perhaps even dead.

She knew now that Peter was capable of violence. She had felt his hands inflict pain on her; she had seen the bruises and blood on Harrison's worry-filled face. And what of the old woman? What had he done to her?

Evelyn's fingers grazed fading marks on both collarbones—rows of perfect prints, each matching a finger on Peter's hands. She felt those hands on her still, pressing harder and harder into her flesh, and she knew he had meant every mark. If he did such things to his own wife, what would he do to some maid with whom he had no connection or care? These thoughts had swirled inside her all those days until they had formed a storm of fear and sadness.

She asked for Lilly on a dozen occasions, directly ordering staff to send her to her rooms, but they always informed her that Lilly was indisposed with some important task, the details of which they were unaware. Sick of being ignored and dismissed, Evelyn tried to enter the staff areas of the house, only to be met with locked doors.

Ms. Winters began to follow Evelyn wherever she went, like some silent, irritable guard dog. Everywhere Evelyn turned, she watched her from the shadows with the same disapproving look fixed upon her stern, harsh face.

It was maddening.

The only privacy Evelyn got was in her chambers, and even there, she had begun to feel anxious, wondering who might be hiding, watching her. The eyes of the portraits followed her closely with every step, and even the crows perched upon the stone grotesques seemed to set their yellow eyes upon her.

She sought solace in Blackthorn's grounds, particularly the walled garden that stretched from her east wing out toward the wild of the moors. A pond was at its center, where mist stubbornly clung to the water throughout the day. Thin sheets of ice had begun to form across its surface, trapping the life beneath—something Evelyn sadly related to. It was the cold and fog that provided her with solitude.

Ms. Winters refused to leave the warmth of Blackthorn,

citing a childhood illness lingering in her chest as an excuse. But Evelyn saw the fear in her eyes when she spoke and noticed how the rest of the staff rarely left the house, as if they feared what lurked beyond the safety of its walls. Evelyn knew what lurked there. She had seen it, had felt it. Unseen eyes stared back at her from the shadows there as much as they did within Blackthorn, but at least outside, they watched her with curiosity rather than malicious intent.

It was by the pond on a cold winter morning that Evelyn was finally reunited with Lilly. A tiny handwritten note was rolled tightly and hidden beneath her teacup. Written in a hurried, child-like hand, it had simply read, "*Pond, one hour. - L*"

Relief flooded Evelyn the moment she read the words, and now she sat, her shawl clutched tight around her, watching tiny creatures swimming beneath the blur of ice. Evelyn's breath fogged before her face, mingling with the mist drifting around the pond. The cold bit at her exposed skin, and she shivered.

She looked around the garden, her ears alert and listening for the sound of any approaching footsteps. Like Blackthorn, the garden was grand and expensive—a clear statement about the status and wealth of the family—but there was a level of neglect and wildness settled there that was not present within Blackthorn's walls. Like the fountain she saw when she first arrived, it appeared to be an afterthought for the Blacks—something overlooked and forgotten.

Moss-covered statues and grotesques, all worn by weather and aged, sat among the overgrown plants and tangles of thorns. Some of the stone forms were so degraded it was difficult to distinguish what they once were. A game she played on her daily visits was guessing what each lump of stone had once been. Some were clear, such as horses and wolves, but there were others whose shapes defied her. One weathered form resembled a horse, yet it appeared to have eight legs like some kind of equestrian spider. Another seemed like the naked form of a woman in the traditional Roman style, which was not unusual in itself. However, the woman, whose beauty shone through the stone even after years of degradation, appeared to have some kind of tail, as well as markings along her back, like scars or perhaps the grain of tree bark.

Evelyn wandered among them now, another lost soul, when Lilly appeared from beneath the shadow of a doorway.

All sense of propriety, of status and titles, fell away. They ran toward each other and embraced, not as a lady and her servant, but as friends—as family. Tears of relief filled Evelyn's eyes, and for the first time that week, she felt something akin to joy. But when she looked into Lilly's tired, sad eyes, relief gave way to concern.

"Where have you been? I have been worried sick!"

"I don't have much time. They'll be looking for me."

"Who will? Are you alright? You're shaking."

Lilly spoke in hurried sentences and shot looks behind her as if she expected something to leap from the shadows and catch them at any moment. "Ms. Winters, the staff—they won't let me near you. They have me working as far from you as they can, and at night, they lock my quarters."

"They lock you in? Dear God."

Lilly's hand shook in Evelyn's, little to do with the weather.

Evelyn affectionately brushed Lilly's hair behind her ear and was shocked to find the faded markings where angry bruises had been. She cupped her chin and moved her face toward the light to find more bruises and swelling, dried blood still clinging around her nostrils, marking unseen wounds now healed. A cut divided her right eyebrow in a straight, deliberate line.

Tears fell from both women's eyes as realization set in.

"Oh Lilly...I..."

"It don't matter, ma'am. I'm fine."

"No, you're not! Who did this to you? Who hurt you?"

Lilly cast her eyes downward. "Ms. Winters."

It was barely audible, but to Evelyn, it might as well have been a scream. Fury overwhelmed her in a way she had never experienced. She had never wanted to inflict pain on anyone before. As a child, she couldn't even hunt, unwilling to hurt or injure some poor little creature. But if Ms. Winters had been present, she would have happily attacked the woman without regard for consequence.

Lilly must have seen Evelyn's thoughts in her anger-filled eyes. "Please don't do anything, ma'am. It will only lead to more pain for both of us. Ms. Winters said if it weren't for you, she'd have killed me, and I believe her."

All at once, Evelyn's bravery and bluster left her, and she simply hugged Lilly. Despite everything, they still had each other, and for that, she was grateful. "The old woman was right," she said. "This place is cursed. I feel it stronger every day."

Lilly nodded. "Which brings me to this." She dug into her apron pocket and pulled out a piece of paper that she unfolded. "I noticed they all wear this symbol on their brooches or buttons. Do you know what it is?"

Evelyn took the paper from her. Scribbled upon it were the strange symbols from the ancient Germanic language she now knew so well, having read and re-read the book with its strange, nonsensical scribblings. It was like a capital H, the horizontal line in the middle askew. Evelyn recognized what it meant immediately. It meant *hail*.

Lilly continued. "I overheard Ms. Winters talking about Harrison. He's dead, ma'am."

At those words, the world felt very far away, smaller and unreal, like a dream.

No, not a dream.

A nightmare.

"They told me it was an accident, that he was repairing the stable roof when he fell and broke his neck, but I don't believe them. I just don't believe them."

Evelyn's mind raced as fast as her heart. She thought about the old woman, about Charlie. "Listen to me, Lilly. When is the food delivered from the village?"

"Fridays, ma'am."

"That gives us two days. I will write a letter to my father and leave it behind the broken urn behind the house, close to the servant's entrance. Do you know of it?"

Lilly nodded.

"I will leave you a few coins as well for the driver's trouble. Ask him to post it, and he may keep them. Do you understand?"

"Yes, ma'am. What if your father is traveling? He has not responded to your other letters."

Lilly was right, of course. Evelyn had sent several letters to her father since her arrival, each more desperate than the last, and she had yet to receive a response. She had already become suspicious of them being intercepted. It was not unheard of for him to travel, but she would have expected him to send something himself, advising of where he was.

"I will write another for my brother, just in case."

Lilly nodded once more.

"Make sure he gives any responses to you and to you only. I will come here every evening at this same time. Meet me if you can slip away."

Lilly looked behind her into the darkness, watching something Evelyn could not see. "I must go, ma'am, before they notice I am gone."

"Lilly? Be careful, please."

"You too."

This time, it was Evelyn who nodded, squeezing Lilly's hand before she hurried off into the darkness. Evelyn looked at the scrap of paper in her hand, the words of the old woman echoing inside her mind. Perhaps the tales whispered about Blackthorn were more than mere children's stories or the imaginings of the superstitious. Perhaps Death did reside at Blackthorn.

Perhaps it was even revered.

Twelve

The hallway was dark, every candle left abandoned. Shadows cast by the moonlight filtering in through the windows resembled the stone creatures from the garden, dancing about her as she walked. Although all was silent, Evelyn swore she could hear them whisper.

The portraits followed her every step with judging eyes. She shivered uncontrollably, fear gripping her body tightly in its grasp, and yet, she carried on. She placed one foot in front of the other, something compelling her to walk toward the door, its blood-smeared carvings as familiar to her now as the blemishes on her own flesh. It pulsed somehow as if it had a heartbeat, a living, breathing thing rather than an object of mere wood and iron.

As she grew near, it creaked open, beckoning her to go inside. The coldness poured from it like water, and the fog licked at her feet. It reached out toward the portraits in the hallway, and the images within suddenly appeared afraid, their eyes wide and unblinking. She saw that same impossible place built of shadow and mist, heard the cries and moans of unseen people, and felt the desperation that dwelt there. Blurred figures appeared and disappeared, never fully forming, moving just before Evelyn could focus on them and determine what they were. Everything was unreal, a blur at the corner of her eye that disappeared when she turned to face it, a story told under blankets by boisterous children, a trick of the light. But it was very real, a place that existed beyond human comprehension, a place that defied description or explanation.

Slowly, the figure emerged from the fog, gradually growing in depth and form, a photograph developing before her eyes. It was her mother again, hanging limply from an invisible rope, her neck jutting at an unnatural angle. Evelyn had known what she would see when she approached—she had the image burned into her mind—and yet, nothing could truly prepare her for the wave of heartache and horror that washed over her. *What have they done to you?* Her mother's eyes stared past her, glassy and unseeing as they bulged from their sockets, covered in veins and burst blood vessels. But the other face she wore—or more accurately, the face which wore her mother's corpse—stared directly into Evelyn's eyes, unblinking and all-knowing.

Evelyn wanted to run with every fiber of her body, the muscles in her legs tensing in readiness for their escape. Yet she remained rooted to the spot as that same strange, duplicitous fear turned her into another of Blackthorn's stone creatures, her own features degrading with age until only a shadow of who she once was remained.

It reached toward her using her mother's arm, twitching and jerking like some kind of grotesque puppet. Evelyn could not move, her mind filling with a scream; her body was too terrified to release as the cold, dead weight of the hand lay on her belly. Maggots writhed on purple tendons, and rotten sinew dangled from exposed black bones. And then, all at once, a voice filled her mind.

Although neither the jaw of her mother's corpse nor the

being that wore her as some kind of rotten flesh suit moved in any way, Evelyn knew the wheezing voice inside her skull came from the creature mere inches from her face. It rasped a single word, a word that finally released Evelyn's scream from her body, a word that sat heavy in the air between both bodies and weighed on them equally.

The word was *blood*.

Evelyn bolted upright in bed. She scrambled and fought with the covers, which had tangled themselves around her legs in the night. The scream, having left her lips within her nightmare, had followed her into the real world and now echoed around her bedchamber. For a moment, the lines between reality and nightmare were blurred, and she believed herself still to be in that terrible place, face to face with the unnatural creature that seemed to dwell within her mind permanently. Thoughts of such a terror ensured that the moment lasted one hundred times longer as Evelyn struggled to focus on her surroundings. Then, all at once, the furnishings became recognizable in the early dawn light, and her breathing and her heart rate gradually slowed as she grounded herself inside the real world.

Her mouth was dry, and her throat was tender with every swallow. She reached for the glass of water on her bedside table with a shaking hand and missed it entirely. It hit the wood with a crack and splintered, peppering the floor with water and glass fragments.

Evelyn held her breath and looked toward the door that separated her room from Peter's. Surely, between her waking cries and the sound of shattering glass, he would come, if not for the sake of her safety, then at the very least with aroused curiosity. But the door never opened, and she heard no sounds beyond her shallow breathing. If he was within his chamber, he had either slept through the commotion or chosen to ignore it.

Either way, she was relieved, which brought a wave of

sadness, settling quickly as an ache within her heart. Once, she had passed each hour without him in agony, yearning to be with him with every fiber of her being. Now, the prospect of seeing him brought her nothing but dread.

She felt trapped in a permanent state of grief, mourning the loss of a love that had seemingly never existed in the first place—at least for him—and the loss of a future she had so happily run toward, which now, she knew, had only been a mirage.

With a heavy sigh, she pulled herself from the bed, careful where she placed her bare feet. She had no broom and dustpan, but she improvised using the small coal brush and shovel with her fire irons. The glass had shattered completely, leaving tiny shards strewn wide over the floor, glittering in the morning light like precious gems. She gathered the remnants into a small pile, then reached beneath the bed to catch those that strayed further than others. She strained to reach the farthest pieces when she noticed what appeared to be a deep score mark in the wood, and then another and another. Some were vertical, others horizontal, some straight, and some curved, but all had the smooth edges of something marked deliberately rather than the roughness of a clumsy mistake.

She could not make out what they were in the shadow of the bed, but she knew they had formed a pattern, and a familiar one at that. A surge of emotion boiled up inside her, and without care or heed, she threw herself against the heavy bed frame, throwing all her weight and strength at it. Slowly and begrudgingly, it moved to one side.

Four times, the broken glass pierced her flesh, her blood mixing with the spilled water, and her footing slipped as she struggled to gain purchase. The pain did not register; her mind was singularly focused on revealing the secrets etched beneath her bed. The bed creaked in protest, scoring the floor with every push, adding its objections to the markings below. Sweat pooled on her brow, and her breathing grew heavy, the physical exertion of moving such a solid piece of furniture causing her muscles to cry out in pain. Inch by inch, it moved aside, her bloody foot marks streaked across the floor, marking the distance it had traveled, until slowly, the secrets were exposed to the light. With one final push, her teeth gritted and her limbs aching, she pushed the bed aside with a determined grunt. Throwing herself at the window, she tore the drapes aside enough to cast light upon the markings before collapsing to the floor, her body spent and her heart racing.

For a moment, the world spun, and her eyes would not focus. She fought to regulate her breathing, the throbbing pain of her feet becoming increasingly pronounced. She knew what she would find when she opened her eyes, and yet, to see those worst fears realized before her still shook her to her core.

There, etched deep into the wood floor, were the same symbols she had seen on the door inside her nightmares. The blood from her feet had painted each with a streak of red, completing the macabre image from her mind. She stifled a wail with her fist as tears fell.

The sight of the carved symbols brought her entire world crashing down around her. Peter did not love her—he never had. He had married her for a nefarious purpose she did not understand—some kind of dark magic. She was there to serve a purpose, an ingredient necessary for a ritual or spell. He clearly meant her harm, perhaps to her body, perhaps to her soul, but harm nonetheless.

The things from her dream were real, just like the beings stalking the moors and the spirits restlessly roaming around the house. Perhaps they were part of the darkness that had been summoned there, or perhaps they too were victims, but they were all very real. She did not know what had happened in that place or what horrors lay ahead, so many questions clouded her thoughts. *Why was Peter doing this? What was the purpose?*

What part was she to play? No answers came, but she knew enough to understand the danger she was in.

Blackthorn still held secrets, but its malicious intent was clear.

She stared at the symbols through a blur of tears and spoke their meaning aloud as if the final pieces of the puzzle would somehow reveal themselves: "Wealth, god, gift, possession, estate."

Just like on the door, the same unknown symbol for which she had yet to find a translation appeared, but unlike on the door frame, the symbol was smaller and formed a circle around another mark. Evelyn recognized it immediately. It consisted of two interlocking V shapes on their sides— one pointing left, the other right.

It was then she understood the nature of the spell scratched beneath her bed, the part she was to play for Peter—her purpose and her end. She knew now why the creature within her dream had placed its hand upon her stomach. She understood fully, and it broke her. She fell to her knees as she choked and sputtered on her anguish, tears falling freely now, her grief broken free. The rune meant *fertility*, and the spell had worked.

Evelyn was pregnant.

Thirteen

"Lord save us!"

Lilly crossed herself, closing her eyes for a moment of silent prayer.

Evelyn watched her through weary eyes. Sleep no longer brought her comfort, so she fought it most nights until she succumbed to exhaustion. It was only a temporary fix, she knew, but she could not face the creature that haunted her dreams and prolonged their next meeting for as long as possible.

Peter did not seem to notice the dark rings around her eyes nor the sense of melancholy that now draped around his wife like a shroud. He barely spoke to her, barely acknowledged her. His evening visits to her bedchamber were the only time they spent together—something she saw now as a task to be completed, a bothersome chore rather than an act of love or affection. Her marriage was a lie, and her husband a stranger. If it weren't for Lilly, she would have succumbed to hopelessness the moment she found the sigils carved beneath her bed.

It had been ten days since her and Lilly's last meeting.

Tonight, they met for an exchange of information—some brought with it terror, and some brought hope. Evelyn told Lilly of her dream, the markings, and, of course, her pregnancy. She could hide it for now, but eventually, her body would betray her, and Peter would undoubtedly claim the child as his and his alone.

She thought of the ghost children that wandered the halls of Blackthorn and shuddered. It was strange how something so small, merely an idea of a child at that stage—a whisper that would grow into a cry out upon entering the world—and yet Evelyn knew in her heart that she already loved it with every fiber of her being. She would do whatever it took to protect it from Peter and his nefarious plans, whatever those might be.

She thought about the creature's rasping utterance: *"Blood..."*

Was it a warning? Or its way of telling her she was with child? She did not know. Regardless of that creature's intentions or origins, Evelyn knew she needed to flee from it. Flee from Blackthorn and its secrets, flee from the staff that wandered its halls, and most importantly, flee from Peter, a man she had given her body and heart to, a man she had loved once so fervently and passionately, but for whom she now felt nothing but disgust and fear.

Lilly's news had been more positive and given them both cause for hope. "Green is his name—Alfred Green. He weren't for taking the letters at first. In fact, he were downright fidgety about the whole thing, not that I blame him."

"Did anyone see you?"

"No, ma'am. I let loose one of the dogs into the kitchen, and Ms. Winters and the others were all a-kerfuffle trying to catch it. I slipped out and caught him as he packed up the empty crates from last week's order."

"What did he say?"

"Well, as I said, he weren't happy about it. It was clear he fears the Blacks like everybody else. He said bad things happen to those who cross them."

Evelyn nodded solemnly—she knew that to be true. She had felt Peter's angry hands, and she had seen what they had wrought on others. A part of her felt bad for dragging the man, a simple grocer, into everything. But they were desperate.

Lilly continued. "But I begged him, ma'am. I said it was a matter of life and death, and I meant it. I said he was our only hope. That seemed to sway him, so he took the letters and the coins. He said he'd post them the very next day. That were four, no, five days ago now. How long should it take for the letters to get to your father and brother?"

"If the gentleman did post them first thing, a week at least, but it also depends on where they are. I have sent the letters to their respective homes, but if they are traveling or are staying in one of their other properties, or with family, or if he didn't post them..."

Evelyn trailed off, unable to complete her answer, fearing it too great to utter aloud. Their very lives could be in danger, and their only hope rested in a few small envelopes, now in the hands of a stranger, a man with no reason to help and good reason not to. Evelyn had seen the terrorized sway the Black family name held over others, and she could not blame the man if he deemed the risk too great and simply burned the letters and pocketed the money. But her hope was real, and she clung to it desperately, but it was also fragile. One word, one small error on their part, and it would shatter into a million pieces, forever lost.

Winter coated everything around them in a glitter of frost, and the familiar wisps of mist drifted above the pond, creating a somber air to the place. It was always so deathly quiet where they stood, as if the house and its gardens were holding their breath. There were rarely the sounds of life Evelyn was used to hearing at her old home, and no birds or other creatures added their voices to nature's normal chorus.

"Did he say anything else when he took the letters?"

Lilly looked down at her hands as she twisted them about one another. She shifted her weight to her other foot and looked at Evelyn like a child caught being naughty.

"Lilly?"

Slowly, she raised her eyes to meet Evelyn, who saw they were now filled with tears.

"Lilly. Did he say something else?"

"I didn't want to worry you, ma'am. Even more so now."

"I need to know, Lilly."

She shifted again before releasing a sigh so heavy she visibly sagged. It wasn't the sigh of a young woman but one of someone older and more world-weary. It was a sigh of resignation. "I asked him about the old woman and the boy."

"And? What did he say?"

"Gone."

Evelyn had never heard a word more weighted and terrible in all her life. It struck her like a fist, winding her. She felt her hands move toward her stomach, a protective gesture for a life only just forming. "Gone?" Evelyn whispered the word, her voice suddenly so small and so meager, she was surprised Lilly had even heard her.

"Gone, ma'am. Charlie and his family packed up and left everything behind. No one knows where they went, just that they left after..." Lilly trailed off once more, her eyes shifting from Evelyn's own.

"After what, Lilly? Please, you must tell me!"

"After they found her."

Evelyn swallowed hard at the horror rising in her throat. "You mean the old woman...he... Tell me, Lilly."

Lilly choked back tears, trying to remain composed, trying to appear strong, but her eyes were so young, so scared. She looked like a child to Evelyn suddenly, like a lost little girl who wanted to go home, something Evelyn mirrored in herself. "A neighbor found her, day after we left. He said she were all blood and bone, that she were barely recognizable."

Evelyn felt as if the world were falling away from her, with the tears that fell from her eyes as she crumpled to the cold, hard earth. Lilly barely caught her arm in time to stop a harder landing. There they both sat, openly weeping as the full weight of everything they knew overwhelmed them. Lilly held Evelyn and stroked her arm, the comforting gesture of a mother to an injured child.

Blackthorn watched them in silence.

"It was us, wasn't it? Harrison, the old woman...we are the reason they're dead. We are the reason that the poor boy and his family have had to flee their home."

"We didn't know. How could we?"

"It doesn't matter if we knew or not. We still caused it."

Lilly said nothing—there was nothing that could be said.

Evelyn turned to face Blackthorn, its large, vast shape creating a void in the night sky where there were no stars, where there was no light. Evelyn hated the building with every bone in her body. It burned within her, a kind of loathing she had never experienced in her young life, and silently, she cursed the house and all who dwelt within. She deeply regretted having ever gone there, wishing it would burn to the ground.

After several minutes passed with regret and grief and terror surging through their veins, Evelyn finally broke their reprieve. Through gritted teeth, she said, "The old woman was right. Death does live at Blackthorn, and we let it out!"

All the grief, sorrow, and self-pity bubbled in Evelyn's chest, hardening it. All her sadness turned to disgust, a black mark on something once pure and unblemished. As the minutes passed, it transformed into something more akin to fury. Peter was a monster, and his staff were either complicit in the horror he wrought or perhaps even actively participated in it. Blackthorn was a trap that ensnared love and life and hope, strangling them until they fell limp.

Evelyn was sick of feeling impotent, a bystander to her own destiny. She was sick of feeling helpless to the whims of a madman. Wiping her tears, she turned to Lilly, the flames that ignited her heart shining defiantly through her eyes.

Lilly seemed to understand and agree without a word or objection. "What is the plan?"

"Could you get a knife from the kitchen unnoticed?"

"I believe I could."

"Good, then do it. Something small enough to be concealed but sharp enough to cause damage if you need to."

Lilly nodded as Evelyn continued. "I still have some money left, though not as much as I would like. I will take some valuables from the house that I believe would go unnoticed, along with my own jewelry, which we can sell or trade if needed. Where is the leather bag in which you brought your belongings to Blackthorn?"

"Under my bed, ma'am."

"When you next get a chance, place it beneath the stone bench at the far corner of this garden. There is plenty of overgrowth to conceal the hiding spot, but be sure to hide it well."

"What about food, ma'am?"

"Steal what you can from the kitchens, things that will not perish quickly, but do not take any unnecessary risks. Everything is lost if you are caught." Evelyn quickly corrected, "If *we* are caught. There is a box of matches on each floor for lighting candles. I will take the one near the library and deposit it in the bag, along with the valuables. We do not know how an escape would go, and we may need to build our fires for heat. There is a quilt in one of the bedrooms, small enough to carry easily but big enough to provide some warmth if required. I will take that, too."

"It might take me a week or two to gather things without anyone realizing."

"That's fine. We will think of this as our emergency plan. If, for whatever reason, the letters go unanswered, we will, upon one of these meetings, simply grab the bag, take a horse, and run from this hellish place and the demons that dwell here."

Lilly gave another firm nod. It appeared both women had had their fill of feeling lost among the shadows, and they now vowed to forge their own path to freedom any way they could.

Any helplessness that Evelyn felt prior had disappeared and been replaced with determined resolve. Both women had regained their inner strength, working quietly to retrieve the items needed for their escape.

Lilly stole a small paring knife from the kitchen, which she now kept on her at all times, stashed within her apron. Evelyn had less luck with Ms. Winters supervising every meal, so Lilly had been attempting to locate one for her, the absence of which would go unnoticed. Evelyn deliberately tried not to think about what they would need such weapons for. But her father, an ever-practical man, had drilled into her since she was a child that it was better to look *at* something than look *for* it. And under their current circumstances, having some kind of means of defense, however small, gave Evelyn the feeling that she had some power over her own life and its trajectory.

Evelyn found removing the other items and depositing them more difficult than expected, given the constant supervision she was under. Still, she learned quickly that by taking them one or two items at a time, they were more easily concealed. The jewelry and cash were simple, slipping easily into the folds of her skirts. The clothing and blanket had been a different matter, and Evelyn had been forced to get creative. She wore the items beneath her clothes or the blankets as capes beneath her cloak to walk in plain sight outside into the grounds. Little by little, in small, invisible acts of defiance, Evelyn felt her courage returning.

Gathering the items for their "escape bag" was the easiest part, however. The escape itself proved far more difficult. Blackthorn House was extremely isolated. It was an hour's ride from the village and much longer on foot. Riding straight to the village would undoubtedly lead to a pursuit, but to wander off the main road could mean disaster. It was surrounded by treacherous moorland littered with sinkholes that could, at best, break limbs and, at worst, swallow a person whole as if it were some black, muddy, yawning mouth ready to accept whatever living creatures dared trespass upon it. Even if they were to avoid such a terrible fate, becoming lost would be just as dangerous, wandering aimlessly until succumbing to the elements. But if it came down to it, they may just have to run and hope for the best, and at least the bag gave them some sense of preparedness, albeit a small one.

On Evelyn's daily walks around Blackthorn, she memorized the corridors and looked for blind spots from the many windows, scouting for items of use. Today, she concentrated on the house's uppermost level, where the rooms remained closed and unused. The furniture had been draped in sheets, creating rooms full of white, ghostly forms. Despite her newfound bravery, they gave Evelyn pause, and she walked slowly and carefully lest they rise up and fly toward her.

As if she, too, felt the potential for hauntings from the many empty rooms, Ms. Winters ceased her pursuit at the stairs and remained hovering at the far end of the corridor. Every time Evelyn emerged from a room back into the hallway, there she would be, lips pursed and toe tapping with impatience and ill ease. Evelyn was torn between her keenness to explore and her trepidation at the eeriness of the space, but Ms. Winters's reluctance to follow her spurred her on.

Many rooms had little within them, so Evelyn made light work of her task. She entered a drawing room, where Evelyn could imagine a Black family member frequenting who appreciated the sprawling view of the wild moorland on that side of the house. Evelyn stared at the harsh, gray landscape in the waning light and shuddered, knowing what creatures moved within the fog. Rubbing her arms, she stared at her reflection, too, and wondered just how desperate things would have to be for her to risk a journey into that treacherous landscape.

While her mind wandered, a small movement in the glass caught her eye. It was fleeting enough to cause her to doubt what she saw, yet enough for her to feel her heartbeat increase. A larger piece of furniture, perhaps a chaise or settee, was draped in sheeting, and beside it stood something slim and taller—perhaps a lamp on a side table, hidden by its gown of white. Evelyn stared at its reflection in the glass, deciding if her mind was playing tricks on her when she saw the sheet grow taller. As if someone beneath stood up from where they had hidden during a game of hide and seek, ready to reveal their clever hiding spot.

Too afraid to turn around, Evelyn's mouth went dry, and her heart beat faster and faster. She gripped her shoulders now, arms clasped in front of her, in part to comfort herself and also to prove it was real that she was not trapped in one of her nightmares. The figure stepped forward, and Evelyn could just about make out the shadow beneath the fabric, distinctly human in shape and considerably larger than her own petite frame.

Her initial instinct was to run, but the sheeted specter stood between her and the only exit from that room, and she could see no way past where it could not easily intercept her.

She stared at it, not daring to turn around, as if acknowledging its presence would make it real. Once more, she was a child with her covers pulled up around her head, hoping that if she did not acknowledge the things outside the safety of her bed, then they could not hurt her. The room grew cold, and goose-flesh blossomed on Evelyn's skin, small puffs of mist escaping her quivering lips with every shallow, panicked breath.

If she were not so terrified, she would have laughed at the image. How many children had played ghosts by placing a white sheet over their heads, chasing their younger siblings until they were scolded by their parents? It was an infantile image of a ghost drawn by young hands. Yet now, as it loomed behind her, it filled her with nothing but dread.

How long she remained like that, she could not say, but it felt like minutes rather than seconds passed. Slowly, the figure raised its arm, shifting the sheets to point toward the wall to its left. Evelyn stole a quick glance in that direction, daring not to remove her gaze from the specter for too long. But it seemed to want her to look away, for the moment she did, it ran at her full speed, giving her no time to think or react beyond gasping and turning to face it as she fell back hard into the window frame. Just as it reached her, its hand still extended, the shape vanished. The sheet covered Evelyn as it fell toward the ground, lifeless and ordinary.

Evelyn quickly pulled the sheet off her and threw it away as if it were aflame. It fell in a crumpled heap. She placed her hand on her chest and took deep, slow breaths, trying to steady her shaking hands and racing mind. All the while, her eyes darted between the still, fallen sheet and the several other covered objects in the room in terrified anticipation of another such attack. But no attack came, and no other sheets stirred.

Slowly, Evelyn rose from the floor. Her hip ached where she had slammed into the stone window sill, and her hands moved protectively to her stomach. Her arms felt weak and tired after being tensed for so long. She looked from the sheet to the wall where it had pointed. The wallpaper was a red velvet damask pattern, and on it hung what Evelyn assumed was artwork of some kind, also covered to protect them from the sun. One sheet hung above the other, and if you were to enter the room in just the right light, their shadows made it seem like the paintings were not attached to the wall but instead simply hovering there, specters all their own.

Evelyn pulled the sheet from the top item first, revealing an oil painting of a fox hunt. Hunters wearing red jackets and shining black boots sat atop horses with their rifles aimed and ready. A pack of hounds was ahead of the hunters, and to Evelyn's horror, she realized they had already found and set upon the fox, with one having torn a deep wound into its bright orange fur. Two dogs held the poor creature in their sharp, bared teeth as bright red paint flowed about them.

Evelyn immediately hated it.

The second item was a box frame, which displayed an old-fashioned musket-style pistol with a small hunting knife, no doubt a trophy of such a hunt. They were exactly what Evelyn needed, and as she glanced back at the crumpled sheet behind her, she silently thanked the spirit who had shown her where to look. Thinking fast, Evelyn wrapped the sheet that had covered the frame around her hand and pounded on the glass with her fist until she heard it shatter and give way beneath her hand. Carefully picking out the remaining shards, she removed the handgun and was immediately dismayed to find its barrel blocked and its chamber fused shut, a common practice where guns were used in displays. Hope began to fall away as she dropped it with a thud. Would the knife be similarly useless? She pulled it from the frame, and thankfully, it was as sharp as the day it had been placed there and the perfect size for her to conceal.

There was no time to celebrate this small victory, however,

as Evelyn heard the creaking approach of footsteps. Ms. Winters's impatience had overcome her fear, and she was coming to see what her mistress—nay, her prisoner—was up to. Quickly and carefully, Evelyn deposited the knife within the folds of her skirt and placed the gun back inside the frame. She lifted the larger pieces of glass, tossed them beneath a nearby armoire, and kicked the smaller pieces beneath the rug. She rehung the sheet just as she heard the door handle turn behind her.

Evelyn strode toward the window, kicking the loose sheet toward a covered chair as Ms. Winters stepped inside. Evelyn feigned surprise and turned as if startled. No doubt, the old woman was curious as to why Evelyn was standing in a dark, cold, empty room, staring out into the fog, but whether it was due to propriety or a lack of care, she said nothing.

"Ms. Winters, you startled me."

"Apologies, milady, 'twas not my intention. I grew concerned, given how long you had been in here, and wanted to check that all was well."

Evelyn merely smiled and said, "Have I? I was just admiring the view. I must have lost track of time. Lost in thought, I expect."

Ms. Winters eyed the dark, fog-obscured world beyond the glass dubiously and then stared at her with eyes full of doubt. Evelyn's anxiety began to rise. She'd had only seconds to disguise her true activities, and even from the corner of her eye, she could still see small shards of glass lying within the gaps of the floorboards. She knew all too well that, should Ms. Winters inspect the room, she would discover the broken frame and the missing knife.

Slowly, Ms. Winters turned her gaze from one side of the room toward the wall in question, searching for any small thing out of place.

"I think that's enough exploring for one day. I expect it is almost dinner time, Ms. Winters?"

Ms. Winters either had not heard or had chosen to ignore, and Evelyn began to panic. "We wouldn't want to keep my husband waiting, now would we?"

It was the use of *we* that seemed to snap Ms. Winters's suspicious gaze back to Evelyn. For a moment, the housekeeper seemed to wrestle with her thoughts, an internal fight between her suspicion and distaste toward Evelyn and the fear of incurring the wrath of her employer. Seemingly, fear won out, and Ms. Winters turned and exited the room, walking quickly back toward the stairs. Evelyn followed her, grazing her hand over the lump where the knife now sat among the folds of fabric in her skirts. It was a modest victory, but a victory nonetheless, and even though the blade was small, it gave Evelyn a great sense of comfort.

Evelyn would escape Blackthorn, or she would die trying.

Fourteen

The following day found Evelyn back at the library. Pleased with the way she'd gathered supplies unnoticed and how their escape plan grew more real, she now felt moved to explore more about the runes. It was also the only time Ms. Winters left her alone, apparently unaware of the clues hidden within the faded tomes. Evelyn searched for hours until her back ached, and her eyes were dry and tired. Occasionally, she would slice a finger on the edge of a book page, dotting the pages with blood. Every time it happened, she couldn't help but think of the scribblings left within the book of runes.

She thought of how some people, when they die, leave great marks on the world. They have statues carved in their image or books written about them, not unlike the ones she frantically searched through. They had streets named in their honor and roads lined with weeping mourners during their funeral march. But others died quietly and without consequence, with no one noticing their passing. They were drawings etched into wood by childish hands. They were a pile of random items, discarded and forgotten. They were scrawled words in the pages of a book left unread. Those people left behind little to no marks of the lives they led, and in the morbid thoughts consuming her of late, Evelyn wondered: if she were to perish within Blackthorn, would the only sign of her existence be the red fingerprints smudged on the pages of a handful of books?

She was tearing her way through a section of thick leather-bound legal journals when she finally found something of interest. It was a thin, small book hidden behind the others that appeared much older than the rest of the library. Its spine was naked and exposed, its fragile pages barely clinging to their stitching. It smelled of mold and age, and its pages, once white, were stained a mucky brown. The barely legible title, its gilding long since worn, simply stated, *Gods of the Old World.* This in and of itself had not caused her to pause and examine the book. What had made her heart beat a little faster upon finding it was the runic symbols etched into the well-worn leather, all of which were now as familiar to her as the letters in her own language.

Slowly and carefully, she read through the book's delicate pages, absorbing every piece of information she could. She learned about Odin, the all-seeing god of war and ruler of the other gods; his son, Thor, the hammer-wielding god of thunder and protector of man; and Freya, the beautiful goddess of fate and destiny. With every page, she discovered new worlds of myth and magic, of powerful beings once worshipped and revered.

Upon turning a page, she was greeted with a drawing that caused her face to drain of color. Although faded and worn, the etching still captured the terrifying visage of Hel, the fierce and formidable goddess of the dead. She sat on her throne at the center of a gray world of smoke and fog, grinning with a face half-flesh and half-decayed.

She appeared to be alive yet dead all at once, her skull just visible beneath her porcelain skin, too pale to belong to someone living. She was beautiful but also fierce and terrifying, her eyes staring at the reader with the intensity of a warrior, and it was those dark, knowing eyes that Evelyn recognized immediately.

It was the woman who haunted her dreams, the creature who wore her mother's corpse like some kind of suit. It was the creature who called out to her and to whom she seemed powerless to resist.

Frantically, Evelyn read the chapter, desperate to find some kind of revelation and understand what was happening at Blackthorn and what was happening to her. Hel was the daughter of Loki, appointed by Odin himself to rule over the underworld. There, she would provide lodging to those who have died, providing a life beyond this one. Hel was Death itself, a fearsome queen who ruled over her realm with fairness and neutrality. All souls who pass must one day walk Helvegr, the road to the afterlife. It is a cold and lifeless road, filled with shadows and mist. Evelyn knew immediately it was the place she had seen in her nightmares—the world beyond the door.

Helheim, however, the afterlife itself, was said to be exactly that. A life after this one, a world where souls continued to love and learn and laugh. It was a world of simple pleasures, like good food and strong ale, but most importantly, it was a life free of suffering or cruelty. Helheim was not the Hell of fire and brimstone she had been force-fed at church, nor was it the white clouds and beautiful angels of the Bible's Heaven. It was merely another, kinder life, where Hel ruled with fairness and benevolence. Where, then, was this realm? Why was the cold and misty road of Helvegr all she could see? And why were souls stuck there and not passing on to Helheim?

A dozen questions flooded her mind as she struggled to understand what she was reading. Why was Hel at Blackthorn, and why was she reaching out to Evelyn? Was the door she had seen a portal to Helheim, the realm of the dead, and if so, who had opened it? What did it all mean for Evelyn and her child? Were they fated to die? To have Blackthorn be their tomb? Why was her mother now a victim of Blackthorn, along with countless other souls who did not subscribe to that faith?

Nothing seemed to make sense to her, yet somehow, it all fit together, another piece of a broken image that brought everything into focus. She knew the runic language carved on the doorway and beneath her bed was used by the Germanic people who had once believed in deities such as Hel. And she knew the Black family had been one of them, conquering the natives of that small part of England and carving a place of power for themselves from the blood and bone of its indigenous population. The words the old woman had uttered muddled among her own thoughts and realizations. She had said the Black family had brought their magic and combined it with that of the local people. Had that magic opened up the door? For what purpose?

Everything seemed too impossible, so ludicrous. It went against everything she had ever been taught—in church, in school, by her father. But how could she have created an image of a being so exactly aligned with the one in the book when she had never read of or heard of such things? How could she so accurately conjure a language in her mind that she had never seen? It fit—it all fit—and yet she still felt so completely clueless as to what was going on and why. Every piece of information she learned only served to create more questions rather than supply answers, and she felt exhausted by the fog of constant confusion and anxiety in which she now permanently existed.

As she stared at the image, she noticed splatters of ink and the shadow of bold script on the other side of the thin paper.

She was about to turn the page when she heard a sudden flurry of activity behind her. The library door flung open, and someone strode toward her. Judging by the brusque, impatient manner of the entrance, Evelyn had no doubt it was Ms. Winters.

As quickly as she could, she shoved the small book inside another from atop her pile and turned to find Ms. Winters laying a tray on the desk. Evelyn's eye flashed toward the clock on the mantel, and she realized she had been inside the library for over three hours. It was not the first time she had lost track of time in Blackthorn. There was a strange sleepiness to the place, as if it always lay in wait. Time seemed to move at its own pace, with hours slipping like sand through fingers.

Ms. Winters eyed her suspiciously. Evelyn had no doubt it was an odd sight. Here she was, the lady of the manor, sitting on the library floor surrounded by piles of books she had removed from the shelves in a desperate search for understanding. Dust peppered her dark purple dress, and small smudges marked her face and hands like a child playing among the fire's ashes. Dismissing the lady's maid assigned to her in Lilly's absence, her hair had been roughly pinned to her head by her own hurried hands, and several strands had fallen loose about her face. Once more, Ms. Winters had caught her at her task, acting suspiciously and inexplicably startled by the appearance of a woman who followed her as closely as her own shadow and who was, by now, just as familiar. She felt like a child caught with her hand inside the chocolate box.

Ms. Winters sniffed at the air, perhaps irritated by the disturbed dust, but to Evelyn, she was a bloodhound searching for a scent. Evelyn began to put the books back onto the shelves in as nonchalant a manner as she could muster. Among a handful of books on the flora and fauna of England, she carefully placed the brown leather hardback, which now bulged with the small tattered tome she had discovered, taking note of where it had been placed. She did so with little time to spare as Ms. Winters tutted loudly and marched toward her, grabbing the books from their piles and shoving them onto the shelves impatiently.

"I couldn't decide what to read next," Evelyn offered weakly.

If Ms. Winters remained suspicious, she said nothing. When the books were back on the shelf, she returned to her task with the tray, unloading the last of its contents without waiting for Evelyn to rise before marching back out of the library as quickly as she had entered. The woman had not said a word, but her detestation for Evelyn radiated from her in waves, and for once, Evelyn was glad to be disliked so fervently.

When the housekeeper had closed the door with a sharp bang, Evelyn breathed a deep sigh of relief. The presence of every single member of staff within Blackthorn made Evelyn feel on edge, like extensions of the house itself, the moving parts of the giant, immobile creature that had so successfully swallowed her whole. Ms. Winters was the epitome of that.

If the staff were the limbs of Blackthorn, reaching out at Evelyn as she tried to escape, then Ms. Winters was its brain, controlling their actions. Evelyn hated her as much as she hated the house, and she hated both of those almost as much as she hated Peter. If Blackthorn was a creature, then he was its blackened, hollow heart.

She waited several breaths, ensuring the housekeeper was truly gone, before finding the book's hiding place. Evelyn hurriedly leafed through the pages until she came to passages which had been defaced by the same panicked scribbles as she had found within the rune book. The ink was thick and hurried, giving the impression that the scrawled words were bleeding ink. It was two short sentences, yet the desperation and terror of the writer somehow came through in every frantically scrawled letter:

"Hel, forgive me! You cannot have them."

The old woman had been right. The Black family had done something terrible. They had opened a doorway between the land of the living and that of the dead. They had let Death into Blackthorn House, and now, she called for Evelyn.

Fifteen

Days blurred into weeks, which then turned into months, and still, no reply from Evelyn's family. Hope, already fragile, had started to crumble and crack, and it became more difficult to pretend with every passing day. Every night, Evelyn was beckoned toward the door within her nightmares. Every night, she was faced with the terrible, deformed figure of her mother's corpse and the rotten flesh of Hel monstrously entwined together, rasping the same cryptic warning—*blood*.

When she awoke, she was greeted with the now-familiar nausea of morning sickness passing through her body in waves. She was glad of Peter's animosity toward her and the fact that the staff barely interacted with her, for she was sure they would have discovered the secret growing within her womb. As it was, she had managed to keep her pregnancy hidden, although she knew her body would betray her soon when it began to swell with the precious life it carried. Already, she had noticed her clothes feeling slightly snugger and her shoes rubbing her where they hadn't before.

Daily, she asked Ms. Winters about the mail, and daily, she was given the same response: "Nothing today, milady."

Evelyn couldn't understand why her father and brother would ignore her. Even if, as suspected, her letters were not being posted, she still should have received something from them by now. She had left their lives months ago, a period longer than she had ever gone without having some form of contact with them. They should have become curious—concerned even—and yet nothing arrived at the house outside the Friday morning food delivery, and no one ever called to visit.

When she lived with her family, every day brought something or someone to their door; the clang of the bell echoing around the halls was as familiar to her as the sound of her voice. But Blackthorn sat silent and unloved. The halls and rooms were devoid of life and laughter, a museum exhibit of what a grand house could be rather than a lived-in family home. The only people she saw, beyond the unfriendly staff and the cold stranger that was her husband, were the dead who wandered its halls, their world detached from and yet still a part of Blackthorn at the same time—a world within a world.

Ghost children's laughter echoed as footsteps without owners pounded toward her, then passed by, to continue their game elsewhere. Shapes visible in the corner of her eye vanished when she turned to face them. Once terrifying to Evelyn, these instances had become commonplace and almost welcomed. The beings never interacted with her directly and had become almost comforting. They helped her escape the unbearable weight of loneliness outside of the few evenings she could sneak time with Lilly.

Lilly's attempts to contact the man who had taken Evelyn's letters had proven fruitless. On the rare occasions she was told to assist with the delivery, the man was not there, replaced by others, different in looks, but similar in temperament and attitude toward her. They would not speak to her when she tried to engage them and would not answer her questions regarding their friend or colleague. Both women feared he had taken their money and simply thrown the handwritten cries for help into the fire.

Evelyn so desperately wanted to take ownership of her own life, yet she felt helpless, a body caught in a rip tide, slowly being pulled out further and further from shore. Her meager attempts to regain a modicum of dominion over her own existence felt childish. The small knife she still carried, wrapped snugly in her skirts, felt like a leaden weight, a constant reminder of her entrapment. A fly caught within a web can struggle all it likes, but it will not escape its fate. What if she were but a fly?

That evening's dinner served as nothing but a reminder of how precarious her position was and how threadbare the veil of lies she had created, stretching daily along with her clothes. Peter was in particularly foul form. She did not know why, nor did she care to know, having as little regard for his feelings as he had for hers. He slashed at his meat with a disturbing ferocity and chased every mouthful with a large swig of red wine. Evelyn stole glances at him as he attacked his plate. His eyes were blurred and heavy, and when he called for more wine, his words were slurred.

He's drunk. Perhaps, she thought, *the alcohol will send him into an early slumber, and I can escape his nightly visit.*

She shuddered.

Even the thought of his hands on her skin made it crawl, her stomach twisting and turning.

She picked at her food, pushing it about the plate with small, unenthusiastic motions. The smell made her feel ill, and her appetite had fled as soon as they had set the lamb and potatoes in front of her. Lately, red meat caused bile to rise, and lamb, in particular, brought with it waves of nausea. Perhaps it was merely the pregnancy affecting her sense of taste and smell, altering her in new and strange ways. But in part, the idea of eating something killed so young seemed at odds with the life she grew up in, and so the meal went untouched.

"You're not eating."

Evelyn suddenly sat to attention, her body rigid at his address. She had been so lost in thought that she hadn't noticed his attention becoming fixed on her. How long had he been watching her? Long enough, apparently.

"I...I'm not hungry." She spoke so meekly, even she was surprised. She hated how weak she sounded. She hated how afraid she was of him. She tried to appear normal, but every fiber of her body was screaming a warning that something bad was going to happen, and she needed to be prepared to fight or flee.

He rose with a jerk, knocking his chair down behind him with a thud that echoed in the cavernous room. Out of the corner of her eye, Evelyn saw the two maids quietly leaving, obviously as aware as she was that danger was present.

Bastards! Cowards!

He stood, a hand on either side of his plate, his eyebrows knitted into an angry, vicious look that rested squarely on Evelyn. "Not hungry?"

It was a loaded question—a trap. Evelyn knew that from his tone, just as she knew there was no right answer or response that would satisfy the tempest of anger that now swelled within his puffed-up chest.

"I...I feel a little...unwell. I might be coming down with something...I..." She tapered off into silence, her gaze shifting from his eyes. His stare was far too intense to hold, and it bored into her being.

He moved from behind the table, strolling toward her almost casually. But his gait betrayed his inebriation, as he swayed slightly with every step. His face remained contorted with an anger Evelyn could not understand but feared greatly, having felt the sting of its tail more than once. Instinctively, she moved her hand toward her stomach, a weak attempt to protect the child within.

"Feeling unwell? Coming down with something? *You're weak!*"

The last words were spat at her like venom, every syllable laced with hatred.

"Your body is weak, and it fails me nightly. What use are you? Almost six months and nothing. One thing—all your kind are good for—one thing, and yet you can't even manage that, can you?"

He was beside her now, so close she could feel the heat radiating from him. She didn't dare move, didn't dare look into his face for fear of setting him off. She recalled reading a book about the animal kingdom and how, for many species, direct eye contact was seen as a challenge. Now, here she was, afraid to make eye contact with her husband lest he attack her like some kind of beast. How had her life become this?

He lowered his face to her own, the stink of the wine and meat hitting her in force, causing her stomach to churn. "My patience is wearing thin, my dear. Don't let it run out."

She could feel his ragged, angry breath, feel the spittle as he spat every word at her. Her breathing was heavy and quick, and her body tensed, ready for a blow or worse. She felt the hardness of the knife within her gown and began to move the fabric, ready to use it if she had to, ready to kill to protect her child.

But no blow came. Instead, he huffed angrily in her face before flinging her plate across the table, meat and gravy splashing the linen. And with that, he stomped away, yelling at his staff to ready his horse. She did not care where he was going; the relief of his leaving overwhelmed her. All at once, her emotions bubbled to the surface, and she wept loudly, choking and sputtering into her hands.

When the maids entered again, they ignored her and cleaned up as if she weren't there. She wanted to scream in their faces, to throw things, to shake them, and ask what was wrong with them. But she knew it was futile. She watched the gravy slowly drip from the table like an hourglass, its sands falling with every second that passed. She needed to escape Blackthorn—she needed to escape Peter—and she was running out of time.

Restless and unable to quiet her mind or calm her ragged nerves, Evelyn simply started walking. She wandered the halls, doing multiple laps of the same corridors, trying to work off the nervous energy that coursed through her body. For once, Ms. Winters was nowhere to be seen. Perhaps the woman felt awkward pity after undoubtedly hearing the altercation. But, more likely, she assumed Evelyn would return to her bedchamber, broken and sad, to cry herself to sleep like a scolded child.

Evelyn was unsure how long she had walked around the house when, quite by chance, she found herself along the third-floor corridor, where Peter kept his study. It was a room she had seen only once, albeit briefly, during Ms. Winters's tour. She had good reason to avoid it, fearful that she might bump into Peter after his outburst. But, she had heard him yell for his horse and listened to the stomp of his feet recede as he marched indignantly into the night, so surely there was no harm in looking around? Perhaps the one room she had been unable to explore contained answers to the many questions that plagued her daily.

Her curiosity and desperation outweighed her fear as the awareness of how precarious her position was pushed her on. And so, without hesitation, she placed her hand on the cold brass handle and pushed.

Locked. Damn.

Like the other hallways, this one was lined with portraits. However, they appeared to be much older in both style and subject. The men were just as stern-faced and stiff in their poses as the more modern portraits downstairs, but their dress and hairstyles spoke of a past long since gone. She moved from picture to picture and wondered if every Lord Black had been as distant as her own. As noted before, there were no women, no children, only the lords themselves. It was as if the line of male heirs existed in a vacuum, detached from the mothers who had birthed them and the wives who produced their progeny.

She moved her hand over her stomach and tried to imagine what gender her child would be and what it would look like. Of course, no mother ever cares what gender their baby is, as long as it is healthy and happy. Yet, she couldn't help but feel sadness for the unborn baby if it were to be a girl, doomed to be overlooked and forgotten, never to have their face added to the halls of her family home or to have any purpose in life other than to produce children, preferably another male to add to the Black family history.

Then again, if it were male, would he be like his father? The idea of her son seeing her as worthless beyond her ability to provide children, or that he would be as cold and distant toward her as his father, pained her as much as if it were already happening. She imagined another portrait—a young man whose features resemble her own, his steely gaze and arrogant gait added to the other Lord Blacks whose faces watched from the walls of Blackthorn. The thought made her stomach twist.

As she moved through the past, the corridor filled with the scent of lavender. The hairs on her neck rose as a shiver snaked its way up her spine. The temperature dropped by several degrees, and she enclosed herself in a hug in an attempt to stave off the sudden cold. She looked around, knowing something was with her, that someone long dead was present.

There were no playing children this time, no disembodied laughter or faceless ghosts in the fog, but there was an energy there—something feminine, something sad. The figure appeared more like a blur, with the outline of a body moving through water and the features indistinct. It came in and out of focus, vanishing before reappearing seconds later, a couple of feet further down the hallway.

Evelyn felt anxious but unafraid. Despite how unnerving the presence of such beings was, she sensed sadness and longing from this one, nothing threatening. She tried to discern her features, to learn who she was, but it was like trying to grasp at the fog itself. The specter was definitely a woman, a little older than Evelyn, perhaps? She had a curl to her hair, but Evelyn struggled to tell if her hair was short or styled up. She had delicate features and a slender frame and was clearly wearing some kind of floor-length gown not too dissimilar from Evelyn's.

Evelyn's eye was drawn toward the locket around the woman's name, the CB initials as elegant as a spider web. Evelyn wondered if one day she would be like this—a whisper in a quiet room, barely audible, or a movement caught in the corner of one's eye. A feeling rather than a being. The thought made tears edge their way toward her lashes, though not quite fall—after all, she still hadn't given up on the idea of escape.

She followed behind the specter, and it paused beside the door to Peter's office before vanishing along with the strong scent of lavender and the feeling of overwhelming sadness. The door, once locked, creaked open slowly, revealing the darkness of the office beyond. Without thinking or questioning, Evelyn walked quickly inside, closing the door behind her.

Not knowing where to begin, she started opening drawers and rifling through them, unsure of what she was looking for. There were legal documents, contracts, and papers, which meant little to her and were of no interest. Some drawers were locked, so she moved on, trying to look through quickly and decisively, but also to leave everything as it had been before. She didn't want to imagine what Peter would do if he discovered her there.

As she moved to the shelves, she was startled by the bottom drawer shooting open behind her. Her heart sank as she reached inside, pulling out every one of the letters she had written to her father or brother. Dozens of pages of her writing, every one opened and read, were cast aside as if they were nothing. Months of her life stuffed into a drawer to be forgotten.

Her tears fell and blurred the ink of her words, causing them to run in long, black lines. Sadness turned quickly to fear as she found the final letters were all too familiar. Unlike those passed to Ms. Winters, these letters were handed to a stranger in desperation. These letters represented her and Lilly's last hope, and worse than finding them there—worse than knowing they, like the others, were never posted—were the red brown spots encrusting their edges, the bloodstains stark among the other white pages.

As she lifted them out, she realized they were wrapped around something solid, but the dried blood had caused some of the pages to stick together, creating a morbid seal. Slowly, she pried the edges apart, the faint smell of something putrid growing ever stronger with every layer peeled. With shaking hands, Evelyn revealed the grotesque contents of the hastily wrapped package.

It was teeth—human teeth—some of which even retained lumps of the gums from which they had been so viciously wrenched. Horrified, Evelyn dropped them, retching not just at the sight and smell of them but at what they represented. It did not take an expert in human anatomy or dentistry to understand that the package contained a full set of adult teeth.

Tears fell as she realized that the kind grocer had not failed them, had not deceived or betrayed them. He, like the others, had died for no other reason than showing her kindness. He had been murdered, just like Harrison and just like the old woman—but worse, he had perhaps been tortured first, each tooth pulled from his begging mouth. And more than that, her husband, the father of her unborn child, was not only responsible, but he had chosen to keep the teeth as some kind of trophy. It was too much to bear!

But there was more to come, the drawer offering further revelations. Beneath the letters were page after page with writing like her own. The handwriting was hers, but the words were not—her signature written over and over again, the same words repeated by a hand growing more confident and competent with every pen stroke. Phrases and sentences practiced until they were perfect, looking as if she'd written them herself: "I no longer wish to see you," "I have tried to forgive you for Mother's death," and "Please do not contact me again."

Together, they formed a letter and a deception that severed her connections with her family, cut her off from everything she had ever known before Blackthorn, and destroyed any hope that remained within her heart.

They were alone.

No one was coming for them.

The walls of Blackthorn seemed to move inwards, closing in around her as she left the office. Evelyn's breathing shallowed as she struggled to draw enough air into her lungs. She felt a weight pressing in on her from all around, and the world began to spin and turn, fading in and out of focus. She scrambled along the corridor, using the walls to stop herself from crumpling, desperate for air, desperate to escape Blackthorn and the dour faces that judged her from the walls. She wasn't sure how far she got before her vision clouded completely, the world turning on its head, but the pressure became too great, eventually pulling her down to the carpet where she fell, and the world faded to black.

When she opened her eyes, she sensed she was walking within the thin veil between her world and the next. Everything seemed to dull somehow, as if she were in a painting, faded by age and sunlight. The doorway was only a few feet away, already open, tendrils of fog snaking their way toward her prone figure, reaching out to take her from the land of the living.

She shook, the coldness pouring forth having already taken hold. She could see them there among the mist, just as she had out on the moors. Spectral shapes moved at speed, appearing and disappearing, sometimes resembling a human form and sometimes something far more terrifying. Their faces were reduced to shadows, their expressions pained and sorrowful. She could feel its regret and dejection as real and measurable as the cold.

Evelyn dared not move, watching and waiting for the now familiar figure to appear. She didn't have to wait long. Slowly, it emerged as it always did, twitching and jerking in a wholly unnatural, sickening movement. Her mother's glassy eyes stared straight at her, never seeing, just fixed and vacant. The other face, rotten and decayed, met Evelyn's eyes and fixed her with that same knowing gaze that always filled Evelyn's chest with fear and her throat with bile. It stopped mere inches from Evelyn, her mother's lifeless feet hanging close enough that Evelyn could reach up and grasp them. It remained upright, standing over her, the decayed face staring down at her knowingly.

"What do you want from me?"

Her voice sounded so meek and childlike that she barely recognized it as her own.

The specter seemed to struggle to speak—the rasping, wheezing voice that emerged sounded pained and forced. *"Blood..."*

"I-I don't understand."

"Blood…made…blood…destroyed."

"My blood? What did it make? Please, I don't understand."

"B-B-Bl…"

Pain shot across her face and through her head like a bullet, pulling her sharply from the in-between and back into the waking world. She couldn't understand what had happened for a moment until she saw him looming above her, his face contorted with rage. She moved her hand to her cheek to find it warm and already swelling, throbbing with every beat of her heart and stinging like she had been burned. His hand was still open-palmed and stiff as if ready to land another blow. Tears filled her eyes, both from the pain and shock as well as from the fear that held her tight in its grip.

"You insolent bitch!"

He spat the words out at her, venom injected into every single syllable. She saw the door open behind him, felt the carpet at her back, and understood that she had only gone a few steps from his office. He raised his hand once more, and she tensed instinctively, readying herself for another blow. Hatred burned within his eyes, and she feared that he might kill her, that he might kill their child.

"Please… I'm pregnant."

Peter's hand stopped suddenly in mid-air, his expression shifting quickly from rage to confusion and, finally, softening to form an unnerving smile. The hand lowered to his side, and his stance relaxed. He bent down toward her, and she flinched —anticipating more violence, more pain—but instead, he took her hand and pulled her up off the ground and into his arms, swallowing her slight figure in a forced embrace.

She became rigid and still, letting him hold her a moment. Being in his arms felt wrong. Being so close to him filled her with revulsion, mixing and churning with the fear already inside her. She wanted to scream, to run, to lash out. Instead, she simply stood there, silent tears wetting his jacket. Her body was there, trapped within the unwanted embrace, but her spirit—her soul—was somewhere else, somewhere far away from Blackthorn.

Eventually, he pulled away and placed his thumb beneath her chin. He had done this so many times, always before he kissed her softly. Once, she had yearned for the feel of his hand there, the taste of his lips. Now, as he moved his lips toward hers, she instinctively jerked away from him. The thought of his lips on hers filled her with disgust. He was repugnant, and any lingering feelings of love left clinging to her heart vanished the moment he laid his hands on her in anger.

He didn't force the kiss or seem angered or upset by her actions. Rather, he seemed overjoyed, the same disturbing smile painted across his face of someone crazed, someone disturbed. He released her and stepped away, giving her the space she so desperately craved.

"You have no idea how pleased I am! I shall have the doctor come at once to check everything is well and to estimate how long it will be before my son arrives."

She hated how he called it *his* son, as if she were not its mother. She hated that he had assumed its gender—that it would somehow be a disappointment if it were a girl. She hated how he had immediately taken ownership of her body, of her pregnancy. She wouldn't look at him—couldn't look at him—lest her expression betray her and earn her another slap.

"I will get Ms. Winters and have the staff informed. You must have all the rest you need. Please go to your bedchamber, and I will have someone come to you."

Evelyn didn't have the strength to argue. She simply turned and swiftly walked away, putting as much distance between herself and Peter, between her child and Peter. And it was *her* child, not his. It would never be his.

As she ran back to her room, she made a vow to the small life that grew and formed within her. "I will never let him have you. Do you hear me? Never. I will protect you, and I will never let anything happen to you. We will escape this place. We must!"

Evelyn had been summoned from her room by a flustered Ms. Winters for an urgent visit with the doctor. Evelyn had hoped that some medical malady had struck Peter, but when she saw him standing beside the red-faced Doctor Wells, who dabbed at his face with his handkerchief, she knew the poor man had been summoned for her.

"Lady Black, please sit. Tell me of these symptoms from which you are suffering?"

Evelyn stared at him, confused. "Symptoms?"

"Yes, is there bleeding? Birthing pains?"

"No, nothing like that."

"Oh?" Doctor Wells looked at Peter. "What is the nature of the emergency, Lord Black?"

"The emergency is that she is pregnant with my son and requires a thorough examination to ensure his safety and health." He spoke through gritted teeth, pointing at her when he said the word "she" as if she were no longer worthy of a name or a title. She was merely a womb now, a carrier for his true prize, and as such, she held no value beyond that. In the past, such a slight would have wounded her, but now, she felt nothing.

"I see. I had been told the matter was urgent and to come here posthaste, hence traveling overnight."

Peter moved closer to the doctor until he loomed over the man. "It is urgent to me, Doctor."

Doctor Wells swallowed hard and straightened to his full height, albeit a full foot shorter than Peter. "I understand that pregnancy can be a difficult time for both parents. I can conduct regular examinations throughout to keep everyone's minds at ease and to prevent any similar misunderstandings in the future."

Before Peter could respond, Doctor Wells turned to Evelyn and led her to a nearby chaise, where they sat.

"How are you feeling, Lady Black?" He smiled warmly as he gently took her wrist in his right hand, removing a silver pocket watch from his waistcoat pocket with his left.

"A little nauseous, but apart from that, I am well."

"Good, Good." He looked at her eyes. "Any shortness of breath? Dizziness?"

"She fainted last night," Peter barked.

Wells did not turn away from Evelyn or acknowledge Peter, just continued speaking in the same kind, soothing tone. "Had anything happened prior to the dizzy spell which may have caused you stress?" His hand brushed Evelyn's swollen cheek, and she flinched. They both made eye contact, and an understanding passed between them. He did not wait for her answer. "How much are you eating?"

"A little less than usual. I feel nauseous."

"That is perfectly normal. Just make sure you eat as much as you can, after all, you are now eating for two." He removed a glass thermometer from a small black box and placed it beneath her tongue. "Make sure you are eating well and drinking plenty of water."

Peter stood over them both, scrutinizing every movement Wells made. "Never mind all that. Is my son well?"

Wells sighed. "We will see once my examination is complete. The mother's health is extremely important during this time and will dictate the health of the baby."

Peter's jaw tensed. "Yes, of course. Please continue."

Doctor Wells nodded and put a hand on Evelyn's stomach,

applying gentle pressure. "Have you experienced bleeding? Any pains?"

Evelyn shook her head.

"Check for any defects, Doctor, any possible issues. I must know my son is well."

"Everything seems well, Lord Black, for both child and mother," the doctor said patiently. He smiled at Evelyn, a kind of sad, knowing smile.

"Well, check again. If any medicines need to be taken or measures put into place, I need to know. Ms. Winters and I will ensure he is provided for."

"Of course, Milord."

Being so blatantly overlooked and dismissed by her husband had begun to grate on Evelyn. She wanted to scream at him, to tell him that the baby would never be his, that it was hers. But she remained silent and resentful, the pain in her cheek reminding her of what happened when she disobeyed.

The doctor seemed to sense her frustration and placed a reassuring hand on hers. It was a small gesture, but one that Evelyn was incredibly grateful for. It made her feel less alone, even if just for a moment.

"Mother and child are physically well," the doctor declared.

Peter smiled broadly.

"She will need to keep her strength up," the doctor continued. "I recommend exercise, though nothing too vigorous; a short daily walk will suffice. Mother must eat plenty of good food, drink plenty of water, and, of course, rest."

Peter nodded along with each direction.

Wells continued. "How is her psychological health?"

"What does that matter?" Peter snapped.

"Well, as we discussed during my last visit, emotional and mental issues can have physical effects. Your wife has already displayed symptoms in the past, and I would hate for them to affect her now."

Peter seemed unmoved.

The doctor added, "And the baby as well, of course."

"It could harm my son?"

If the doctor had been surprised at the gendering of their baby, he did not show it. "Of course. As before, I recommend plenty of rest and fresh air, perhaps a trip—"

Peter cut him off. "Absolutely not. She must remain here at Blackthorn, where she is safe."

"Perhaps a visit from family—"

"No. She has everyone she needs right here."

Doctor Wells coughed awkwardly. He looked at Evelyn with sympathy before changing his tactic. "Mothers often have a dedicated lady's maid, someone to assist with everything from dressing to bathing. Perhaps..."

Peter waved a hand at Ms. Winters, who eagerly shuffled toward them, ever the lap dog for her master.

Evelyn's face wrinkled with loathing.

"Ms. Winters, you can tend to Lady Black."

The women eyed each other with silent disdain, both remaining silent. The hatred was clearly mutual.

Perceptive as ever, Doctor Wells seemed to pick up on the tension immediately. "I'm sure the housekeeper of such a grand manor as this has her hands full. As the lady grows with child, she will need more and more attention—for the baby's health, of course. Ideally, a little closer in age, perhaps an already-established rapport...? Is there anyone on staff who fits that bill?"

Evelyn bit her tongue. If she were to ask for Lilly, she was sure Peter would outright reject it, purely out of malice and spite.

Surprisingly, it was Ms. Winters herself who suggested it. "Pardon me, Milord, but what of the orphan girl? She can split her time between the kitchen and attending to Lady Black. Her poor cleaning skills surely won't be missed."

Evelyn resented Ms. Winters's implication about Lilly's

competence but thought better of saying anything aloud. The woman was, after all, helping her. Evelyn felt Peter's eyes move to her. She could see him in her peripheral vision, weighing the options, considering the possibilities. She didn't dare look, but she sensed he was unconvinced.

Apparently, so did Doctor Wells. "Of course, it is up to you, Lord Black. You know best. However, I have seen mothers who were prone to attacks of the nerves suffer terribly in pregnancy, even losing the child in extreme cases."

Peter shot him a terrified look as he continued.

"If leaving the home is impossible, then having the appropriate support here would be imperative, in my professional opinion."

That seemed to do it.

"Ms. Winters, fetch the girl at once."

Ms. Winters nodded and hurried out of the room.

Evelyn's heart began to beat a little faster. She missed Lilly so much, and the idea of seeing her at long last filled her with hope.

Doctor Wells gathered his various instruments, hat, and coat. "I shall return in a month for another check-up."

Peter frowned. "A fortnight." It was not a request but an order.

Doctor Wells eyed the man before nodding in agreement. Evelyn felt pity for the man. Whatever Peter was paying him, it was not enough.

When Lilly entered a few minutes later, with black soot marks on her apron and chin, it took all Evelyn's willpower not to jump up and embrace her immediately. Both women smiled at one another as Ms. Winters barked a series of orders at Lilly, including her new duties to "the future Lord Black."

Once business was done and all parties satisfied, the doctor departed with a friendly wink. Evelyn mouthed the word "thank you" and smiled at him gratefully. Peter and Ms.

Winters followed behind him, and Lilly and Evelyn were alone at long last.

All decorum and propriety were thrown out the window as Lilly fell on the chaise beside Evelyn, sobbing. Both women embraced tightly, tears of gratitude and relief falling from their eyes. They sat like that for a long time, crying and holding one another tightly, before Evelyn withdrew from Lilly's arms and kissed her forehead.

"Oh, how I missed you, Lilly. I cannot navigate this place without you."

Lilly returned the kiss with a gentle one of her own on Evelyn's cheek. "You won't have to ever again." She placed her hand gently on Evelyn's stomach. "Either of you."

Evelyn smiled. With Lilly by her side, she truly believed they could escape Blackthorn. Her face fell as she remembered her perilous circumstances. She took Lilly's hands in her own, shifting her tone and posture. "I have much to tell you..."

Ever since Evelyn had revealed her pregnancy to Peter, he had treated her as if she were a breeding dog, only worthy of the offspring she could provide. He never spoke with her except during the doctor's fortnightly visits, where he would ask the physician questions as if she were not even in the room. Thankfully, this new attitude meant the nightly visits to her room had ceased. The thought of him touching her in that way caused bile to rise in her throat, and she found herself grateful to no longer be worthy of his attention.

After nearly three months, her belly had swollen, and her body had begun to feel as if it were no longer her own. It betrayed her often, making demands she could not meet, giving in to weakness when she yearned for strength. She felt exhausted, physically and emotionally, and the more she desired quiet, the louder the voices of the dead seemed to scream.

Almost daily, Evelyn would hear voices without an owner or would see blurred images of what once were people, mere reflections of who they used to be. Some would act as they had in life, as if she and the other residents of Blackthorn went unnoticed or perhaps disregarded—something existing around it but apart. On occasion, however, something would seem to breach the veil between both worlds, reaching out toward the living with desperate hands. These instances proved to be the most unnerving—their cries for help breaking Evelyn's heart each and every time, giving rise to her deepest fear that one day, she would become one of them, trapped within Blackthorn forever, despairing and alone.

Squealers—that's what Lilly called them, naming them after the pigs that she had heard being killed at the slaughterhouse near her home as a child.

"They want summit."

She had said this so casually as if that were obvious to anyone who lived there.

"But what?" Evelyn had cried in response. "What can they want from us?"

Her response had settled over Evelyn like a cold, damp blanket. "I don't know, but it will only get worse. If we don't find a way free of this place, I fear what they may do to make us understand."

The doors of their prison had been constantly locked and bolted. No longer could Evelyn wander the grounds or gardens; no longer could she visit her favorite spot by the pond. She was restricted to the house alone, and what had once seemed so large and grand suddenly felt uncomfortably small.

Their escape bag, so carefully hidden, lay untouched, the food within it rotting and decaying along with their hope. They had been naive to think they could so easily walk free of

Blackthorn's grasp—Evelyn saw that now. No one was coming to rescue them, and they would never have been able to simply sneak away unnoticed. The two women were on their own, and any escape would have to be something they took—Blackthorn would not give it through chance or circumstance.

Blackthorn not only seemed smaller to Evelyn since her imprisonment, but also transformed. The shiny veneer had worn off and exposed the rot beneath. Everywhere she looked, she could see flaws. Cracks spiderwebbed across walls while the black stains of damp and mold crept their way up others. Windows allowed drafts that whistled through the halls and invited in the foul British weather. Fabrics frayed at the edges, unravelling piece by piece, or were faded and washed out from exposure to sunlight.

The longer Evelyn spent within the walls of Blackthorn House, the more she saw it for what it really was—a lie. The house was, on first appearances, extravagant and expensive, luxurious and enviable. But it was an optical illusion, a mirage, and by the time one realized the truth, it was far too late to escape. She took comfort, however, in knowing that whatever happened to them, they would be together—cell mates in a prison of the damned.

It was the dead of night when Evelyn awoke from a restless sleep. There had been no nightmares that night, no visits from Hel or her mother's lifeless body, yet still, she had been unable to sink into the comforting black of solid sleep. She always seemed to skirt the edge of that blissful oblivion—close enough to reach out and touch it—but it was just beyond her grasp. Instead, she would have strange, fitful dreams, as if one foot were still planted firmly within her bed while the other was in the subconscious world. It was frustrating, now more than ever. The small bump that now protruded from her made sleeping more difficult as it was, and summer had brought with it humidity, making Blackthorn seem all the more suffocating.

She stared up at the drapes surrounding her bed, trying to remember what had stirred her from that dissatisfying rest. It was not Peter, the door between their rooms now remaining firmly shut. To make sure he could not sneak in while she slept, she had inserted her own copy of the key from her side of the door and broke it off inside the lock. She decided it would be worth suffering his wrath for the sense of safety it would bring, and she had prepared her own alibi—a story of feeling a pain in her side and wishing to rouse him for her help, which had accidentally caused the damage in her panicked haste. But she had never needed to utter her excuse as he had ceased using the door the day he had discovered her pregnancy, the day he had struck her down like she was nothing to him.

The night was silent and shadowed, but in the fog of first waking, she was sure that some kind of noise had awakened her, the details of which seemed lost now among a jumble of other thoughts and feelings left to linger from dreams she could no longer recall.

As if Blackthorn heard her thoughts, it answered them in kind. The noise sounded again, low enough not to cause panic or fear but loud enough to be noticed. It was like a scraping of one object being dragged over another, something hollow. Evelyn lay still, pretending not to notice, as if ignoring it might simply make it go away. She felt like a child again—hiding under the covers and pretending to sleep, hoping that whatever had scared her would disappear, that by reacting to it, she would somehow make it manifest, make it real. But unlike the imaginings of her childhood, this did not vanish with closed eyes.

She hoped it was an animal, perhaps a mouse or rat trapped beneath a floorboard or a bird at the window pane, but something about the consistent rhythm, the clear and deliberate pattern, made that seem unlikely. Part of her wanted to remain there, hiding from the world outside her bed. Hiding from

Peter and Ms. Winters, from ghosts and specters. But she knew now that some of the souls wandering Blackthorn's halls wished to reveal its secrets.

When she asked Lilly why the beings did not simply speak to her, Lilly told her that spirits were often unable to do so. That breaching the veil was difficult and draining for them, and that sometimes, they could only come through in part. They communicated how they could—hence disembodied voices, knocking, or the movement of an object or door. Often unable to speak or write, they moaned and cried and threw things around, their frustration at being misunderstood or ignored only adding to their eternal suffering.

Evelyn had decided then that she would answer their calls, however they came—if not for her own sake, then for the sake of the poor wretched creatures doomed to wander Blackthorn for all eternity. So, with a heavy sigh, she slowly and ungracefully sat up and peered into the darkness, trying to see who peered back.

Nothing stirred within the darkness of her bedchamber, but the sound came consistently every thirty seconds or so from the far wall where her dresser stood. Evelyn forced herself out of bed, rubbing at the constant pain in the small of her back—yet another annoyance added to her list of discomforts and bodily changes. Slowly, she walked toward the large, solid piece of furniture, ears alert for the continued *scratch, scratch, scratch* that grew in volume with every step.

The sound was coming from the bottom drawer. She knelt down and took a deep breath before opening the drawer, preparing herself for what she might find. There was nothing remarkable there—just some of her night dresses, neatly pressed and folded. As she shuffled them about, checking if perhaps something was within the folds of fabric, the scratching came again, and she realized the sound was not within the drawer but *behind* it. With some difficulty, she pulled the heavy wooden drawer free, revealing the dark space behind it. Fearing what may lurk there, she lit the candle atop the dresser and brought it down with her. The flickering light revealed little but cobwebbed, wooden corners until something glinted.

Reaching inside, she felt something hard and thin, and when she pulled it out, she noticed she held a key. It had the same head as every key in Blackthorn—a *B* within a circle—but unlike the others, which were plain on the other side of the head, this one had another marking. It was covered with dirt and rust, so Evelyn took it to her washstand and rubbed at it with hurried fingers.

When she revealed the symbol beneath, her heart beat fast, and her breathing shallowed. Simultaneously, she felt the child within her stir and flutter for the first time, as if the baby were as disturbed as she was. It was the symbol she had seen dozens of times within her nightmares, the one carved above that damnable door which haunted her day and night.

She stared at the strange character—part cross, part crosshair, part something else. What did it mean? Could it be possible that this key somehow fit the door inside her dreams? It was such a preposterous idea. The door was not real—it was a metaphor, a symbol. She struggled to picture the door as she tried to remember whether it had a lock or not, but from what she recalled, it did not. Besides, such a large door with black iron hinges and a handle would have a key to match. This was an ordinary key—something to fit an ordinary, earthly lock. And yet, the key held some kind of importance, some link to that ungodly place and the creature that lived within.

Regardless, whatever had revealed it to her had done so for a reason, just like that specter had revealed her letters in Peter's office. For that reason alone, she placed it around the same chain from which the crucifix hung, hidden within her breast and always near her heart. She would try every lock in Blackthorn if she had to. She would do whatever it took to escape that godforsaken house and the people within it.

The scent of lavender washed over her, and she felt the room grow colder. As the hairs on her arm rose, she instinctively wrapped her arms around herself, scanning the room to find the specter who had already reached out and offered help, but nothing stirred. Despite this, she knew the woman was there.

Evelyn whispered, "Thank you," into the darkness, knowing she was heard.

Sixteen

"Ms. Winters almost caught me today. I will have to be more careful."

Evelyn nodded before she sipped her tea. It tasted strange to her, metallic as if a penny had been stewed in the pot along with the leaves. Everything seemed to taste off-putting to her now, the pregnancy bringing with it strange and unpleasant side effects. She sighed heavily, mourning the loss of one of her favorite things.

Lilly continued. "But I did manage to get that whole corridor checked before she did, and it doesn't open any doors there, either."

She handed the key back to Evelyn, who quickly deposited it in her breast pocket. Between the two of them, they had tried almost every door within Blackthorn, both internal and external, and the key had not fit a single lock. It was another frustrating blow.

The Lavender Lady, a nickname Lilly had given to the helpful specter, had obviously shown her the key for some reason. The symbol had marked it as important and linked to both Hel and the runic symbols carved beneath her bed, as well as those worn by the staff and carved upon the door depicted in her dreams. But despite tearing the library apart and reading every book on language or Germanic culture they could find, they were no closer to understanding what the symbol meant.

Everything was beginning to feel too much for Evelyn. It felt as if she and Lilly were mice trapped in some giant maze, part of a game they didn't understand. Every time they seemed to make progress, every time they made a discovery or found a piece of Blackthorn's puzzle, the rules of the game changed, the walls of the maze moved, and they were back at the beginning again, more lost than ever. Escape felt impossible, and it took every ounce of Evelyn's strength not to give up. If it weren't for the child that grew inside her, perhaps she would have.

Lilly tried her best to encourage Evelyn and give her hope, but it was obvious that she, too, feared they would never escape Blackthorn's clutches. While she was allowed to wait on Evelyn again, privacy was rare. Ms. Winters continued to follow Evelyn's every move. Both women felt eyes on them everywhere they went—both from the living and the dead—making Evelyn's fanciful maze analogy feel very real. Only in her bedchamber did Evelyn feel truly free of observation—ironic given that the dead had already violated its space. They had even managed to permeate her dreams. The fact that this room felt like her only safe space was, in itself, a sad reflection of their dire situation.

"I shall have to get back, ma'am. I'm only s'posed to drop the tray to you and leave. They'll be wondering where I got to."

As if Lilly's words had summoned her, Ms. Winters burst into the room, announced by a single knock with no pause left afterward to allow Evelyn to permit her entry. All the staff entered like that now, as if her permission were no longer required. It was clear from several interactions with Ms. Winters and the other staff that Evelyn's status as Lady Black no longer held much weight with them. Any pretense they once held was dropped the second they discovered she was pregnant. She was treated now like a guest who had overstayed her welcome.

Lilly shot out of her seat like a soldier standing to attention, a look of panic crossing her face. Evelyn felt anger bubbling inside her.

"I thought I would find you here," Ms. Winter snapped. "Why are you incapable of following the simplest orders, girl? Get out of here and go about your other work before I lash you."

Lilly quickly marched toward the door, head down, as Ms. Winters entered Evelyn's space, examining how much she had eaten as she always did. She lifted the tray and sniffed it in disapproval. "You are eating and drinking for two. This simply will not do! You must eat more for the sake of the child."

Evelyn's anger rose higher, boiling into a rage. She was sick of Ms. Winters and her constant intrusions. She was sick of the staff treating her as if she did not matter. She was sick of Blackthorn and its secrets. And she was sick of people telling her what to do with *her* body. Something took her over, and she smacked the tray out of Ms. Winters's hand, sending it to the floor with a clatter.

Ms. Winters froze, her face painted with shock. Lilly stopped short of the door and turned to look at Evelyn, her face aghast. Evelyn rose from her chair, eyes seething, fists clenched and filled with fury. She stepped toward Ms. Winters, who suddenly seemed small and weak beneath the bulk of Evelyn's newly rounded body. She had several inches over Ms. Winters and towered over her, glaring down with disdain and fury. "You will address me as Her Ladyship. You will stop telling me and *my* maid what to do. You will keep your opinions to yourself, and you will never enter my chambers again unless explicitly invited. Do I make myself clear, Ms. Winters?"

Ms. Winters shrank away from Evelyn, her face pale and mouth agape. It was clear that no one had ever dared to speak to her in such a manner before, and she was unsure how to process it, never mind how to react. She simply nodded meekly, her bottom lip quivering, before practically running from the room, leaving both women behind.

Lilly walked toward the shards of broken china and the tea-stained rug and stared up at Evelyn. "Where on Earth did that come from?"

Evelyn smiled weakly as she fell back into her chair. The adrenaline had already worn off, and she now felt exhausted but also proud and powerful. Perhaps she did still have a fight left in her. "I have no idea."

"Well, wherever it came from, I liked it."

"So did I."

The door was familiar to her now, forever etched in her mind like a scar. It opened slowly, deliberately, once more letting the cold pour forth into Blackthorn and wash over Evelyn. It felt like being plunged into cold water. Evelyn held her belly protectively, painfully aware of just how vulnerable she was in her present state.

The figure emerged from the fog once more, with the same jerking motion as always, except that instead of her mother's body, another emerged. She was older than Evelyn, but only by a few years, with fair, curly hair pinned up into a chignon. Her delicate features were wholly obscured by the rot and decay that had set into her flesh. Her skin and lips were blue, and along her neck, where a gold oval locket hung with the initials *C.B.* engraved on it, was a large gaping wound that opened and closed as she moved, reminiscent of an angry mouth gasping for air. Sinew and fat hung from its edge, wiggling and vibrating with every awkward motion. Her dress, an ivory gown not dissimilar from many hanging in Evelyn's own wardrobes, had been stained red and brown by the blood released from that very wound—dark and intense at the neck, then gradually lightening toward the hem, a gradient of gore. The woman's eyes had no color other than milky white, and they stared through Evelyn, unable to see anyone or anything ever again.

As usual, the body was worn like some kind of mask by the being Evelyn now knew as Hel. Her face was rotten and decayed, and her teeth were visible through her fleshless cheeks, gray and black chunks of festering flesh clinging desperately to the bones beneath.

Evelyn couldn't help but shriek with horror. She did not recognize this woman—did not know her—but she understood instinctively that her tortured, twisted fate was inextricably linked to her own and that of her unborn child.

Before she had a chance to try to run, the woman's hand grabbed her arm as Hel spoke through the corpse like a depraved puppet show. Just as before, every syllable was pained, every word born of insurmountable effort. The words were forced and agonized, the audible manifestation of desperate struggle.

"B-bl-bl...ood."

"Please! I don't understand...please stop!"

"Oth—others... B-Be...Before."

"Others? What others? What do you want from me?"

"B-B-Bl..."

"I won't let you hurt my child! I won't!"

Evelyn jerked her arm free and awoke with a start, struggling to catch her breath, perspiration beading along her face. She rubbed her arm where the creature's hand had held her, as if trying to erase the event from existence, to make it into a simple dream and not some prophetic vision. And yet, she could already see the bruises forming, already feel the pain from its vice-like grip. It had been real, just like the others, and just as before, she didn't understand what the creature wanted from her.

She wrapped her arms around her head, trying to block out the daylight that had begun to creep beneath her drapes, and wept. She cried from frustration as much as fear. She cried for herself as much as her child and for Lilly and every soul, dead or alive, trapped within Blackthorn. But then something caught her attention, causing her tears to cease and her mind to still.

Her arm had a lingering scent of death about it, the same smell she had found so nauseating upon visiting her mother's open casket the day of her funeral. It was a sickly smell that instinctively induced caution in all who came upon it. But there was another scent there, too, faint but perceptible. It was the unmistakable scent of lavender.

The locket!

How she had not recognized it the moment she saw it, she did not know. Perhaps it was fear or shock—perhaps that was how dreams worked, with a perceptible lag in time and understanding. But now, outside of the dark crevice of her subconscious, she could see plainly that she did know the woman whose body Hel wore. She had met her several times within Blackthorn. The woman had helped her and guided her to answers on more than one occasion. Although Evelyn did not know who she was in life, in death, the Lavender Lady was her ally.

She mulled the words over in her mind, combining them with the previous messages desperately passed to her through agonized, rotten lips: *Others before, blood created, blood destroyed.*

What did they mean? Was it the blood of this woman? It

could not be her mother's blood, for she had no wounds. Perhaps it meant bloodline, as Evelyn was born of her mother's blood. But then, what did this CB have to do with Evelyn's bloodline? There was an answer among the jumbled thoughts; she could sense it, real and tangible, but just out of reach.

The baby kicked as if it, too, felt and understood Evelyn's frustration. She cradled her belly and smiled sadly, painfully aware they were all running out of time.

Seventeen

Evelyn stared out of the window at the moors beyond. Despite her breath fogging the glass and obscuring the wilderness, it was a bright, cool morning of early autumn, the clear skies tinged with gray. She longed to feel the breeze upon her skin, the earth beneath her feet. Blackthorn had her trapped behind its thick stone walls, and the air within had grown stagnant and oppressive. She felt isolated from the world beyond, like the insect specimens her neighbor once collected and preserved, pinning them into position and confining them beneath glass forever. She was still alive but trapped, desperately flying into the glass over and over again, trying to reach freedom.

She felt sure that if she remained at Blackthorn too long, she would become entombed there, forever among the other dead who wandered. Perhaps they knew they were dead, and perhaps they continued to aim themselves headfirst at the glass, but either way, they were trapped forever, never to feel freedom again.

Her child moved inside her, stirring and shifting as if in

tune with her thoughts and fears. She cradled her stomach tenderly. Lately, she had felt sure it was a boy. There was nothing to confirm this—she did not believe in the old wives' tales, which stated that the way her bump lay or its size could somehow predict the gender—it was more of an intuition.

She was reluctant to reveal her beliefs to Peter or Ms. Winters, who had begun to refer to the child as male the moment her pregnancy was discovered. Unlike them, however, she would feel no disappointment should her prediction be incorrect. He shifted again, this time pushing a foot or hand forward so the shape protruded through her skin. It had taken her a while to get used to such sights. Even though she knew it was normal and natural, there was something unnerving about seeing something pushing outwards from inside you. Now, she welcomed every shift and kick—even those that brought discomfort or pain—as it let her know her baby was healthy and growing.

His movements always seemed to coincide with moments of heightened emotion or discomfort for Evelyn, and she wondered if her mood could be influencing him so strongly and what the implications of that would be. She tried to remain calm and find comfort and happiness when she could, but those moments were so few and far between. She worried that she was somehow making her child sad—or worse, affecting his health. The slight movement she felt now as she stared through the fogged glass was as slow and half-hearted as her sadness. In the few moments when she felt an inkling of happiness, usually when she was with Lilly, the movements were quicker but far less forceful. They were little flutters like a butterfly frantically beating its wings.

The presence of people also seemed to affect his movements, as if he sensed who was there and their intent. When Peter approached her, and Evelyn had to swallow the bile that rose inside her throat, the child would kick and push violently as if it were in distress. In comparison, when Lilly was nearby, singing one of her ditties to pass the time as Evelyn embroidered or helping Evelyn bathe or dress, he would push his little hands and feet out with calm determination as if trying to reach out to her. When Ms. Winters entered the room, he would lie still as if hiding. He'd become a barometer for Evelyn's inner thoughts and feelings. This brought with it a certain amount of comfort as well as anxiety, for he must surely know and feel how loved he was already.

She looked at her bump and forced a small smile, a fruitless attempt to fool the babe into thinking she was happy when a bang at the window jolted her free from her thoughts. She wiped the fogged glass to reveal a small crack, spiderwebbing from the center of the glass pane. There was, however, nothing and no one outside to indicate what had struck the pane or how it had been struck.

She wiped her finger along the crack. It was as thin as a hair and barely noticeable. Before she could form any logical explanation, something black suddenly struck the same spot, scaring her so much she fell backward, landing on her behind with a painful jolt. She rose from the floor while rubbing her lower back, cursing whatever animal or weather event had caused her to fall. She noticed that not only was the crack slightly more prominent, but it was also marked on the other side of the glass. There was a brownish-red smudge there, left by whatever had struck it. Once again, as she peered outside, she saw nothing and no one.

She moved a little closer to the glass, this time with trepidation, when another black blur struck the window with a thud, causing the crack to expand to reach two of the window's edges. Despite trying to prepare herself, the bang still caused her to jump back in shock. Her heart beat fast now, her breathing shallow and hurried, and she could feel her baby shifting from one side of her belly to the other as if it were a worried adult pacing a room.

This time, there was no need to guess what had smacked into the glass. A raven lay still on the stone sill on the other side, the only movement from it the ruffling of its plumage in the breeze as its neck lay at a painful, unnatural angle, broken from the force of striking the glass. Evelyn's hand moved toward her pearls, the image immediately reminding her of her mother.

Evelyn stared sadly at its lifeless body. The crazing on the glass created a horrifying kaleidoscope of black feathers and gray legs, its toes curled in a spiky fist. The poor creature must have become confused and believed it could enter through the glass—or perhaps it was ill or mad, for why would it strike the glass more than once? She was reminded once more of her earlier thoughts, of the insects butting helplessly against the invisible, impenetrable barrier, and her heart sank further still.

Despite her fear subsiding, her child still made its journey back and forth inside her, apparently still anxious. She rubbed her hand around her belly, following the child's tiny form from side to side. "There, there, my darling. It's alright. It was just a—"

Before she could finish her sentence, another thwack came from the window, then another, and then another. Great black shapes sped toward the window, graceful in flight but clumsy in death as they crumpled against the glass. She backed away, one hand protectively on her bump, the other rising to her lips to suppress a gasp of shock and fear. She knew it was only a matter of time before the huge birds shattered the entirety of the window pane.

A fourth raven struck, this time punching a hole through the glass as its wing protruded out and into the room, twitching and jittering as it died. A fifth struck the quivering corpse of the fourth, absorbing the thud but sending both birds tumbling inside her room as the glass shattered. It tried to right itself as the other lay still, twitching and bleeding on the rug. Its wing hung at a sharp angle, and it appeared confused and dazed as it circled its dead friend.

It was then that Evelyn saw that these were no ordinary ravens. Impossibly black, they were living shadows, spaces cut out of the room, of the world itself, in the shapes of birds, revealing the dark of the nothingness behind. Their eyes were more extensive than any bird's should be, bulging and shining like wet glass beads, rolling around inside their cavities as if unattached. But their beaks filled her with the most dread—sharp, thick, black needles stabbed into their faces, ready to tear away at flesh and fur. They snapped together with an almighty crack, the sound of bones breaking or whips cracking, hungrily biting at the air as if seeking something to feast upon.

More birds continued to fly headfirst at the window, some tearing feathers and flesh from their bodies as they drove across the jagged glass, while others tumbled straight into her room.

There were a dozen birds in the room now, both dead and alive. Those trapped in the opening now blocked out the daylight, so all she could see were feathers and blood. Their painful, terrified cries filled the room, increasing in volume as more and more birds threw themselves at the window, building to a cacophonous scream.

Evelyn put her hands over her ears and ran for her door as bird after bird barreled into her bedchamber, beginning to strike the second smaller window as well, causing it to crack and break. She threw her body out into the hall before slamming the door shut behind her. She slid down the wood, panting, her heart beating so hard she feared it might burst.

Her baby was still moving back and forth within her as the sound of the birds only increased behind the door. To her horror, she felt a solid thump against the wood behind her, then another and another. The creatures were now throwing themselves against the door as if all along, they had been trying to get to her. She frantically shuffled away from the door, fearing it too would somehow shatter, and pressed herself against the opposite wall.

"St-stop..." It was a whimper, barely audible above the choir of squawks. "Please...stop!" Tears fell helplessly as she put her hands over her ears, feeling like a child trying to mute the sound of violence, helpless and afraid. Her baby's movements had not slowed, but her tired body was wracked with pain. She closed her eyes as tightly as she could and pressed her hands harder against her ears, but the squawks and thuds kept coming. All at once, all of her grief and pain and heartache built up inside her and poured forth in a pained, desperate roar.

"STOP!"

All activity halted. There were no more bangs or thuds. The frantic flapping of wings ceased, and the caws silenced. All she could hear was her own heartbeat throbbing through her temples. The child, too, stilled completely, and all was calm once more.

She wasn't sure how long she had sat there. It was several minutes before she felt brave enough to lower her hands and longer still before she dared open her eyes. Eventually, with great effort, she heaved herself off the floor and slowly opened the door to her room. Inside, everything was how it had been before. There were no birds—alive or dead—and no feathers. Both windows were intact and unharmed, free of any cracking or marks.

Evelyn looked outside the window and saw nothing. It was as if the last fifteen minutes had been but a dream, merely her nightmares bleeding into reality. The only indication that anything had passed—and the reason Evelyn did not immediately question her sanity—was the presence of a single black feather in the center of her bedspread.

Part of Evelyn wanted to collapse on the bed and cry herself to sleep. She was constantly on edge, living her life as if walking the blade of a knife, fearful of her existence and dreading what might come to be. But she knew she did not have the luxury of succumbing to her emotions. Lives depended on her holding things together—her own and her child's.

She wiped her tears with a hurried hand and ran to the dresser, under which she had hidden the books she had found in the library. The memory of something she had read sat at the edge of her consciousness. Within the book on the old gods and myths, she had located the passage on the imagery and symbols used by that ancient culture and found a section regarding animal symbology. There, she found the entry titled "Ravens."

The passage spoke of Odin's raven companions, Huginn and Muninn, who whispered secrets to him. Each evening, they flew around the world and returned at first light to report to him all that they had seen. It read, "Ravens symbolized death and rebirth in Norse tradition. The scavenging nature of these birds meant they would often be found on the battlefields long after the last warrior had fallen, feasting on the remains of the dead. To this culture, they represented the cycle of death and life, as well as the presence of Odin on the battlefield. They would seek out the bravest warriors to join Odin in Valhalla, for death was not the end but merely a stepping stone to their afterlife, where the bravest would be rewarded. As such, they were seen as a connection to the realm of the dead, acting as intermediaries between this world and the next and as messengers for Hel, Goddess of Death, and Odin's Valkyries."

So, the ravens could have been sent to her by Hel, but why? What was she trying to tell her? Every time she had encountered Hel, she had strained and struggled to tell her something, but Evelyn remained in the dark. The birds were terrifying and violent, so perhaps it was a threat. But that did not make sense based on all she had encountered so far. Perhaps then, they were a warning—an urgent warning about some imminent danger. But what?

Evelyn was sick of feeling like she was a guest in her own life, walking blindly toward her own fate. Secrets surrounded her at Blackthorn House, and with every day that passed, she felt sure they would consume her.

Night fell, and the light slowly faded from her bedchamber. Evelyn stared at the ceiling, watching the shadows shift and transform, shapes from a world just out of reach, separated only by a pane of glass yet somehow so far away. She was tired, her strength and conviction beginning to wane. Her body was no longer her own. The clay of her flesh had been squeezed and molded into something only resembling her true form, transformed into something else entirely. As she stared up at the ceiling, the thoughts she had been fighting all day began to overwhelm her, and she succumbed to hopelessness. Tears began to fall—slow, solitary tears at first, but soon, they came in waves. Her heart ached as if truly broken, and her tears escaped into the world in a torrent of pain and fear.

She cried for her baby, so innocent in everything. He had made none of the choices that had led them here—that was all Evelyn's doing—yet he was doomed to suffer from their consequences. She cried for her mother, whose hugs had solved so much in her youth and whose gentle kiss had cured every ailment. She cried for her father, whose wisdom she so desperately craved, and her brother, who had always protected her growing up. She cried for Lilly, another innocent soul dragged to Blackthorn by her actions. And finally, she cried for herself. For the life she had so desperately wanted and the love she thought she had found, both a lie. For the things she wanted to say and do and may never get a chance to, the woman she could have become, as well as the young girl she had once been, so pure and naive in her innocence. For her independence and autonomy, both stripped from her and locked behind stone walls and bolted doors. She wept, finally and completely feeling every ounce of fear she had suppressed deep inside her heart. She let the grief pour from her until she trembled with the exertion.

As she lay there, drained after all of her deepest and darkest thoughts and feelings had escaped its broken walls, she thought of the souls that inhabited that same world of hopelessness, and she called out to them. “Please...I do not know who you are or why you remain here. I do not know what terrible fate befell you or what you want from me. But I know you understand my position better than anyone else. I know you, too, feel this sorrow, to be caged here. I beg of you, help us! Some of you have tried, and I am more grateful for your efforts than you know, but I need you again. To those who are angry and lost, I understand, for I feel that same pain in so many ways. But we did not harm you, and we did not trap you here. My child and I are innocent. Lilly is innocent. So please...help us! Help us. Help us.”

She uttered those last two words over and over, her voice growing weaker as she succumbed to exhaustion, slipping willingly into the black void of sleep. She put every ounce of her remaining strength and will into them, and although she could hear no response and could see no acknowledgment, the faintest smell of lavender flitted through the room.

Eighteen

Evelyn's regular pacing of Blackthorn's halls proved more difficult as her stomach continued to swell. Her feet ached, along with her lower back, and she lost her breath easily as she found herself struggling with the slightest incline. Nevertheless, she continued her jaunts, unable to sit still for fear of going mad.

Today, she walked with the purpose of meeting Lilly in the library. As she followed the winding corridors, she recalled a time when she was a child, when her father took the family to the London Zoo. It was the first of its kind in England, a place to see wild beasts and animals from foreign shores in person and up close. The thought of seeing the creatures from her picture books standing before her was the single most exciting thing to happen to her, and she was so overwhelmed by the excitement that she barely slept the night before.

She had looked forward to seeing the giraffes the most, and she happily lined up with all the other visitors to marvel at the strange but beautiful animals. But even as a young child, she was soon struck by how sad and diminished they seemed within their cages. These majestic creatures once roamed the wide-open space of the Serengeti, and now they stood behind bars inside a straw-lined concrete box. Everything about the sight had been unnatural and wrong, made all the more heartbreaking by the goggling crowds. These animals' lives had been completely upended. They had been ripped from their homes and families, and for what? To act as entertainment, to become a display to be ogled.

Evelyn burst into tears and refused to go to any other exhibits. Her brother had berated her for ruining his fun, and her father had been cold with her for the rest of that day, angered at his ruined plans. Only her mother had understood the pain seeing those animals had brought her because she, too, had seen the loss in their eyes. Evelyn had never returned to the zoo since, and now, pacing back and forth within her own cage, she understood the animals' heartbreak more than ever.

Lilly met her in the library with a tray of tea and sandwiches. She frowned at the sight of her. "Ma'am, you must try to rest."

But Evelyn felt too agitated, too filled with anxious energy to enjoy anything of the sort. She was one of her brother's tin toys—wound until the spring might break and set off down the corridors of Blackthorn, shifting and clicking forward until she stagnated and stopped, never to move again.

"It's not good for either of you to get yourself wound up so."

"It's not good for us to be caged either, and yet here we are. My child will be born in a house I hate, to a man I loathe, surrounded by the dead. He may never meet my father or brother, and I may never see them again. I cannot bear it any longer!"

"Well, at least eat something. If you're to pace around like some mad woman, you'll need your strength. You are due to give birth at any moment."

Unable to fault Lilly's logic nor her jab, she fell indignantly into the wingback chair opposite Lilly, the chair creaking beneath her weight. Lilly poured steaming tea into the cups and handed one to Evelyn. The smell and taste almost immediately calmed her, and she felt her agitation slowly dissipate with every sip. Unfortunately, without her frustration, she was free to feel the other emotions whirling around inside her. Emotions like anxiety, sadness, and fear, the latter having an ever-tightening grip on her heart, the closer she came to her due date.

Evelyn stared blankly into the fire as it crackled beside her. Lilly sat opposite, absently stroking the black feather, the gift from beyond. She looked tired, sad, and resigned. Evelyn understood that feeling all too well. Her baby was due in a month—or was it a week, or a day? Time seemed to have lost all meaning to her. Days bled into night, seasons shifted, and always, she remained within Blackthorn. She wondered if this was how prisoners felt, isolated from the outside world so long that it seemed to no longer exist in the real one, reduced to a mere memory one reminisced about regretfully.

They tried the key in every door they could find, but it opened none. They had checked every book within the library and found no clues of hidden entrances revealed. They had planned and schemed, but they were always watched, guarded by the many staff who skulked about the corridors and followed them like shadows.

Even if they somehow managed to give them the slip and smash their way free through a window or veranda, what then? Blackthorn was isolated. It lay in the middle of wild moors, treacherous to those who did not know where to step. They would have to stick to the main road in and out, and inevitably, as soon as the alarm went up, they would be chased down, hunted like animals. How far would they get, especially with Evelyn's delicate state? She moved slower than ever, her walk becoming more of a waddle. And again, even if they made it to the village by some miracle, would anyone help them, given the risk? After the deaths so recently linked to those who had assisted them, Evelyn doubted very much they would receive any kind of assistance. It all felt so hopeless.

Now that she was so close, every twinge of pain or particularly forceful kick was met with the fear that she was giving birth. Both women were acutely aware that they were now on a countdown of sorts, and while neither was quite sure of what would happen when it reached zero, they knew it was nothing good. The impending arrival of her child meant another life to worry about, another person to try to smuggle out or escape, but worse, someone who did not know why or how to be quiet when needed.

Evelyn was terrified of what Peter would do to her child when it arrived. The markings beneath her bed, the way he had treated her like some kind of broodmare rather than a wife, the shift when he discovered her condition—it was clear that her being pregnant was something he had deeply yearned for. But beyond that, it seemed to be a step in a grand scheme in which he was the architect and she an unwilling participant. She did not know what he wanted from her baby, but she knew in her heart that it was something she must protect.

Both women still carried their knives, tucked neatly in an apron or pocket. Lilly had a cross she wore daily. She muttered prayers as she worked or repeated the Lord's Prayer over and over like some kind of spell to be cast. Evelyn wore the crucifix about her neck, along with the key, a talisman alongside her mother's pearls. She had tried to pray but found what little faith had remained after her mother's death to be disappearing quickly.

Nothing in her childhood days of church and Sunday school would explain what she had seen at Blackthorn. There was no such thing as ghosts in the Bible—every soul was sorted and filed appropriately as if humans could be easily understood and categorized. As if life were merely black and white, with none of the myriad shades of gray in between. Good and evil were such definite concepts; few things in life fell completely into one without straying into the other.

Even if she had set aside these philosophical debates she had been having so regularly lately, the God she knew did not exist at Blackthorn. The god that resided there was something dark and ancient. How could she trust her fate to prayer and trinkets when her life was driven by forces she did not know or understand? The only way she would escape Blackthorn was through her own actions, and she knew time was running out. Her child kicked as if to emphasize the thought and confirm their grim reality.

"Are they still out there?" Evelyn asked.

"Of course. I counted at least five as I passed. They don't even try to hide why they're there anymore."

Since Evelyn had entered her last trimester, the staff who had been watching her and Lilly so closely, always finding something to clean or tidy near them, had increased in both number and scrutiny. They no longer pretended to fluff pillows or brush clean floors but stood sentinel, watching. Where one had once sufficed, several now hovered near, often outside the doorway, listening. It only added to Evelyn's feelings of being caged.

Lilly leaned in to speak, as if conveying gossip, "Ms. Winters was not among them today."

"Oh?"

"Unless she was trying to remain out of sight, but I can't see why she would start that now. She's never been shy with her intrusions."

Lilly was right. Ms. Winters was Peter's right hand. She seemed to be the only one who conversed with him directly, received the orders and requests, and delegated them to the rest of the staff. Of course, it was the normal role of a head housekeeper to do this, but these scenarios went far beyond the domestic chores of a household and moved into something far more insidious.

She seemed to be his general, the overseer of his venerating army, eager to perform whatever nefarious task he entrusted her with. All the staff treated Peter with reverence and approbation beyond what his title and social standing demanded. It verged on the veneration displayed by a congregation to its adored leader, and if Peter was their Papal master, then Ms. Winters was his Cardinal. She had been following and encroaching on the women with eagerness enough for all the staff, and yet, today, she was elsewhere.

Evelyn could not decide if that was good news or a bad omen.

While lost in these thoughts, her mind circling her fears like a whirlpool, the overpowering scent of lavender washed over her. As Evelyn scanned the room for the now familiar specter that accompanied that scent, she noticed Lilly was also still. Both women were suddenly alert and aware of their surroundings, apprehensive of what might happen. Like the animals in the London Zoo, trapped behind Blackthorn's bars, they still had their instincts. They were creatures aware of a branch breaking or grass moving—all the signs of a predator approaching.

The scream rose from the silence like a siren, increasing in volume and pitch. It was coming from beyond the library door, but somehow, it was loud enough to be by their side. Both women quickly rose from their seats and moved toward the door. The original scream weakened as other voices, all yelling in panicked tones, joined it, along with the heavy thumps of many hurried footsteps. Lilly placed her hand upon the door's brass knob, and after seeking an approved nod from Evelyn, opened the door a crack to peer outside. Smoke entered the library in a haze, along with the acrid smell of burning hair. Someone ran past the doorway with a blanket outstretched as the panicked voices twisted and knotted together to form one unintelligible garble. Staff came and went, rushing past them and in the opposite direction, some barking orders and others following those orders. Both the smoke and the smell originated from a room down the corridor and to their left, along with the wails and whimpers of someone in great pain.

The noise of feet and yelling grew louder once more as a door was flung open. Someone was crying like a wounded animal, and the smell of burned hair and fabric grew in strength. There was a mass of action as the group left the room and moved quickly away from the library down the corridor in a panicked crowd. They were carrying something towards the servants' quarters. A cloud of black, acrid smoke exited along with them, as if desperate to escape the room, remaining after they were gone as wisps only visible in the bars of light from the lamps.

As the footsteps and shouting diminished, the two women looked at each other, and something passed between them. It was as if their thoughts sought each other's out and converged on a single idea—escape. Evelyn reached out to Lilly, who took her hand and squeezed it. In response, Evelyn gave a slight, sharp nod. It had been decided.

Whatever had happened, every staff member who had been so closely watching them, along with many others, were distracted with their tasks, and Evelyn and Lilly were free of scrutiny for the first time in many months. On cue, the lavender smell appeared once more, mingling and mixing with the scent of burned flesh and hair. It breezed past them in the opposite direction from the chaos and disappeared behind the open door of a nearby bedroom. Without saying a word, both women quickly and quietly ran from the library into the open room. Lilly quietly closed the door, carefully moving the handle to make as little noise as possible.

The burning smell seemed stronger inside, and scorch marks were clearly visible on the hearth rug, where wisps of smoke rose from the blackened carpet, and coal lay smouldering outside the safety of their hearth. A piece of singed fabric lay nearby, which resembled the aprons many of the maids wore, but it was the heavy set of keys that lay discarded by the fireplace that made the fire's victim obvious to both Lilly and Evelyn—Ms. Winters. The idea that Ms. Winters, so sure and confident in her abilities and experienced in her role, would have leaned too close to the fire and caught flame seemed too out of character, too foolish for a housekeeper of her knowledge and skill. But Evelyn knew in her heart that the spirits of Blackthorn had heard her cries for help. The Lavender Lady and perhaps others had brought flame to Ms. Winters and given them the opportunity they needed so desperately.

Lilly grabbed the set of keys and used them to lock the door to the hallway before opening the door to the adjoining suite. Both women hurried into the next room, and Lilly locked the door behind her as they went. It benefited them to keep everything as it had been, leaving no clear trail to track them, and if anything, it would slow their pursuers down. There would be no trail of breadcrumbs left to follow. They moved as quickly and quietly as they could, placing an ear to each door before moving through the corridors and various rooms until they had reached the door to the staircase used by staff.

As they hurried down the steps, the shouts and footsteps surrounding Ms. Winters's tragic "accident" grew fainter until they could only hear their own footsteps and hurried, ragged breathing. Evelyn held her bump as she ran, trying to ease the pressure she felt. She hoped the baby would hold still, that he would understand through some kind of psychic connection what they were trying to do, that her body would remain as strong as her will, and that they would find their way to freedom unobstructed. It had been so long since she had felt any hope at all, and it spurred her onward.

At times, Evelyn and Lilly struggled with what direction they should take. When two options presented themselves—right or left? Back or forth? Through that room or this one? They would spy the swish of a spectral skirt ahead or feel unseen hands guide them toward the right path. The Lavender Lady was there. Evelyn could smell her and see the outline of her form just ahead. But there were others also, a flash of a petite figure or a whispering voice on the side they should turn, leading them safely through the house and out of sight. The spirits had heard her cries, and they had answered in kind.

The further they got from the chaos, the more conscious Evelyn was of how easily they could be caught and how quickly their escape attempt could be curtailed. Regardless of how stealthy they were, there was only one door to that staircase on each floor, and if a staff member were to enter as they moved along that floor, they would come nose to nose, and the alarm would surely be sounded.

As if the house itself had heard her thoughts, Evelyn heard the door open on the floor above them. Both women halted suddenly and pressed their bodies against the wall, trying to make themselves smaller and less conspicuous, something Evelyn found nearly impossible to do in her current condition. Lilly looked at Evelyn with wide, panicked eyes as both women tried to control their breathing not to betray them.

The door opened slowly above them, and footsteps on the boards above their head unsettled the dust and cobwebs, which then fell onto them like confetti. There were only two ways for the unknown person to go: either they could go up the stairs to the floor above them or beyond. Or they could come down the twisted, narrow staircase to go to the next floor, where they would quickly come face to face with both fugitives.

Time seemed to slow, and seconds stretched into minutes. It felt as if the stranger above could not decide in what direction to go, and the creaks of every slow-motion step echoed inside her mind like the clanging of an alarm bell. Evelyn's heart thumped ferociously inside her chest, and her stomach churned as it threatened to evacuate her tea all over the floor. What if they were caught? Should they fight? Should they run? Fear clouded her mind, and she could only close her eyes tightly against the world outside, hoping upon hope that they would remain undiscovered.

The steps grew closer and louder, and Evelyn's heart began to beat so fast that she feared it would burst free. The stranger was walking toward them. Evelyn's eyes began to fill with tears.

Not now, not when we are so close!

Lilly removed the small knife from her apron and nodded to Evelyn to do the same with her own. The idea of violence seemed so ridiculous, so foolhardy, and yet what could they do? They needed to escape—there was no doubt about that—but could they really hurt another person? Even if it were one of Blackthorn's loyal staff? Even if it were Peter? These thoughts formed and reformed again and again in her mind. She envisioned a struggle—blood being spilled and skin split—and she felt her legs weaken and shake.

Both women readied themselves as the steps grew closer. When society was cast aside, humans were just animals, hairless apes beneath their fancy garb. When a threat was presented, when they were backed into a corner or caged, their fight or flight responses were triggered just like any other creature. This was Evelyn and Lilly's choice: fight or flight? Whatever they did, there would be no going back. They had crossed that line the moment they took Ms. Winter's keys. Evelyn's palms were sweaty, and she had to regrip the knife. She held her breath as she waited for the person, whoever they were, to take the corner and come eye to eye with both women.

But just before the person reached the turn in the staircase, a door frantically opened from a couple of floors above them. It was thrown open with such force that it hit the wall hard, reverberating on its hinges and freeing dust and debris from the bare boards above them. The person directly above them immediately stopped as a panicked voice screamed from above. "Anyone below, we need help! Ms. Winters's skirts caught fire! She is badly burned."

Without a word, the thump of the steps changed direction and moved quickly up and away from them, heading toward the cry for help. Briefly, they could hear voices asking what had happened and what her injuries were before the door banged closed once more, and Evelyn and Lilly were left alone in the stairwell.

Evelyn let out a long, relieved sigh. She had not realized she had been holding her breath, and she inhaled deeply, trying to slow her heartbeat and calm her shaking. They looked at each other and, once again, silently agreed to continue, squeezing each other's hands for courage.

Within seconds, they had reached the ground floor. Lilly's hand reached for the handle just as it was turned from the other side. Both women instinctively threw themselves to the side, shrinking into the shadows behind the flung-open door. Three male staff members ran urgently up the stairs, too distracted with the task at hand to look back. If they had, they would have seen both women there, eyes wide with fear.

There was no time to express their relief or marvel at their luck. Lilly stuck her head out into the hallway beyond, and with a quick gesture of her hand, both women barrelled toward the nearest exit—the veranda doors in the salon. Banging and raised voices above them all came together to form some kind of frantic choir. Evelyn wasn't sure if the chaos was due to Ms.

Winters's unfortunate "accident" or if the staff had noticed their absence, but she did not care to find out.

Like every other in Blackthorn those days, the salon door was locked, and Lilly frantically tried several keys, hands shaking, before she found the correct one. Evelyn kept watch, her head constantly moving from one end of the hallway to the other, a rabbit twitching its nose for the scent of hunters. When the familiar click came, they quickly moved inside, closing and locking it quietly behind them.

The salon was eerily quiet, as if the sounds of chaos in the house beyond could not penetrate it. It was a room as large and grand as the others at Blackthorn, in the same rich red, black, and gold color palette. Velvet sofas sat atop a huge red Persian rug, all angled to face a black marble fireplace carved to look like a lion's head, the hearth within its great, roaring mouth. Evelyn froze before its gaping yawn. Its stony eyes seemed to watch her, and for a moment, she swore she could hear its breathing and smell its acrid breath. Something about it sent shivers down her spine. It looked so desperately hungry, and Evelyn felt so small. If she were the prey of Blackthorn House, then this fireplace was its mouth.

Lilly grabbed her arm hard and brought her back to reality.

"Are you alright?"

"Yes...I just... Yes, I'm fine." She shook the feeling from her mind and focused on the task at hand, yet as she stared out of the glass doors into the gardens beyond, she could still feel the creature's eyes upon her back.

"From here, no matter where we go, we are on open ground. There is nowhere to hide."

Lilly was right. The grounds on this side of the house were open. There were no trees or structures for cover. If anyone happened to look out of Blackthorn's many windows as they ran, they would be easily spotted. The nearest structure was the walled garden, but it was back toward the rear of the house and in the opposite direction from where they wanted to go. Their best bet was to run for the stables. Although a short distance away, it seemed to Evelyn that it existed in another world. The distance seemed insurmountable—a mountain too steep to climb, a river too deep to cross.

But what else could they do? Going on foot was the straightest line toward the village, but there was nothing but open ground with nowhere to hide until far beyond Blackthorn's grounds. From the house, you could see the road for several miles. The stables were the most logical choice. Not only was it less distance to run in the open, but they could also retrieve horses and significantly quicken their escape.

"Are you ready?"

Evelyn rubbed her bump, a gesture she did often now that she was so round with life. She liked to reassure herself that her child was still in there, still safe. She knew she could not run at the speed she could have before. Lilly would have no difficulty outrunning her in her current state. The idea of slowing her down pained Evelyn, and she worried that if they were caught, it would be because of her. She took a deep breath and removed her heavy bed coat. The white cotton nightgown beneath was not thick enough for the cold October morning, but she knew the layers of fabric would slow her down, and she needed all the advantage she could muster. She looked at Lilly and squeezed her outstretched hand in a silent yes.

Then, they ran.

The wall of cold air hit Evelyn and left her struggling to breathe. But she didn't have time to process it. She could not worry about the dampness immediately settling over her skin, soaking the hem of her nightgown. She had no time to think about the pain shooting up her legs every time her swollen feet hit the earth, nor the throbbing in her back. Her skin erupted into gooseflesh, yet she quickly felt too hot as sweat beaded on her forehead and upper lip.

Lilly was several feet ahead, darting across the lawn like a bullet fired from a gun. Every few feet, she glanced back at Evelyn to make sure she was still behind her. Evelyn slowed with every step, but dared not stop—not until they reached the stables. The structure seemed further away somehow, as if it, too, was running, fleeing from the pursuing women. Evelyn ran out of breath quickly, struggling to fill her lungs with ragged, frantic breaths.

The feeling hit her like a blow, almost physical in its immediate realness.

She stopped abruptly and turned to face Blackthorn, knowing in her heart what she would see there.

Peter stood at the large picture window on the second floor, staring at her with such hatred, such venom that she feared the old expression was somehow true and his look would somehow kill her. That she would drop dead on the spot from the poisonous energy he exuded through his gaze. He locked eyes with hers, and he began yelling and gesturing wildly.

Their warden had seen them and raised the alarm.

With newfound energy, Evelyn ran as fast as her legs would carry her. She held her belly as if trying to carry it somehow or alleviate the weight, as if her womb were a bag of books she could simply pick up and carry. Her body felt so heavy, so uncoordinated, as if it weren't her own. Her lungs burned and her feet ached, but she ran on, putting every ounce of strength and willpower she had into making it to the stables.

Ahead of her, Lilly slipped inside and out of sight. It was a painful thirty seconds before Evelyn made it in behind her. In the distance, Evelyn could hear yelling now, barely audible over the sound of her own jagged breathing but slowly growing in volume. Lilly had already untethered a horse and was reaching for a saddle.

"Forget the saddle; we haven't time."

Lilly nodded and ran to fetch another animal. Evelyn stared

at the chestnut-colored beast before her. It was at least fifteen hands tall, and without stirrups, she was unsure how she could possibly force her hefty weight up onto its back. She improvised, using nearby bales of hay and a wooden bench to throw herself upon it.

The horse stirred and whinnied, clearly a little agitated at having such weight thrust upon it so abruptly, but it remained calm, allowing Evelyn to fix her seating. She hadn't ridden bareback since their visit to see the old woman just outside of the village, and she hoped she would have the strength she needed to do it now.

Lilly mounted the mottled gray horse behind her. She looked anxious and out of place, but her face was also set with a dogged determination that made Evelyn confident she would hold her own.

"Buttress yourself against her neck and hold on using her mane," Evelyn said to both herself and Lilly. "Kick your heels firmly into her sides to make it go or to urge her onwards at speed. Move your body up and down with her natural run, and keep your grip with your thighs. Whatever you do, don't let go, and don't look down, just ahead. Alright?"

Lilly looked at the beast beneath her nervously, but nodded in understanding.

Before they could utter another word, Evelyn clipped her heels and sent her horse flying forward, straight out of the stable doors and out into the open gardens beyond. The cold wind rushed past her, stinging her ears and face and causing her eyes to water. The autumn chill wrapped itself around her and held firm, further dampening her white nightdress, which clung to her shivering body.

To her right, Blackthorn loomed like a great, stone demon, its glass window eyes following her as its doors opened, roaring in anger at the escape of its meal. More than a dozen staff members poured from inside, all at various places across the lawn. Like a bloodthirsty mob descending upon a village, they held brooms and rakes aloft like weapons as they shouted at the women flying past. Evelyn thought of Black Skull and Peter's ancestors, and she understood the terror they must have felt to see such a horde intent on murder and mayhem descending upon them.

She glanced back at Lilly, who seemed to be holding her own on her horse. Though thrown about and bounced around like a toy being played with by invisible hands, she was steadfast and determined, her eyes focused ahead on Evelyn and the road beyond.

Evelyn's horse moved into a gallop easily, and both were soon in sync. Her thighs burned almost immediately, and her arms ached, but she pressed on. She worried about what such an impact and roughness would do to her child, but she knew she had no other choice, so she banished those thoughts to the back of her mind.

The stables were soon behind them as they left the soft, damp lawn and reached the hard gravel path of the driveway. The shock of each hoof landing grew in intensity and force, and the pain increased in Evelyn's back and legs. Still, she held firm, and a quick look behind confirmed that Lilly had, too. She was slower than Evelyn, but the creature instinctively followed its friend, matching its pace and direction.

Fog held fast, thick and unwavering in the moorland beyond Blackthorn, obscuring the way ahead. Evelyn had only traveled the road through the moors three times, and she was painfully aware of how fatal a misstep could be. The fog made their journey all the more perilous, although she took comfort in knowing its veil of gray would quickly consume them, rendering them invisible to the gathering forces behind. She had no choice but to put her faith in the animal beneath her, who must have traveled the road dozens of times in its life, hoping it knew its way well enough for both of them.

By now, Evelyn imagined the Blackthorn staff had mounted their own horses in their pursuit. Would Peter be among them? Or would he remain in his castle, sending others out to do his bidding for him? She swallowed her fear and anxiety and tried to focus on the road ahead—or at least, what she could see within the smoky haze of fog.

As they neared the end of the long gravel drive, Evelyn saw shapes and forms materialize in the fog. Black silhouettes resembling human forms, their arms outstretched, desperately reaching for something they could never grasp. She realized they moved, revealing the occasional open mouth and set of eyes, gaps through which the fog poured. It gave the impression that the beings were aflame from within, smoke escaping where it could. The dead, it seemed, were the audience to their escape.

The horse spooked and slowed considerably, beginning to huff. The straight, sure line it had been running became a waveform as it veered left and right, its head constantly scanning its surroundings. Evelyn knew a frightened horse when she encountered one and knew how dangerous it could be. If it were to buck and throw her from its back, she could be killed, or she could lose her child. Lilly's horse caught up with her and began the same hesitant trot forward, both women trying desperately to reassure the creatures and encourage them forward.

"They fear the spirits!" Lilly's voice was filled with panic.

Both horses had slowed to a walk now, and the noise of approaching voices and hooves in the distance grew worryingly close. The shapes began to fly and veer from one side to the other, moving around them in a blur.

Evelyn felt surrounded. Both the living and the dead were following them. She suddenly thought of the Lavender Lady answering her cries for help, of the invisible hands and shapes that had kindly guided them to safety. With nothing to lose, she yelled into the fog, "Please, I implore you: leave us be. If you must scare horses, scare theirs. Help us! For the love of God, help us!"

Silence hung in the air as both women waited with bated breath. The sound of pounding hooves was growing louder. Their pursuers were close enough now for Evelyn to discern words and voices.

"*Faster, you idiots!*"

It was Peter.

Evelyn's heart had already been pounding so hard and so fast that she was sure it would fail, and yet it somehow increased as he approached. "Please, please..." It was a tearful entreaty she feared would go unheeded, yet all at once, the shadowy figures began to back away from them and moved in the direction of their pursuers.

The horses relaxed almost immediately, as if waking from a dream. Evelyn encouraged hers onward once more; she could hear the high-pitched whinnies of the horses behind them, panicked and frantic, among the equally panicked screams of their riders. A singular horse emerged from the fog behind them, running full speed ahead and passing them, riderless and alone. Its appearance meant two things: one, her pleas had worked, and the spirits in the fog were now deliberately scaring their pursuers' horses, and two, their pursuers had caught up to them and were far closer behind them than Evelyn realized.

She nudged her horse, encouraging it to gallop faster. Lilly did the same, and they matched the speed of the lone horse ahead, the three beasts falling in sync with one another, chasing their freedom through the autumn fog. The wind rushed past Evelyn's face and sang in her ears. The cold no longer bothered her as her mind focused solely on the path ahead and their freedom. She dared to hope, to believe that they would make it.

Something whistled past her, breaking through the fog.

The riderless horse unexpectedly let out a pained screech

and bucked violently. Evelyn's horse was the closest to the creature, and it narrowly missed being clubbed by the other's hooves. It veered suddenly left, causing Evelyn to slide dangerously to the side. She gripped the horse's mane until her fingers ached and tried to tighten her legs around its belly, but she was slipping, and every pound of its hooves brought her closer to letting go.

"Evelyn!"

Lilly appeared beside her. Clumsily and shakily, she reached down with one hand, trying to pull Evelyn upwards while both their horses continued on. Evelyn made the mistake of looking at the ground as it passed her in a blur. If she were to fall, she would not survive. Evelyn screamed as she almost lost her grip. Her position was so precarious, so tenuous, she was sure she would fall at any moment.

"Hold on!"

Lilly let go of Evelyn and instead reached for the horse she rode. She kept steady, pulling back on both horses until they began to slow. "Whoa, whoa..."

By some miracle, both animals responded, and their gallop turned into a trot, allowing Evelyn to right herself with Lilly's help. She hugged the horse, trying to calm her ragged, hurried breaths. Sweat coated her skin, and every muscle in her body hummed with pain.

"What happened?" Lilly cried.

"The other horse...it bucked. It..." Evelyn pointed at the other mare who had followed their lead and trotted alongside them. It was white with black spotting, except for a patch of bright red, which glistened on its hindquarters. Something long and thin jutted unnaturally from its flesh as blood congealed around the object.

Evelyn realized too late that it was an arrow.

The whistling sound came again, and this time, it was Evelyn who screamed. The arrow emerged from the fog and struck Lilly square in her back, embedding itself deep in her flesh. She didn't cry out or scream; she didn't even whimper. She just fell forward before sliding off the horse, hitting the ground with a painful thud. Evelyn brought her horse to a halt and slid from its back. She ran to Lilly, who lay still as Evelyn fell to the cold, wet earth beside her.

"Lilly! God, no, please!"

Lilly's eyes were half-closed, her pupils hidden by her eyelids, leaving only the whites visible. Her skin was drained of all color, so even her freckles seemed to have faded away. Blood bubbled at the corner of her mouth, and her breathing was shallow and labored. Evelyn cradled her head on her knee and wiped the blood from her face with the sleeve of her nightgown.

Tears choked Evelyn as she tried to speak—to say something, anything, to the young girl in her arms, to her closest and dearest friend. She wanted to tell her how Lilly was family to her, a sister chosen rather than inherited through blood. She wanted her to know how much her counsel and support had meant to her, how she had kept her from giving up hope so many times. How she was an inspiration to her and a true ally. But mostly, she wanted to tell her how much she loved her. She so desperately wanted to tell her all of those things and more, and yet, the words would not come. Her grief and pain were so profound, so intense, that they overwhelmed her completely. Her heart was breaking, and she felt every crack with a painful intensity she had not experienced since that day in the barn. So instead, all she muttered was, "Lilly...no..."

Lilly's body went limp in her arms. Her ragged breathing slowed until it stopped altogether, and her chest stilled. Evelyn pulled Lilly close, cradling her. Grief forced its way from her body in a long, tortured scream that echoed around the moors. Evelyn held her, rocking back and forth while she sobbed and wailed, releasing her pain into the world.

Nineteen

It was as if time went still. Shackled to the earth by intense grief, she wailed as she cradled the body of her only true friend. As if the world itself understood her pain and matched its ferocity, the heavens opened in a torrent of heavy rain, which mingled with Lilly's blood and created a pool around them both. The creatures of the moors, both alive and dead, answered her cries with melancholic calls of their own. They came together in a beautiful, awful choir until the air was filled with anguish, a death song for Lilly.

Evelyn didn't notice them approaching her. She was lost to her pain, oblivious to anything around her. The men surrounded her with slow, deliberate steps through the mud. Some broke off to catch and calm the horses, who were skittish from the smell of blood and the lamentations echoing around them.

A crowd gathered around Evelyn, silent observers of her bleeding heart, as they waited for their leader to catch up. Unlike the others, he was on horseback, and as they parted to allow him and his black horse through, the screaming moors were silenced. Peter dismounted and handed his crossbow to one of the servants, who dutifully took it with a bowed head and averted eyes. No one dared meet his furious gaze. Rage pulsed from him, a haze of heat charging the air around him. He was a human storm, and they feared his lightning strike.

Peter paused above Evelyn's crumpled figure, staring down at her in disdain. He seemed to take pleasure in her anguish and the fact that he had been the one to inflict it. He reached down and grabbed her hair in his fist, yanking her up hard. Lilly's limp, lifeless body fell from her arms, landing in the mud with a wet thud. Evelyn screamed in both physical and emotional pain as she scrambled to keep hold of Lilly.

Peter merely yanked her harder. The mud was too wet to gain purchase, and she slid as she tried to find her footing. Her scalp flared with pain as hairs ripped free. She gripped his fists, trying to alleviate some of the pain, but it was no use. She was a fly ensnared in a web, and the spider had come to claim its prize.

He dragged her toward his horse as if she were a heavy sack, an object without importance, without any need for regard. The other men continued to stand in silence, their heads bowed. No one tried to help her; no one raised an objection. They, too, saw her as nothing—something they demonstrated with their complacency.

Once he reached his horse, he abruptly released his grip, and Evelyn landed hard on her back, the wind knocked out of her. Peter tended to his saddle, adjusting straps and buckles, while his wife lay sputtering and gasping in the mud. When he went to grab her once more, she swatted helplessly at his hands above her, screaming her objections, but it only served to anger him further. He punched her hard in the face, her nose cracking beneath his knuckles, as the warm copper taste of blood filled her mouth. With a single blow, he knocked all the fight from her body, and she fell defeated on the ground, choking on her blood.

Everything seemed so far away.

She could hear Peter's barking at the other men and their mumbled responses, but she could not discern what they said. She could see them move around her and feel their many hands on her body, pawing at her, grabbing at her, and finally lifting her from the earth below. She stared up into the gray sky and felt herself floating away. It was as if the force of his blow had sent her through the ground below, to be absorbed by its darkness, and she could only see the world from the entrance above her, far down the tunnel of black. Everything moved out of sync, out of time, and in slow motion. Nothing was real. It all blurred and twisted together until it was turned upside down. At first, she fought the darkness, scrambling to reach the end of the tunnel, to reach the world beyond. But the exhaustion and hopelessness soon took hold, and she let the darkness claim her.

Evelyn was in the moors, the fog so thick she could only see a few inches around her. She was alone in the gray, surrounded by a deathly, unnerving silence. She no longer hurt, but the echo of the pain remained just below the surface of her skin. She was still in her nightgown, although she was now dry. The crimson of Lilly's blood and mud had created stains like klecksographs on her nightgown, but all that had vanished. The cloth was white again, as if freshly cleaned. Her feet were bare, and she could feel herself sinking into the wet, cold mud with every footstep. She knew she had to be dreaming, yet it felt real. That place where she ventured in her sleep was a world between dreams and reality. A plane that existed in both realities while simultaneously existing in neither. It was the in-between.

She knew the dead were watching her from behind the thick, gray curtain of fog. She could sense their eyes on her, yet they never intruded, remaining distant observers only. The now-familiar shape of the door slowly appeared before her. Every knot and stain was etched inside her mind like the lines of her own hand. She reached out and felt the roughness of the wood and the hardness of the iron. Somehow, it brought her comfort after all that had just happened. Perhaps she was dead as well, and she could finally enter and be with her mother and Lilly.

The door opened slowly. Both sides were equally cold and foggy, as if the two worlds were merging, the veil growing thinner by the day. Multiple figures emerged, black blurs growing more distinct as they approached. The ghosts became bodies, their faces frozen in death.

She recognized them all, their vacant, glassy eyes looking at her, but not fully seeing her. The old witch from the village with her purple and swollen face and her jaw hanging off-center at an unnatural, sharp angle, dried blood crusting her mouth and nose. Harrison, with a thick line of bloodless sinew and empty veins along his throat, his arm dangling out of its socket, his leg twisted and foot facing the other way.

On the other side, her mother hung from an invisible rope, her neck broken and protruding, her eyes bulging and blood-shot. Next to her, the body of a woman, strange yet somehow familiar, the "C.B." engraving on her locket the only clue to her identity. Like Harrison's, the Lavender Lady's throat lay halved and open, an angry mouth silently gaping at Evelyn.

In the middle was Lilly. She had more color than the others, but only slightly, the blue-gray of her surroundings already leaching into her skin. Unlike the others, her eyes were half-closed, just as Evelyn had last seen them. The blood around her mouth had dried in little bubbled clouds, and her head lolled like a well-played-with doll.

Lilly jittered and shook as she walked toward Evelyn, the others flanking her on either side in a vile parade of violence. But, unlike before, Evelyn was no longer afraid. She had watched the life drain from Lilly and held her as her body fell limp. She had seen death in all its forms, and it no longer frightened her.

Death was no devil or demon; it took no sides and inflicted no pain. It did not choose who came to its world, nor when or how it happened—it merely came when needed. Nothing was fairer in the world than death—it was the great equalizer, coming for the rich and poor alike. Everyone had to face it eventually, and Evelyn was ready to face it now.

Death wore Lilly as it had the others, a grotesque puppet theater playing out in front of her. The bodies were not the people they had been in life—they were merely vessels—and in death, they left those vessels and moved on elsewhere.

At least, that was what was supposed to happen.

Yet, there was no peace within Blackthorn; all those who died remained there, trapped forever. Her worst fears were realized. Lilly was trapped there too, a figure among the shadows in the fog, and soon she would be too, along with her child, destined to remain unborn, dead before he had a chance to live.

The second face superimposed on Lilly's was opaque and somehow solid. What little flesh it had hung from its exposed bones. Unlike the bodies around it and the one it wore, its sunken eyes stared directly into Evelyn's. It stood there, observing her, waiting patiently for Evelyn to speak.

"Are you Hel?"

It shuddered and quivered, Lilly's head lolling back and forth in a macabre nod.

Evelyn spoke louder. "Are you Hel, the ruler of Helheim, who presides over the dead?"

Again, Lilly's corpse trembled in a nod. Every movement seemed to take so much painful effort. Death was an unwavering, undefeated force, yet Hel seemed weak somehow.

"Am I dead?"

This time, Lilly's body jerked clumsily from side to side to indicate no.

What had happened to bring this being to Blackthorn? Why did she remain? There were so many questions, and Evelyn wasn't sure where to begin. From her previous encounters, she had learned how difficult it was for Hel to communicate with her, so she tried to make her inquiries as simple as possible.

"Are you trapped here?"

Another jerking nod in the affirmative.

She remembered what the old woman had told her—that the Black family had brought their own gods with them to this land—but how had they managed to bring such a powerful being as Hel? But the woman had spoken of a deal between Hel and the Black family, a contract she had said could not be broken.

Evelyn moved her eyes briefly to the old woman's corpse and wished she could speak with her once more. Their time together had been frustratingly short, thanks to Peter. She turned back to address Hel. "Did the Blacks trap you here?"

Another nod.

The old woman had spoken of magic from the cold, fjordic lands from which the Black family had come, and the pagan magic of the local population, blended together, defiled into some unholy dark working.

"Did they cast some kind of spell? Some kind of dark magic?"

Hel manipulated Lilly's body: another yes. Power had been their purpose—that's what the old woman had said. Evelyn suddenly understood why Hel was so weak and why she was trapped within Blackthorn.

"They took your power." It was not a question but a statement, a realization.

Although Hel did not stir, Evelyn could see pain within her dead, unblinking eyes, along with something else, something darker—fury. Somehow, Peter's ancestors had combined their magic with that of the pagan locals to create a spell that defiled nature.

Hel had come to this land along with Peter's ancestors to gather the dead and lead their souls to the afterlife. Instead, she had been taken and stripped of her powers and strength. They had perverted their own culture and religion and twisted it into her prison. Unable to return to Helheim, souls remained trapped like her, stuck in Blackthorn's grip like an insect trapped in amber. But beyond that, the soul of those who fell at Blackthorn or the surrounding area, regardless of their faith or customs, were also trapped, unable to pass on to their own hereafter. And Peter's ancestors had ensured there was death in abundance, an entire village stripped bare and burned. The doorway to the underworld was permanently open, as trapped in stasis as the souls themselves, and so, the dead had remained, growing in numbers and sorrow as the centuries passed with Hel herself among them, a queen without a kingdom.

Disgust and anger bubbled within Evelyn's chest. The Black family had desecrated Death itself, harnessing and twisting it for their own selfish needs. Centuries of souls were now trapped, doomed to remain in the void between life and death, a weary and painful existence in a limbo not of their making.

She thought about the Black family's riches, their status, their grand estates—all stolen, taken from Hel and the thousands of trapped souls that surrounded the epicenter of their wealth, Blackthorn House. She felt physically ill at the thought of now sharing their name and becoming part of such a vile and contemptuous legacy.

Her hand moved to the child within her belly, the next generation of the Black family. If Peter were to take it, he would corrupt it just as his family corrupted nature itself. He would twist and mold it in his own image, perpetuating the cycle of villainy its ancestors had started. She could not—would not—let that happen.

"Can it be stopped? Can you all be freed?"

Lilly's body moved up and down in a violent, wrenching dance, Hel indicating a very firm and enthusiastic yes.

"How?"

"B-b-bl-blood." She spat the words through her exposed, yellowing teeth, each syllable labored, torturously tugged from within her and forced out with great, painful effort.

All at once, Evelyn felt hands on her shoulders where there were none, shaking her, but somehow, she did not move. She felt split in half—her mind here and her body elsewhere—being touched and manipulated without her consciousness or consent. She could hear muffled voices that sounded far away and right beside her. The fog began to shift and move as if blown away by invisible winds, and the door, as well as its inhabitants, began to fade in and out of existence.

"What's happening?"

Hel gripped Evelyn's arm with a strength that almost immediately began to wane. She hurriedly spat out words, each one in an aching, tortured rasp. "Bl-Blood...cre-cre-created... bloo-blood des...troyed."

"I don't understand! Please tell me what to do!"

The hand on her forearm vanished and reappeared along with Lilly and Hel. The door was gone, as were the other bodies, and the fog had almost entirely disappeared to reveal a black, empty nothingness, which scared Evelyn more than the realm of the dead ever had. Everything was being erased before her eyes, removed from the world, leaving nothing but emptiness.

Hel muttered the word "blood" once more, barely more than a whisper, before she too faded into nothingness, leaving Evelyn alone in the black. The invisible hands shook her harder, and the muffled voices grew louder until, with an abrupt burst of light and noise, Evelyn awoke.

Twenty

The world gradually came into focus. Evelyn's nose and jaw throbbed, and she could no longer breathe through her nostrils. She tasted blood, her throat dry and sore from her mouth hanging open as she lay unconscious. Everything ached with a level of pain Evelyn had never felt before, and she realized this would only be the beginning of such pain, the agony of childbirth only a short time away. Her mind was a whirl of images, thoughts, and noises, none of which made sense. She wanted to scream, but it was as if her mind and her body remained disconnected somehow, the link only slowly forming as her mind processed the world around her.

She was lying on a cold, damp stone floor and could see only the feet of people nearby. One wore Peter's leather riding boots, and she heard his voice somewhere, irate and argumentative. She saw a skirt made of long, charcoal-colored wool, with one side scorched, still smoldering slightly.

Ms. Winters.

There were other boots and shoes off in the distance that she didn't recognize—an audience of strangers. Where she lay was too dimly lit to see much else. She smelled fire and an unknown stench—something rotten, festering.

Her head throbbed as she slowly faced forward, trying to take in the room she'd never seen before. The curved walls were bare stone, with intermittent torches attached to iron holders. The ceiling, which rose into a dome shape, was made of identical stone slabs, and at the center hung a chandelier of bones and antlers.

Bile rose in Evelyn's throat when she realized human skulls were among the collection, adornments to a trophy celebrating death. There were over a dozen, some with their jaws still attached, empty mouths hanging agape in a silent scream. For others, the human jaw bone was missing, replaced with the jutting jaw bone of another creature—a sheep, perhaps? Whatever it was, it created a grotesque hybrid creature that terrified Evelyn, even in its inert state of death.

Antlers tangled and roped together with jawbones, and skulls of all shapes and sizes stared with hollow, unblinking eyes. It was like a dungeon from a medieval castle, and Evelyn couldn't help but imagine what hideous torture and bloody deaths had occurred in such a place.

Markings adorned the walls, which appeared to be random lines and scratches, perhaps the marks of age and decay. However, as her eyes adjusted to the dim torchlight, she could see they were runes—thousands of them—some small and repeated over and over again, others large and gouged into the stone. She recognized most of them from the book, but she saw the same unknown symbol carved over and over, and it was one she knew all too well, having seen it etched on Ms. Winters's brooch and Peter's tie pin. All the staff wore it, though she still did not know what it meant.

Below the bone chandelier was a rectangular stone slab on which there appeared to be more carvings. It reminded Evelyn of a sarcophagus, and she wondered if she were in the Black family crypt. It was a darker stone than the rest of the room, a deep gray with a blue tinge similar to slate. Massive dark stains covered its surface, though Evelyn's already fearful mind refused to dwell too deeply on what those stains might be and what they might mean for her.

Fogginess clung to her mind, and she couldn't form cohesive thoughts. Everything remained blurred and far away, and she struggled to focus. All she could feel was her own aching body crying out with every movement she made.

A loud smacking sound caught her attention, and Ms. Winters's charcoal-skirted figure fell beside Evelyn. Half of her face was a raw, shining red, peppered with a few angry blisters, and a fresh spray of blood emitted from both nostrils. Her twisted, mutilated visage screamed in agony mere inches from Evelyn's own, and immediately, everything came into focus.

Evelyn scrambled to get away from the woman who clawed at her with desperate, pleading hands, both of which were a patchwork of red, angry skin. She reeked of burned hair and fabric.

Before Evelyn could fully process what was happening, unseen hands pulled her roughly off the ground and yanked her to her feet to face Peter. He wore his signature twisted smile —part amusement, part fury—an expression of barely veiled insanity.

"Ah, darling, so glad you could join us at last."

A flurry of emotions swarmed inside Evelyn—rage, disgust, anguish, fear—she could barely contain them. She wanted to attack him and claw at his eyes, to scream out, "Why?" But she swallowed them down through gritted teeth. She needed her strength for the fight that was to come.

Ms. Winters continued wailing from the ground, chipping away at Peter's façade of control. He swiftly kicked her once in the ribs. "Ms. Winters, do stop that caterwauling, or I will end you!"

The wailing quickly ceased, but she still wept and wheezed quietly from the floor.

Evelyn felt little pity for her.

Peter continued, talking to her as if she were an insolent child. "If you hadn't gotten so clumsy by the fireside, none of this would have happened. You're lucky I don't kill you where you lie!"

His head snapped back to face Evelyn. "Where were we? Oh, yes, now that you're back with us, my dear, we can begin. It's a tad earlier than I would have liked, but needs must!" He was wearing some kind of cloak made in a coarse, black fabric that Evelyn had never seen before. There were a myriad of patches and repairs about its length, which indicated it was old but well maintained, something precious to repair and retain rather than discard, and as such, it was a stark contrast from the pristine, modern black suit he wore beneath. Peter was not the sentimental type, and he cared deeply about his image and style. This cloak represented something worth preserving, though for what reason, she was unsure.

Evelyn stared at him, silently seething. There were parts of the puzzle still missing, and she didn't fully grasp what he meant—she just knew she was prepared to fight for herself and her unborn child until her last breath.

Amusement settled around his face, and he tittered under his breath as if laughing at a joke that Evelyn was not privy to. "You still haven't quite figured it all out, have you? All that poking around, sticking your nose where it doesn't belong, and all you accomplished was getting people killed."

Guilt swelled inside Evelyn, her tears threatening to burst forth in a torrent.

Peter smiled again, clearly pleased that he had touched a nerve, before continuing. "This..." Peter raised his hands, indicating the room, his face awash with manic pride. "This is our church, where my ancestors used blood magic to conjure and trap a goddess of the old world! We took her strength and power for our own, and now *we* are the gods!"

They were penned in on one side by a crowd as all of Blackthorn's staff stood side by side. Some held torches similar to the ones adorning the walls, and the dancing flames illuminated their faces, all of which were focused solely on their Lord and Master, expressions of rapturous mania painted on every one.

Evelyn could not look at them. They seemed on the cusp of frenzy. It frightened her beyond anything she had experienced at Blackthorn, though she knew in her heart there was worse to come.

Peter seemed to revel in his speech. He had an audience, and he was putting on the best show he could. His face was animated, like an excited child recounting a happy memory. He was a mad priest, preaching to his zealous congregation. This was the true, real Peter. He had no reason to wear a mask of respectability and decorum any longer, a façade of caring, of humanity. He was an evil man, just as cruel as his entire family had been before him.

Evelyn looked around at the faces of the staff who encircled them both. They wore faces of devotion and admiration. Peter was their Pope, and they were his parishioners, fanatics who for generations had done the bidding of the Black family. Finally, Evelyn understood that the dead and Hel were not the things to be feared within Blackthorn. They were not the monsters—Peter and his followers were. The Black family and their greed.

Peter continued, almost rapturous in the face of his devotees. "For generations, we have prospered as the unseen forces, the hands that moved the pieces on the board, out of sight and out of reach. We have been advisors to kings and clergy alike. We have fought and won wars, toppled regimes, and corrupted governments. We have wealth that never diminishes, and a well of influence and power that never runs dry." He lowered his arms slowly, fixing his gaze on Evelyn, his eyes wide and excited.

"But such magic requires sacrifice, my love—blood and death—and that's where you come in."

He pointed at Evelyn, and the men holding her arms forced her toward him. She tried to struggle, but it was useless. They were physically stronger, and even if she were to escape, what would she do? She could not fight them all. There were dozens of people now, all gathered around them in a circle, staring gleefully at Peter's display of power. She recognized them as staff—people she had lived with for a year—yet they looked at her as if she were inhuman, just another lamb to be sacrificed in the Black family name.

Peter cupped his hand around her chin, forcing her to face him.

She loathed him with every fiber of her being. She never thought it was possible to hate someone so thoroughly, but she could feel her rage burning through her veins, and she knew right then, with certainty, that if she got the opportunity to kill him, she would not hesitate.

She spat in his face, a burst of bile and venom. His face briefly shifted from one of controlled confidence to that same expression of disturbed madness. With one swift, blurred motion, he slapped her hard. A burst of white spun across her vision, the sharp, sudden pain sending her reeling.

She tasted blood again as the cut on her lip reopened. She slumped slightly, the two men having to shift their hands to keep her upright, before she righted herself, the searing pain of her cheek gradually diminishing to a dull, throbbing ache. His touch, even in the form of a strike, disgusted her enough that it gave her strength.

Peter chuckled under his breath as he wiped the spittle from his face. "They are always reluctant, are they not? For how can a mere lamb understand the importance of its slaughter?"

The staff stepped aside, parting to make room for their

admired leader, which revealed an alcove in the wall. At first, Evelyn could not make out what she was looking at. It was a hulking mass of differently sized objects carelessly thrown together, twinkling in the flickering candlelight.

Peter knelt and lifted something small from the pile. He held it before him as if admiring it. "My stepmother Charlotte tried to fight as well, but how can one defy fate itself?"

He gestured for the men to drag Evelyn forward and dangled the object in front of her face. Like the pendulum of an unwound clock slowing to a stop, it came into focus, and Evelyn gasped. It was a gold locket with the initials "C.B." engraved on it.

The Lavender Lady.

She had been his stepmother, Lady Charlotte Black. She had died in that cold, damp dungeon, and now her soul was trapped within Blackthorn, with the very people who had murdered her.

"Murderer!" Evelyn struggled against the men who held her tight. What she would have done had she broken free, she did not know, but she was consumed by the urge to strike at Peter, to claw at his eyes and tear at his face with all her might. She wanted to hurt him as he had hurt her, as he had hurt God only knew how many before her.

He snickered again. "I didn't kill her—my father did, just like he had killed my mother before her. They both served their purpose after all—they produced sons. But make no mistake, my father was a weak old fool. Once my half-brother came, after the mistake that was my half-sister, he struggled to finish the deed. Two sacrifices were to be made, for what use does a man have for a daughter?" His voice turned colder as he continued, his words tainted with an edge of bitterness.

"He should have done it sooner, but something snapped in him. He killed both children and himself, said in a note, he did so to 'save their souls'—how ridiculous! The girl was of no concern, but the boy was to be my second, my spare! He was to carry our family forward into the twentieth century by my side. Fool!" He slammed his fist into the objects before him, spilling several onto the stone floor beneath.

Slowly, what she was seeing dawned on Evelyn. She thought she had become accustomed to horrors. She had seen festering, putrid death in every form—she had seen the bodies of her loved ones worn and used like old clothes. But this made her truly understand the extent of the Black family's reign of terror and the danger she was in.

It was jewelry. Hundreds of pieces of jewelry thrown atop one another in a pile with no regard or care. Gold and silver chains and pendants, brooches, beads, and even a small silver tiara, tarnished and dusty. Adornments of the dead.

In one swift motion, Peter tore her mother's pearls from her throat and threw them onto the pile with the locket. There were so many pieces, she couldn't count, of different fashions and different eras. A Celtic brooch, blackened and greening with age, ripped off a woman centuries before. A garnet necklace, caked with dirt, from a decade not far from her own.

Each piece of jewelry represented a woman. They represented her dreams, her life, and eventually, her murder. They were mothers and daughters and sisters and friends. They were wives, betrayed and murdered by the men they trusted and loved. They represented sacrifices, a debt paid in their blood, and now, Evelyn was to be added to the pile. Another necklace whose owner would be forgotten in time, another soul to add to Blackthorn's collection, another lamb brought to slaughter to ensure the Black family's power. Everything that had happened had been leading her to that moment, to that place, to her death.

"But...the baby!"

"Yes, it's not ideal. I would prefer to let you nurse it for a while and ensure its health before you die. But your unacceptable behavior has meant a change of plan. I will cut the child free now. If it is female, she will also die, for I have no use for either of you. If it is male, I will ensure he thrives and grows strong. Either way, your blood will seal our power until I find another to take your place. Wives are easy to find when you have money and power, especially when they are as desperate to be loved as you." His laugh echoed around the stone walls, mocking her and all those who came before her.

Evelyn struggled to think straight, rendered speechless by her terror. She knew that the child in her womb was a boy, but that offered little comfort. He would be taken from her arms as she lay dying, to be raised by a sadistic madman and his hellish cult. Raised to be an image of his vile forefathers and to continue the cycle of murder.

Evelyn slumped against the men who held her, defeated. She had fought so hard to escape, to save herself and her baby, and to foil the dark plans of Blackthorn House, and now, as she stood surrounded by emotionless men, facing death, her worst fears were becoming realized. She would be trapped within Blackthorn, another lost and lonely soul, endlessly wandering its halls, impossibly trying to escape and find peace where there was none. She looked at Peter, and the only outward expression she could muster was a half-whisper. "Why?"

Peter moved so close she could smell his musk and feel the hotness of his breath upon her cheek as he gently, almost affectionately, whispered, "Your blood, my darling. Black family blood."

She looked at him, confused as he continued. He spoke loud enough that his audience could hear, but kept nose to nose with Evelyn, his eyes burrowing intensely into her own. "The magic can only work with Black family blood—that's the payoff, you see? The very thing we want is for our family to thrive and prosper, and yet the price for such blessings is our lives. Our blood created the seal; thus, it is needed to maintain it. But there is always a solution if one is intelligent enough to find it. Wives marrying into the family become Blacks by name. They can provide an heir, and their blood maintains our hold over Hel."

Evelyn wanted to scream. She wanted to lash out, to run—anything—but she was exhausted. Her mind and her world began to spin, the pain from fingers digging into her arms the only thing preventing her from falling unconscious.

Peter straightened to address the room. His voice turned serious and stern, booming throughout the stone chamber. "It is time."

Twenty-One

Electricity hummed in the stagnant air, a metallic scent filling Evelyn's nostrils. The staff surrounding the altar were elated, staring at her like a starving man stared at a piece of meat, desperate and hungry. They had dragged her there, kicking, screaming, and fighting with every ounce of strength she had, but her protests had been futile. Their strong hands, rough from a life of hard labor, held her firm, and her attempts to resist only tired her further.

She felt so weak, so helpless. She was afraid of dying and even more afraid of what came after. She couldn't die here, not like this. But what could she do? Her mind scrambled to find an answer—there had to be something. She thought about the small knife hidden in the hem of her nightgown. If she could reach it, perhaps... Perhaps? What could she do? Fight an entire room of people? It was a ridiculous notion, but it could, at least, buy her some time. Yet the firm grip of the men holding her made reaching for it impossible.

Peter barked orders as servants hurried around the room, producing towels, bowls of water, and rags—the instruments of her demise and, perhaps, her child's. Tears of fear, frustration, and grief for a life she never had and would never know forced their way down her cheeks. Her eyes fell on the pile of jewelry, already forgotten in the corner, a collection of trophies taken by hunters. Her heart ached for every woman whose blood had been spilled on that stone as much as it ached for herself.

There were hundreds of pieces there, each one a woman—each one now a trapped soul. Alone, she may not be strong enough to escape, but together...

Evelyn closed her eyes in concentration. She summoned the souls haunting Blackthorn House, bidding them to come to her. The room began to fade, the sounds around her becoming muffled as she felt herself slipping out of her body.

She thought of Lilly and Charlotte. She thought of the women who had owned each piece of jewelry before her. She thought of the unnamed daughters who had died because they were not male, and of the old woman who had tried to help her. She thought of Hel and even her own mother, of their collective despondency and fury. She felt them reaching toward her as the veil between worlds thinned.

With every ounce of strength left in her body, she yelled, "Help me end this!"

Peter whipped around, furious at the interruption. He sneered before letting out a derisive laugh. "No one here will help you, Evelyn. You are alone."

But she was not alone—she had never been alone. Her mother had walked with her every day since she had died. Lilly had followed her back from where she lay now, growing cold and stiff. The wives of Blackthorn were all around her, and they were *angry*.

At once, every weak flame that surrounded her grew with violent intensity, then died, leaving trails of smoke retreating into the darkness. The smell of smoke sullied the air, and the hairs on Evelyn's arms stood up as a shiver snaked its way down her spine. The staff shifted nervously, rubbing their arms and looking anxiously around at each other. Evelyn's ears popped, and the atmosphere of the room shifted as shadows darkened and multiplied.

They are here.

Peter had noticed the shift and, for the first time, seemed to be concerned.

Everyone stood still. The world had paused—a great game of statues played with invisible opponents. The room seemed to collectively hold its breath, waiting for something, though they had no notion what it was.

Then, it started.

The staff jumped and yelled as invisible hands assaulted them. The bone chandelier above them began to sway—slowly at first, but quickly building into a full swing. Objects fell over, hitting the stone floor with loud bangs that mingled with the ever-growing noises of fearful discourse. The stone table holding the jewelry shook violently, and those surrounding it backed away. Their fear was contagious, passing between everyone in the stone chamber until chaos erupted. The chandelier swung higher and higher as Peter stared at it, his mouth agape. It quickly reached its apex and smashed violently into the stone ceiling, causing the bones and skulls to crack. The shards scattered across the people beneath them like macabre confetti.

Peter jumped back just in time to avoid an antler, while another hit one of the staff square on the forehead, slicing away a chunk of skin. Panic escalated, and soon, everyone knocked into each other, scrambling on top of one another to escape the mayhem.

In the shuffle, one of the men holding Evelyn released her, and she quickly tore the knife from her nightgown, slashing at the other man. He stood confused for a second, holding his bleeding hands, but his features shifted to anger as he raised a fist, determined on revenge. The torch behind his head exploded as if someone had tossed fuel onto it, and his hair and clothes instantly caught fire. He screamed in pain, his howling surpassing the din of the other panicked people, but quickly incited them to louder, more frantic protestations. He thrashed, knocking over others who tried to move away, but he seemed trapped. Another torch rolled toward one of the maids and immediately burst upwards like a small bomb, sending her skirts aflame.

Pandemonium raged around Evelyn. She crouched behind the altar, her knife raised toward Peter and her eyes darting wildly as she tried to find a way out. The stench of burned flesh and hair filled the chamber, and black smoke began to gather, a sinister imitation of the fog outside.

Peter had been standing in the center of it all, slack-jawed and unsure as he sought the source of the disruption. Finding none, he focused all his anger on Evelyn. He lunged for her just in time to avoid the chandelier that fell to the ground and cleaved the heads of the two men who had been standing beside him.

Evelyn threw herself backward to avoid the blade he swung in a clumsy, hurried arch, and it struck the stone altar with a spark. She realized she was trapped by the altar—a stone wall behind her, and Peter on the other side, his face twisted in fury. She coughed and sputtered in the thickening smoke, and, using all her strength, held the knife out and pointed at Peter, prepared to defend herself and her child until she collapsed.

All of the staff clustered toward the far corner of the room, crushing each other in their desperation to flee. In the smoke, Evelyn could see a woman lying face down, the back of her skull now pulp beneath the scrambling feet. If it weren't for the singed, burned gray dress and blistered hands, Evelyn would never have been able to recognize her as Ms. Winters. The crowd hammered at the door, screaming for help.

Evelyn's heart sank, knowing it was the only way out.

Peter, as if sensing her thoughts, pulled a key from his waistcoat pocket and held it up to show her. "Only I have the key. If I die down here, so do they."

Evelyn instantly recognized it as the same one that hung around her neck now, the key the Lavender Lady, Charlotte, had led her to find. But it was useless when the door was obscured by dozens of screaming people, even if she somehow got past Peter, who stared at her, incandescent with rage.

"I don't know how you did this, but it won't matter. You will die down here, you and your brat. I possess the power of Death herself! At Blackthorn, I am God, and you are nothing but a lamb for slaughter. I will walk out of here unscathed as you lie in a pool of your own blood."

With that pronouncement, everything that had once seemed blurred came into focus, her jumbled mass of thoughts all coming together to form one clear realization.

Blood.

That was what Hel had been trying to tell her, why she had used every ounce of strength that remained to visit and plead with Evelyn. Blood magic—that was what his ancestors had used to control Hel. It was blood that gave them their power and status, but the same blood had to be spilled to maintain the spell.

Blood created, blood destroyed.

The curse that trapped Hel at Blackthorn, that trapped all the lost and tortured souls there, was forged in blood, and only in the same way could it be broken. Hadn't Peter himself told her that through marriage and pregnancy, she was now a member of the Black family, that its blood coursed through her veins just as it did his own? He hadn't realized when he was gloating that he was telling her exactly how to stop him and end it all forever.

Evelyn held her hand out, slicing a large, angry gash across the palm. A few droplets fell as she spoke, dotting the gray stone with bright red as she cried out, "Blood created..."

Peter's look of bewilderment shifted quickly to panic as realization dawned on him. He lunged toward the altar, his arms outstretched and his eyes wide and frantic, just as Evelyn slammed her hand down onto the smooth stone, shouting, "Blood destroyed! I release you, Hel! I release you all!"

Everything shook as the earth vibrated violently, sending Evelyn reeling backward into the wall. The followers' cries crescendoed as Blackthorn seemed to shift on its very foundation. Dust fell in waves from the roof above, churning with the smoke below. The fire had taken hold of a set of velvet curtains nearby, and flames climbed the wall, setting an apocalyptic scene, complete with panic and death. Evelyn feared the house would soon collapse and entomb them there forever.

Without reason or warning, it stopped.

Silence fell over the room, save for the crackle of flames as they climbed. It seemed everyone held their breath in anticipation, knowing the earthquake had been only the beginning. Peter looked around, his hand splayed just in front of Evelyn's bloody handprint, showing just how close he had come to stopping her.

With a loud crunch, a crack appeared at Evelyn's bloody signature and began spiderwebbing out. Peter jumped up and away from it as if fleeing the approaching fissure. He stared, eyes wide with fear, as the stone was cleaved in two by an invisible force. With an enormous snap like the sound of a whip, the stone lay in two halves, dust settling around it.

"What have you done?"

Twenty-Two

Evelyn stared at the stone, waiting with bated breath to see what would emerge. Mist poured from the crevice of the stone like liquid smoke, flowing around the room with snake-like quickness. The fires that had roared around them diminished, their small flames turning a pale blue and casting the room in an eerie sapphire shadow. Apart from Evelyn's ragged breathing, she heard someone weeping along with the crackle of the shrunken flames. No one knew what to do or what to say, so they waited, watching. A blueish-green light pierced the black, seeping from the stone as a figure rose, giving off the same ghostly light.

It was a woman with two faces—one of life and one of death. The living face was beautiful—an ethereal vision with dark, knowing eyes and sharp cheekbones. The dead face was horrifying. A skeletal grin smiled through what little pieces of rotten tendons and festering flesh had remained attached to its face. The sockets were empty, black caverns where eyes had once been, and the same sharp cheekbones protruded, bare and defined. Worms crawled around what was left of her tongue and ears, and putrid skin dangled, barely attached.

Both faces existed, yet did not exist all at once—like some kind of optical illusion, visible yet not really there. She was beautiful and terrible, alluring and terrifying—the embodiment of mortality in all its stages, the inevitability of death, the fate all living creatures shared, and the single equalizer in the world. She was Hel, ruler of Helheim, queen of the dead, and a powerful goddess.

Her body was opaque, and through the blue-tinged light, Evelyn could see Peter's face contorted with terror. She was glad. She wanted him to be afraid the way she had been, to feel the horror Lilly had felt in her final moments. He opened his mouth to speak, but before he could utter a word, mist rose like tentacles emerging from a foggy sea. It entered his mouth, causing his eyes to bulge and widen in panic. He began to claw at his throat as the fog split into dozens more strands, each one entering the terrified bodies of the servants, their screams only allowing it faster, easier access to their bodies.

Evelyn stood paralyzed as their bodies jerked, writhing in muted agony. Each only uttered choking, suffocating coughs as they clawed at their skin as if trying to burrow out of the mist. Blood pooled in their eyes before falling in red, streaming tears. Their mouths opened and closed like fish brought to land, gasping desperately for air but finding none. Soon, blood leaked from their mouths as they choked on their own insides. Darker blood, almost black, streamed from their ears before they finally stopped their desperate, twitching dance, falling like marionettes whose strings had been cut. Every one of Blackthorn's devout staff lay still, contorted in pools of their own blood and excrement, their faces permanently trapped in an agonized death mask.

Only Peter remained alive. Hel, it seemed, had a slower death in mind for the master of the house. He stood choking, bloodshot eyes bulging. He had clawed deep gouges along his own neck, desperately trying to breathe as he twitched. The color leached from his skin, as it retracted and tightened around his bones. It continued to shrink until it split open, exposing almost bloodless flesh beneath.

His eyes soon popped out of their sockets entirely, dangling from their stalks, swelling until they ruptured, yellow jelly oozing out until only two wrinkled sacks of dried tissue remained. Thick, black blood dribbled from the empty sockets as his lips and cheeks retracted and split, revealing a skeletal grin. Even his gums seemed to shrink, exposing the bone beneath. His tongue, now hanging loose in a slack-jawed skull, seemed to be sapped of all fluid as it dried and shrank.

Evelyn watched in disgust, unable to look away as the man she had once loved mutated, his life force draining from his body. By the time Hel was done with him, he was a mere skeleton, covered in patches of rotten skin and sinew. When he fell to the ground, he shattered like porcelain in a cloud of dust. All that was left of her husband—of the last Lord Black, the father of her unborn child—was a pile of clothes and fragments of bone.

Evelyn walked toward the pile. She reached down and plucked out his ruby tie pin, the same symbol etched on its surface as she had seen the other staff wear—their very own rune, a marker representing the defilement of their culture and religion, of their murderous, blood-soaked history, and their insatiable hunger for power. She tossed it onto the pile of discarded jewelry that represented the death of so many innocent women. It seemed a fitting place to put it.

She felt little at his loss. She did not mourn the man she had married because he had never existed. He was only a figment, another of Blackthorn's ghosts. A ghost that would live on in the lies she would tell her child—a myth of a kind man who sadly perished before her son was born. Evelyn had learned that sometimes, lies were kinder than the truth.

Evelyn noticed movement behind her and turned to find a woman. She was intensely, unnervingly beautiful. Her eyes were striking—one white and dead, the other a blue as bright as a springtime sky. Her nearly transparent skin exposed the winding threads of purple and blue veins visible beneath. Her cheekbones, raised and sharp, protruded a little too much like her collarbone and jaw, as if someone could cut themselves if they dared to touch her. Her hair, as black as a raven's wing, went far below her waist. She wore a long, simple white gown, almost bridal in style, with long, flowing sleeves that grazed the tops of her bare feet. A pale glow emanated from her, reminding Evelyn of an autumn moon.

Hel.

For several heartbeats, both women stared at one another knowingly. Nothing needed to be said, and so, no words were uttered—only a deep understanding and gratitude passed solemnly through their eyes. The light around Hel grew momentarily brighter, and figures appeared behind her, entering through a door Evelyn could no longer see. There was the Lavender Lady—Charlotte—who Evelyn had only known briefly in death, but to whom she owed so much. Gone was the angry wound which had marred her throat. She looked as beautiful as Evelyn had imagined and was flanked by two children, one a boy and one a girl, who smiled at Evelyn with wide, toothy grins. There was the old woman, no longer hunched over, pained by age and its many afflictions. She appeared strong and healthy—perhaps even younger.

Then she saw Lilly—her beautiful, beloved Lilly—alive and healthy again, smiling with eyes full of grateful tears. The sister she had chosen, her dearest and kindest friend. Evelyn smiled back, her tears falling freely. She was happy to see her friend at peace, but saddened by the knowledge that this would be the last time she would see her. Her gratitude could never be expressed in words, especially with so little time. Instead, Evelyn gently placed her hand on her heart, a gesture which Lilly immediately reciprocated. It was a simple movement, yet it said so much.

Finally, Evelyn stood to face her mother. She had never left Evelyn's side, watching her as she had grown, and finally following her there to Blackthorn to be trapped as she was, as they all had been. But now, they were free. Her neck was no longer bent and broken. She stood as tall and beautiful as Evelyn remembered, tears falling from her eyes as she stared at her daughter, now grown.

Evelyn wept as she whispered, "Mother."

She understood now the pain and terror her mother had faced on a daily basis—the horrors of death that she had witnessed and the loneliness that those visions brought. She no longer felt bitterness or anger toward her choice to end her suffering. She no longer felt the guilt she had carried for so long. She took comfort in knowing her mother could finally be at peace and that Evelyn would see her again someday when death came for her, too.

She had been young—she could never have understood what her mother was enduring, nor could she have predicted her reaction. Peace had at last come to both women.

Her mother reached a pale, glowing hand toward Evelyn, who outstretched her own in turn. There was no hand to feel, no solid flesh or bone, but Evelyn felt a warmth, and she smiled, grateful to have the opportunity to say goodbye. The light increased in brightness until it became blindingly light, swallowing the ethereal figures before suddenly blinking out like a candle flame extinguished. The crack in the stone remained, but no longer did the coldness and mists of the other side creep through it. The door was closed, and Evelyn was once again alone.

The fires, which had shrunk away from the cold mists of Helheim, began to come back to life once more, their blue flames returning to the red, orange glow of danger. Heat re-entered the room in a wave, and Evelyn knew that she must find her way out before the full force of the fires returned.

She reached a shaking hand towards the pile of jewelry and retrieved her mother's pearls, careful not to disturb the other pieces. Just as she went to place them back around her neck, she felt something deep within her burst as warm liquid trickled down her legs and onto the stone floor. A wave washed over her body, spreading from her stomach outwards, like a stone dropped into still waters. It wasn't pain exactly, but it was unpleasant and brought with it nausea and a sudden rush of anxiety. Her skin prickled despite the increasing heat of the still-growing flames, and she knew that her child was coming. She needed to leave—now.

Smoke began filling the chamber, and Evelyn found herself coughing and sputtering. Burning embers floated around her in the rising smoke, as beautiful as it was deadly. She covered her mouth with her arm and started to move in the direction the others had run. She had to clamber over their bodies, blood and bile still oozing from their every orifice. But Evelyn did not have the luxury of time—she could not let herself feel disgust and horror—not then. She climbed over them as if they were mere pieces of furniture, trying not to wretch at the stench of feces and urine that surrounded them.

Briefly, she looked back, and through the growing waves of heat and smoke, through the bright, dancing flames, she saw hundreds of women. Some wore the cloaks of Norse settlers; others wore dresses she had seen in old paintings, long since out of style. These were the women of Blackthorn. The women whose blood had sealed generations of wealth and power. Women who had died for no other reason than being women, no longer useful to their cruel, immoral husbands.

They were mothers, each of them having not lived long enough to raise their own children, instead being cursed to watch them be molded and distorted into the grotesque form of their fathers, doomed to repeat their murderous acts of defilement. Generation after generation of women, all beautiful and wonderful, all struck down before their time and all of them now finally at peace.

"Goodbye...and thank you."

It was barely a whisper, but Evelyn knew they had heard her as the light surrounding them pulsed brighter before they all vanished completely. The smoke was now thick and acrid, and Evelyn could feel the heat from every breath within her lungs. Moving was becoming a chore. The cramps in her stomach were beginning to change from discomfort to pain, and every breath felt labored and shallow as her vision swam. The smoke disoriented her, leaving her lost among the corpses of her captors. A part of her wanted to lie down so badly—to rest, to sleep. But she forced herself onward, now crawling among the dead and the foul bodily fluids leaking from each one.

Evelyn had almost given up hope when she saw the door ahead. It was the one from her dreams, exactly as she had always seen it. With shaking hands, she pulled the key from within her nightgown and forced it into the lock. It took her three desperate tries before she managed to insert it properly and turn it. With every ounce of strength she had, she heaved the door open, sending a gust of cold, fresh air into the room.

The momentary relief of breathing clean air was immediately overshadowed by the burst in the fury of the flames behind her. They, too, sought the fresh night air. It fed them as much as it did her, and they exploded with a force and energy that almost pushed Evelyn tumbling outwards into the room beyond. The fire in the chamber was now fully taking hold, and it would not be long until the heart of Blackthorn House became an inferno.

Evelyn used the walls to steady her weak and pain-ridden body. The heat behind her grew in intensity, driving her toward the cold autumn night, and she found herself in a part of the house she had never been in. A long corridor of bare stone led her toward a small winding staircase taking her upward and away from the smoke and heat. It stopped with a wooden door directly above her head. It was heavier than she had expected, and she had to bend over to brace her back against it and use her legs to force it open. More cold, fresh air flooded in, and she heard something explode from below. The temperature sharpened again, and Evelyn could not help but imagine it as something alive, nipping at her heels like a starving predator hunting its final meal.

It led into a damp, dark room, its walls lined with shelves filled with hundreds of dusty bottles of wine. She was in the cellar. She had fought her way into the actual body of Blackthorn house, but unfortunately, she was in its bowels. There were many stairs to climb before she reached the outside world. Pain swept through her body, and her stomach rippled. She bent over, crying out, twisting her soiled nightgown in her fingers until it once again passed. It seemed the baby was impatient to join her.

Slowly and with great effort, she hoisted her aching body out of the hole and onto the damp, earthen floor. She lay there coughing, but knew she had no time to rest. She dragged herself up, limping slowly but determinedly through the cellar toward the wooden stairs. Behind her, she heard the familiar crackle of flame and heard glass breaking and corks popping. The coolness of the cellar dissipated quickly, its dampness becoming an uncomfortable dryness.

The fire had found its prey once more.

Each step took effort, always accompanied by a painful

groan, another ache, another part of her body screaming for her to stop, yet she continued. She emerged from the cellar into the food store, where the corpses of recently caught pheasants stared at her as she passed through to the kitchens. The room was filled with the scent of that evening's meal along with the acrid stench of burned flesh.

She hobbled toward the back door, only to find it locked. She threw the bolt aside with little resistance, but the door remained closed when she turned the handle. She screamed in frustration, picturing Ms. Winters with a large set of keys lying against her burning corpse, red hot with the flames. More glass popped below as she felt the floor growing hotter. Her pursuer persisted behind her, slow and steady, patient in its hunt.

She limped toward the hallways lined with the various staff areas, slowly approaching Blackthorn's grand central hall. She found it in darkness, abandoned. No longer did she admire the sconces or the chandelier—there was nothing of beauty at Blackthorn House. Every piece of furniture, every candlestick and painting, had been paid for in blood. Every velvet drape and elaborately woven Persian rug had cost human lives. Now, to Evelyn, everything appeared ostentatious and boastful. They were all hollow, meaningless trinkets, defiled by how they were obtained. She wanted none of it.

She pulled on the heavy front doors to find them also locked. Tears stung her eyes as she sobbed. She was so tired, so sore. Her determination waned as she faced the possibility of remaining trapped within Blackthorn's walls, as she had been for so many months. Something exploded from beneath her, and she felt the very foundations of the house shake. The doors to the staff area blew open with such force that one broke off its hinges, left to dangle uselessly as the smoke rushed into the room. She could hear the crackle of flame, feel its heat. It was coming for her.

As quickly as her swollen, painful body would allow, she

trudged toward the parlor. The fireplace silently roared at her, teeth bared, its feline eyes staring at her accusingly. Smoke and ash poured from the grate within, giving her the impression that it was breathing fire.

From the glass patio doors, she could see the now-clear night sky. The full moon cast a gentle glow over the moors, seeming so peaceful, so unaware—or perhaps disinterested in the turmoil and violence which now burned below. The doors were, unsurprisingly, locked. Evelyn grabbed a small wooden chair, its arms carved to look like rope, and threw it as hard as she could at them. It smashed against the glass, one leg jutting through the hole it had created, as if it too were trying to escape the house. Cold air streamed in, and Evelyn eagerly used the chair to break away more of the glass until she could safely step outside into the night.

She was so grateful to finally be free of Blackthorn that she barely noticed one of the glass shards drawing a clean, straight line across her forearm. She walked forward, the hairs on her body all standing to attention as she erupted in gooseflesh, the cold autumn air biting at her almost as much as the heat had. Once she reached the grass, she collapsed in a sobbing, heaving heap. Every emotion that had been suppressed, bubbling beneath the skin, burst forth in a torrent. She wept and screamed, and at one point even laughed to herself as she fluctuated between grief and anger, sorrow and horror, and at last, relief.

As if in response, or perhaps as a reminder that she still had a way to go, she felt another burst of pain coursing through her body. While it was not the most painful she had ever endured, it had an intensity and urgency like no other injury or ache she had ever experienced. She knew from the doctor that these waves of pain would grow in intensity as the time between them grew shorter.

She needed to get to the village.

When the contraction ended, she painfully pulled herself up. Blackthorn House was now fully aflame. The dancing orange heat radiated from every window now, thick gray smoke in large plumes escaping where it could. It illuminated the blackened sky like an early sunset, and Evelyn smiled. The house was the embodiment of the Black family, beautiful on the outside, but rotten within its heart. It was built on the backs of corpses, painted in the blood of innocents, and decorated with their bones. Blackthorn House was a graveyard—not a home—and Evelyn was glad it was burning.

The horses in the stables were stirring, anxiously huffing and thumping frightened hooves among the dogs' whimpers and frantic paws scratching at the doors. Evelyn would free them all, taking one horse for her own long trek to the village.

There would be no more death at Blackthorn House.

Epilogue

A chubby hand, plump and healthy, clutched a small silver rattle, noisily banging it against the crib. Evelyn watched him, smiling, amazed that something so beautiful, so pure, could come from so much chaos and pain. George was almost a year old and was big for his age—everything Evelyn never knew she needed. The love she felt for him was unfathomable, and she simply couldn't express it in words. She settled for allowing small actions to tell the boy all she felt—gentle kisses of his tiny, wriggling feet, or the tender brush of his forehead as he slept. He was everything to her and somehow made the nightly terrors she still endured bearable.

He had his father's eyes, but in all other ways, he was the image of Evelyn. Her father even joked that the stern look he would give when his toy was taken from him or when a spoonful of something suspiciously green was produced for his lunch reminded him of Evelyn's own disapproving stare, and that if he could tut, undoubtedly, he would.

Her father and brother spent their days trying to repay a debt which Evelyn had already forgiven. Their guilt at not having tried harder to reach her, at believing Peter's forgeries still ate at them, and she saw it in the sad smiles they would give her and George whenever they thought she couldn't see.

Evelyn held no ill will toward them. As soon as they were notified of the fire and Peter's death, they ran their horses to exhaustion getting to her, dropping everything to be by her side. Their company, their love, plus George's kept her optimistic for the future.

She hadn't told them everything, partly out of fear she would be disbelieved, labeled a mad woman—a hysteric—and partly to save them further guilt and grief. They were aware of Peter's true nature—his cruel abuse and deceit—and, of course, the fire, but nothing more. They asked a few questions and accepted the answers she gave without opposition. Perhaps they could see something in her eyes that told them not to press further, a fragility that should not be pressed lest the cracks spread and cause her to shatter.

The villagers, who had found her bloody, beaten, and in labor, wearing a filthy, tattered nightgown, had asked nothing about what had happened beyond whether they should check for survivors, accepting her answer without a single protest. They clearly had no urge to go to Blackthorn House, nor would they mourn the loss of any therein. They simply nodded knowingly as if they had always expected it to meet a violent end. They had been kind to her and George, but had treated her with suspicion and a small amount of fear, always keeping her at a distance—both literal and metaphorical—as if Blackthorn and its horrors had been a virus, and she were contagious.

Now, that time seemed to be so far away. She saw it through the haze of memory, like a bad dream—a particularly vivid nightmare. Only at night, when she was carried off by sleep, did she see and feel it all as clearly as if it were happening again, reliving the fear and pain over and over again. They had lessened in their ferocity, but she remained haunted by Blackthorn House when night came. She lived in a perpetual state of fatigue, with large, dark circles under her eyes, which, when combined with her weight loss, gave her an almost skeletal appearance. But deep down, she knew that time would heal such wounds and that someday, she would sleep deeply once more. For now, she had George and her family to help her face her ghosts.

"Evelyn, can you help me with this?"

Her father had purchased a new home, somewhere free of hard memories, a way for him to escape his own ghosts. Evelyn had not objected. She understood how a building could retain the pain that had occurred there, absorbed into the walls and floors, and stain it forever. A fresh start was something they could both agree on. He had been enthusiastically renovating and redecorating it, asking Evelyn's input at every step of the way. It was clear he was attempting to distract her, to help her forget a little piece at a time, but he had also made it clear it was her home more than his—something George and Evelyn would inherit someday. She reluctantly accepted his kindness despite Evelyn's protestations and insistence that he would outlive his entire gentleman's club out of sheer stubbornness alone. She began to mold the house into something bright and happy. She reasoned that if Blackthorn's dark, cruel heart affected the emotions of those within, then a home full of light and love would do the same. Today, they were working on the library.

"Coming."

Evelyn smiled at George once more before leaving the room. She made it a few steps down the hall when she felt the temperature drop suddenly and without reason. Her skin prickled, and the hairs on the back of her neck stood up. She halted mid-step. For a moment, it was as if she were back at Blackthorn, standing before that doorway once more. She could hear George babble in the next room, his small rattle hitting the side of his crib. She strained to listen, convincing herself it was merely a residual effect of her trauma—an echo that would pop up every now and then to remind her of what she had endured.

She didn't dare move or speak, lest she make it somehow "real." She held her breath. She heard the rattle drop to the floor with a thud, followed by George's frustrated noises as he lamented its loss.

See, all is well.

Yet she remained rooted to the spot, unable to move. She could hear his frustration, his small protestations building in volume and impatience. She would need to retrieve the rattle for him to avoid tears, but still, she could not bring herself to move. Her heartbeat quickened.

She could hear him on the verge of tears when his tone suddenly returned to contentment. She heard him saying, "Mama" in his sweet, singsong way, and she wondered if he was calling her to come for the rattle when she heard its familiar sounds. He had the rattle again, shaking it joyfully, hitting it off the crib. How had he retrieved it? There was at least a distance of two feet between the bottom of the crib and the floor below, and his small arms would never reach. It was a task that each family member did a dozen times a day, one which George never seemed to tire.

She turned back towards the parlor, straining to listen yet still unable to move. He said, "Mama," a few more times, and Evelyn felt herself begin to relax. He must be calling her. He must not have dropped the rattle all the way.

Yes, that was it.

Then why did her heart still pound within her chest? Why did she sense something had shifted? But, just as she began to convince herself that all was well, she heard the voice. It was a familiar voice, but one she did not wish to hear ever again. It was a voice that had transcended death and imprisonment to reach out to Evelyn across worlds and time, a voice that had haunted her nightmares at Blackthorn for many days since her escape. It was a woman's voice—the voice of death herself.

It was the voice of Hel, and she spoke softly to Evelyn's son.

"*Blood created...*"

Acknowledgments

Firstly, I would like to thank Cassandra L. Thompson, Lisa Morris, and everyone else at Quill & Crow for helping me put my art out into the world.

A big shout out to my wonderful friends and family for always being so supportive. In particular, my beautiful daughter Paige, who inspires me every day with her endless imagination, and my incredible partner Gerard, my biggest cheerleader and my best friend.

Lastly, thank you to all my friends on Bookstagram. Thank you for the book recommendations, the inspiration, and the support. I hope to see this book on your feeds!

About the Author

Marie McWilliams is a horror writer and content creator from Northern Ireland. Her writing has been featured in multiple anthologies, magazines, and book boxes and her first novel, a dark crime thriller *Broken Mirrors* is available to purchase now. Her second book, which accompanies a Tarot Deck, called *Mother Mort's Carnival of Souls,* has just been released by US Games. When Marie is not writing horror, she is reading it and sharing her love for the genre on her social media platforms. You can find them, as well as full details of her various publications on her website.

Thank You For Reading

Thank you for reading *The Secrets of Blackthorn House.* We deeply appreciate our readers, and are grateful for everyone who takes the time to leave us a review. If you're interested, please visit our website to find review links. Your reviews help small presses and indie authors thrive, and we appreciate your support.

Trigger Index

This book contains the following:

Abuse of Women:

- Attempted Murder of a Pregnant Woman
- Gaslighting/Manipulation
- Physical Assault (slapping/hitting)
- Marital Sexual Coercion (non-violent/off-screen)
- Murder (off-screen)

Animal Abuse (ravens)
Animal Death (off-screen)
Child Death/Murder (off-screen)
Immolation (woman)
Suicide (mentioned/off-screen)
Revenge Violence

www.ingramcontent.com/pod-product-compliance
Ingram Content Group UK Ltd.
Pitfield, Milton Keynes, MK11 3LW, UK
UKHW041331210726
13916UKWH00015B/110

9 781958 228913